HOME SCHOOLING

HOME SCHOOLING

stories

CAROL WINDLEY

Atlantic Monthly Books
New York

First published in Canada in 2006
by CORMORANT BOOKS

FIRST AMERICAN EDITION

ISBN-10: 0-87113-994-4

ISBN-13: 978-0-87113-994-8

Atlantic Monthly Press
an imprint of Grove/Atlantic, Inc.

841 Broadway

New York, NY 10003

Distributed by Publishers Group West

www.groveatlantic.com

09 10 11 12   10 9 8 7 6 5 4 3 2 1

For Bob

CONTENTS

What Saffi Knows   1

Home Schooling   21

Family in Black   51

Sand and Frost   83

Felt Skies   109

Children's Games   133

The Joy of Life   161

The Reading Elvis   191

Acknowledgements   219

WHAT SAFFI KNOWS

That summer a boy went missing from a field known as the old potato farm, although no one could remember anything growing there but wild meadow barley, thistles in their multitudes, black lilies with a stink of rotten meat if you brought your face too close or tried to pick them. There were white fawn lilies like stars fallen to earth and bog-orchids, also called candle-scent, and stinging nettles, blameless to look at, leaves limp as flannel, yet caustic and burning to the touch. Even so, nettle leaves could be brewed into a tea that acted on the system like a tonic, or so Saffi's aunt told her. She recited a little rhyme that went: *Nettle tea in March, mugwort leaves in May, and all the fine maidens will not go to clay.*

Imagine a field, untended, sequestered, grass undulating in a fitful wind. Then disruption, volunteer members of the search party arriving, milling around, uniformed police and tracking dogs, distraught relatives of the missing boy. No place for a child, Saffi's mother said, yet here Saffi was, holding tight to her aunt's hand, taking everything in.

All the people were cutout dolls. The sun hovered above the trees like a hot-air balloon cut free. Saffi's shoes were wet from walking in the grass; she was wearing a sundress that tied at the back of her neck and she kept scratching at mosquito bites on her arms and legs until they bled and her Aunt Loretta said she'd give herself blood poisoning, but Saffi didn't stop, she liked how it felt, it gave her something to do. She could see her daddy, standing a little apart from the others, drinking coffee from a paper cup. He was a young man then, tall, well-built, his hair a sprightly reddish-brown, his head thrown back, eyes narrowed in concentration, as if he hoped to be first to catch sight of any unusual movement in the woods, down near the river. Saffi looked where he was looking and saw a flitting movement in the trees like a turtledove, its silvery wings spread like a fan and its voice going coo-coo, the sound a turtledove would make when it was home and could rest at last. But there was no turtledove. Never would there be a turtledove. Saffi was the only one who knew. But who would listen to her?

July 1964, in a town on Vancouver Island, in the days before the tourists and land developers arrived and it was quiet, still, and everyone more or less knew everyone else. There was a pulp and paper mill, a harbour where the fishing fleet tied up, churches, good schools, neighbourhoods where children played unsupervised. Children were safe in this town. They did not go missing. But now, unbelievably, not one but two children were gone, one for nearly six weeks and then three days ago this other boy, his red three-speed bike found ditched at the edge of the old potato farm, where it seemed he liked to play, hunting snakes and butterflies, but never hurting anything, just catching things and letting them go.

His name was Eugene Dexter. His jacket had been found snagged in a hawthorn tree beside the Millstone River, at the far end of the old potato farm. Or else it was a baseball cap that was found. Or a catcher's mitt. You heard different stories. There was a ransom note. There was no such note. The police had a suspect, or, alternately, they had no suspects, although they'd questioned and released someone and were refusing to give out details. But, said Saffi's mother, wasn't that how they operated, secretly, out of the public eye, trying to conceal their own ineptness? She kicked at a pebble. A woman beside her spoke of premonition, showing the gooseflesh on her arms. Some men got into a scrum, like elderly, underfed rugby players, and began praying aloud.

One minute it was warm and then the wind made Saffi shiver. Behind the mountain dark clouds welled up, filled with a hidden, shoddy light. The boy's parents arrived in a police car, lights flashing. But maybe Saffi was remembering that wrong. Maybe they drove up in their own car, Mr. Dexter behind the wheel. In any case, there they were, Mr. and Mrs. Dexter, making their way over to tables borrowed from the high school cafeteria and set up in the field, with sandwiches and donuts and coffee and mimeographed instructions for the search party, so perhaps it wasn't surprising when Mr. Arthur Dawsley sidled up to Saffi's mother and said wasn't this turning into quite a three-ring circus? He was their neighbour. He lived on the other side of a tall hedge. Along the front of his yard was a picket fence painted green and on his front door was a sign that said: No Peddlers. When Saffi was small, less than two years old, she'd mispronounced his name, saying Arthur Daisy, and in her family it was the wrong name that had stuck. It didn't suit him; she wished she could take it back. Her parents teased her, calling Arthur Daisy her friend, but he wasn't. His hair the colour of a cooking pot sat in deep waves above his forehead. Under his windbreaker he was wearing a white shirt and a tie. He said he knew this gathering was no circus, that was merely a figure of speech, and not a good one, considering. He said he supposed he was too old to be of much help in the search, but surely he could lend a little moral support.

"Beautiful weather, all the same," he said, and then walked in his peculiar upright, stolid fashion over to Saffi's daddy, who averted his face slightly and emptied the dregs of his coffee onto the ground, as if the last thing he craved was a word with Arthur Daisy. At the same time the boy's father was handing an item of clothing over to the police, a green striped soccer shirt, it looked like, tenderly folded, and the police let their dogs sniff it and they strained at their leashes as if they'd been given a new idea and the sound of their baying came like a cheerless chorus off the mountain.

Later the wind died down and the clouds built up, dark clouds edged with a beautiful translucent white, dazzling to the eye, and just as Saffi and her mother and aunt got in the car to go home there came a violent drenching downpour, and everyone said it was almost a relief; it was turning out to be such a hot, dry summer.

This could be said of her: as a child she noticed things, she took things in, and to this day she can't decide, is this a curse or a gift? A curse, she thinks, for the most part.

The child she was and the person she's become: in a way they're like two separate people trapped in the same head. Could that be? The child mystifies her. The child with her pallor, her baby-fine, dry hair; her solemn grey-blue eyes, her air of distraction and wariness. Her odd little name that her mother had got out of a book of names: Saffi, meaning "wisdom." *Who are you? I am Saffi, no one else.* She feels sympathy for that child, of course she does, and affection, impatience, anger, shame. And sorrow. Shouldn't someone have been looking out for her? Shouldn't someone have been watching over her? "Daddy's girl," her daddy called her, but daddy didn't have much time for her, not really.

When Saffi was in her yard she made a game out of watching for Arthur Daisy to leave in his car, which he did sometimes, not every day, and as soon as he was gone she crawled through a gap in the hedge into his backyard. She knelt in the shade, looking out at the things he kept there: a wheelbarrow tipped up against a garden shed, a pile of buckets, a heap of steamy grass clippings buzzing with blue-bottles, a mound of composted dirt he made from dead leaves and egg shells and potato peelings, garbage from his kitchen.

At the foot of his porch steps there was a folding chair and an overturned washtub he used as a table, a coffee mug on it. Two of his shirts hung from the clothesline like guards he'd left on duty.

He had painted his cellar window black, but he'd missed a little place shaped like a star and she could get up close to it and see a shaded light hanging from the ceiling and beneath the light a table with a boy crouched on it. He was a real boy. She saw him and he saw her, his eyes alert and shining, and then he let his head droop on his chest. Don't be scared, she said; don't be. He was awake but sleeping, his arm twitching, his feet curled like a bird's claws on a perch. All she could see in the dim light was his hair, nearly white. He was wearing a pair of shorts.

She called him bird-boy. She whistled at him softly, as if he were a wild thing. She had to be careful. Since he'd got the bird-boy, Arthur Daisy never stayed away for long; he'd drive off and then almost at once he was back, slamming his car door and pounding up his front steps. Before he got that far, though, Saffi would have scrambled through the hedge, her hair catching in the branches so that she'd have to give it a cruel tug, but she never cried or uttered the least sound, and at last she was home free.

If Arthur Daisy didn't drive away in his car, if he happened instead to be working in his garden and saw her playing outside, he'd call to her. "Well, Saffi, what do you think I've got?" He kept calling to her. Your friend, Arthur Daisy, her daddy would tease her. She walked to his house on the side of the road, placing the heel of one foot in front of the toe of the other, her arms out for balance. "Hurry up, slowpoke," he would say, pushing his gate open to let her in.

He looked like the old troll that lived under the bridge in *Three Billy Goats Gruff*, one of Saffi's picture books. He wore an old brown cardigan, the pockets sagging with junk. "What do you think I've got?" he'd say, and he'd pull something out of a pocket and hold it in his clenched fist and if she stepped back he'd bend closer, closer, his colourless lips drawn back so that she could see his stained teeth, gums the bluish-pink of a dog's gums. She didn't want to guess, she was no good at it. She covered her eyes until he told her to look and it would turn out to be an old nail or a screwdriver or the sharp little scissors he used for cutting roses.

"Well?" he'd say. "What do you say? Has the cat got Saffi's tongue?" He slapped his hand on his trouser leg and laughed his old troll laugh and picked up his shovel and went back to work digging in his garden.

That summer Saffi's mother got hired as an operator at the B.C. Telephone Co. on Fitzwilliam Street. Her first job, she said, since she got married. Her first real job, ever. If she had a choice, she wouldn't leave Saffi every day, but the truth was, she had no choice, she needed the extra income; she'd lost interest in being poor her entire life. She ran up some dresses for work on her old treadle sewing machine, dark blue dresses, in rayon or a serviceable poplin, something she said she could gussy up with a little white collar, or a strand of pearls.

Saffi remembered her mother wearing those dresses to work for years. When at last they'd gone completely out of style or had simply worn out, she'd cut them into squares and stitched them into a quilt for Saffi, and Saffi had it still, folded away in a cedar chest her husband's parents gave her for a wedding present. When she took it out and ran her fingers over the scraps of fabric, little cornfields, meadows of blue, she couldn't help returning in her mind to those long-ago summer mornings, bright and hot, dreamlike, almost, when she'd clung to her mother and begged her to stay home, and her mother had given her a weary, abstracted glance and pulled on the little chamois-soft gloves she wore for driving. She kissed Saffi on the top of her head and then she was gone, and Saffi heard her backing her car out onto the road and driving away. Aunt Loretta made Saffi sit at the table and eat her breakfast, but Saffi's throat ached from not crying and she couldn't swallow a spoonful. Aunt Loretta rinsed her uneaten porridge down the drain — what a terrible waste, she said — and then she wiped Saffi's face with a dishrag and sent her outside to play in the sun while she got on with tidying the house. Saffi sat on the front steps and looked at one of her books, with pictures of a frog prince, his blubbery mouth pursed for a kiss, a scraggly old witch with skinny fingers reaching out to grab anyone she could catch.

Even though she knew he couldn't see her, she imagined the birdboy was watching, and so she turned the pages carefully. She was good at reading, but poor at arithmetic. It wasn't her fault. The numbers had their own separate lives, their own shapes, and refused to let her touch them. Nine in its soldier's uniform the colour of an olive with a double row of brass buttons. Three a Canterbury bell, a curled-up snail leaving a trail of slime, dragging its little clamshell house behind. Seven had a licking tongue of fire and smelled like a thunderstorm. Four was the sea coming in along the shore, it was a ship sailing, it was blue and white and stood on its one leg.

The numbers said: Leave us be! Be quiet! Don't touch! They kept themselves apart, like little wicked soldiers in a castle. The teacher held her worksheets up in class and said, Is this the work a grade one girl should be doing? Saffi had to cover her ears and sing to herself about the Pied Piper, how he made the rats skip after him out of town and then the children followed and the town got dark and the parents wrung their hands and lamented, Oh, what have we done?

When Aunt Loretta finished the housework she called Saffi inside and read her a story about a turtledove.

"I know what that is," Saffi said. "I seen a turtledove in the cellar at Arthur Daisy's house."

Aunt Loretta said she must have seen some other kind of bird. "All we have around here is pigeons," she said. "You know what a pigeon looks like, don't you? And it's *I saw*, not *I seen*."

"It looked like a boy," Saffi said. "It had white feathers on its head. It sang like this: *cheep, cheep, cheep*."

"Oh, Saffi," her aunt said. "You are a funny little thing."

Outside her house the road was all churned up where her daddy parked his logging truck when he got home. Sometimes he'd swing her up into the cab and she'd sit behind the steering wheel and he'd get her to pretend she was the driver, telling her, "Start the engine, Saffi, or we'll still be sitting here when those logs sprout a whole new set of roots and branches." He made engine noises like a growling cat and she pretended to turn the wheel and he gave directions. "Turn left," he'd say. "Gear down for the hill, now shift into third, that's the way." It was hot in the truck and there was a sour smell of her daddy's sweaty work shirt, the smell of stale thermos coffee and engine oil, the beer her daddy drank. Her daddy always said he was a hard-working, hard-drinking man and people could take him or leave him. Leave him, was his preference. He liked a quiet life. He liked his home and when he got home he deserved a beer, didn't he? "Yes," said Saffi. "Yes, sir, you do."

"Who are you?" her daddy said. "Are you daddy's favourite girl?"

Her daddy. Danny Shaughnessy. He was away in the woods for days at a time, then he'd be home, he'd come into the kitchen, where Saffi was standing on a kitchen chair at the counter, helping Aunt Loretta coat chicken pieces with flour or peel potatoes, little tasks her aunt allotted her to fill in the last hour or so until her mother returned. Her daddy would go straight to the fridge for a beer and sometimes he gave Saffi a taste, the beer making her gag and trickling down her chin and her daddy laughed and kissed it away. Her aunt told him to leave her alone. He said Saffi was his kid, wasn't she? He didn't have to leave his own kid alone, did he? Aunt Loretta said he could at least take off his work boots and wash his hands.

"Don't you have a kitchen of your own to go to?" he'd say. "Isn't it time you got back to good old Vernon, Loretta?"

They fought like kids, the way kids at school went at each other, hands on their hips, faces thrust forward, then they agreed to an armistice and sat at the kitchen table and had a glass of beer together, Saffi with them, and her daddy praised her, saying what a doll she was, a real little lady. On the drive down from Campbell River, he said, he'd heard on the radio a boy was missing, ten years old, a slightly built boy, with white-blond hair, last seen wearing shorts, a blue jacket, running shoes. And then, just south of Royston, a boy who answered that description exactly was standing at the side of the highway. He'd blasted the horn at him, because kids never understood, they had no idea how much room a truck like that needed to stop, they'd run out without thinking. More than likely it was some other kid, but what if it was this Eugene Dexter and he'd just driven on by?

He had another beer. He talked about joining the search party, if they needed more volunteers. He had a sense for these things, he said, a kind of infallible sixth sense, which was why he never got lost in the woods or took a wrong turn driving the truck. He stood up and stretched his arms and said he was going to have a shower. What time was supper going to be, he wanted to know, and Aunt Loretta said it would be when it was ready and not a minute sooner.

"Daddy's girl!" her daddy said, sweeping Saffi off her feet, holding her high above his head, shaking her as if she were a cloth doll, her hair flopping in her eyes, and she laughed so hard she thought her sides would split open and the stuffing would fall out. I'll knock the stuffing out of you, her daddy said when he was angry. But he was teasing. He was never angry with her. She was his girl. He tossed her in the air and caught her safely, every time. His fingers dug hard into her ribs and she couldn't get a breath.

"Can't you see she's had enough?" her aunt said.

If she wasn't laughing so hard, if her daddy wasn't laughing and cursing Aunt Loretta, telling her she was a tight-assed old broad, she could tell him she had this bad secret in her head that hurt like blisters from a stinging nettle. In Arthur Daisy's cellar there was a bird-boy, a turtledove, its head tucked beneath its wing.

It seemed to her a line divided her yard from Arthur Daisy's yard. Even after all these years she saw this line as a real thing, like a skipping rope or a length of clothesline or a whip, taut, then slack, then pulled tight again until it sang like a banjo string and nearly snapped in two. The line or the rope or whatever it was separated the dangerous elements, fire and air, from the more tolerable elements of earth and water. That was how she pictured it. She crept into Arthur Daisy's yard, holding her breath, mousey small, so small and quick no one could catch her. She pressed her hands to the window. She had to see if the bird-boy was still there, perched on his roost. He was. He scared her to death. His skull was luminous and frail as an egg, yet he seemed strong to her, his gaze cold, not beseeching but full of strength, as if nothing could hurt him. His eyes were dark, like a bird's eyes. What did he eat? Where did he sleep? She called to him, whistling a tune she'd made up. She told him not to be afraid. She cupped a black and yellow caterpillar in her hand. It was so small she felt her heart curl around it. She pictured the hawthorn tree near the river, light spilling in tatters through the leaves, the sun caught in its branches. She saw the boy's jacket hanging there still, as if no one cared enough to take it home.

She held the caterpillar up to the window, saying, look at this, look at this.

All around there was fire and air, scorching her hair and clothes, leaving her weak and sick and shaking with a chill, so that her mother would have to put her to bed and take her temperature and fuss over her and say, What have you done to yourself, Saffi? She put a cold cloth on Saffi's forehead and called her dumpling pie and gave her half a baby Aspirin and a little ginger ale to swallow it with.

What did Saffi see? She saw Arthur Daisy in his garden, snipping at blood-red roses and sprays of spirea, telling Saffi he was on his way to visit the municipal cemetery to put flowers on his mother's grave. His dear old mother, who'd passed away twenty years ago this month, almost to the day, dead of a wasting disease, did Saffi know what that meant? It ate her body up, her skin, her flesh, and she never was a fleshy person. She shrivelled up to the size of an old lima bean, a dried pea. She'd scare the liver out of you, he said, and that's a fact. That was what happened when you got to be the age he was, he told Saffi. You ended up having to visit the dear departed on a regular basis. He placed his scissors and cut flowers on the ground.

"What's wrong with you?" he said. "Cat got your tongue, little girl?" He bent over, his hands on his knees. He looked at her. He looked into her eyes and she knew he saw everything in her head; he knew how scared she was.

"Well, well," he said, straightening up and brushing a leaf off his sleeve. "Isn't Saffi a funny little monkey?" he said.

Before she could do a thing — run, or squirm away — he'd reached out and pinched her arm just above her elbow. It burned like a hornet's sting. "There, now," said Arthur Daisy, turning his face away. He picked up his flowers. He pocketed his scissors. Don't think anything, she told herself. Behind her in the house there was the bird-boy crouched in the cellar, eating crumbs from the palm of his hand. She saw him like that in her dreams. She couldn't get rid of him.

Sleep: what was *sleep*? Saffi's mother complained to Saffi that never before in her life had she suffered from insomnia, normally she didn't even dream, and now she was lucky if she got two or three hours of decent sleep a night. It could be the heat, she said. Or it could be that her head was crackling with the sound of voices, her own voice repeating endlessly, *Number, please,* and *One moment, please, while your call is completed,* and then the voices of strangers, people to whom she'd never in this life be able to attach a face or name. She was in her bedroom, the blind pulled down against the evening sun. Saffi stood beside her mother's dressing table, watching her take off her pearl earrings and put them away in a jeweller's box. Her mother pressed her hands to her head. She wasn't used to working, she said; her nerves were shot. She'd lie awake until dawn, her temples throbbing, and a feeling of unbearable sadness, of grief, would descend on her. It haunted her all day. She hated this summer, it was unlucky; it was a trial to her and everyone else.

The real reason she couldn't sleep, she said, was that she worried about life passing her by, about not getting the things she'd set her heart on, like a nicer house, with three bedrooms, in case she and Danny decided to have more kids, which they might, a little brother or sister for Saffi, or maybe one of each. Wouldn't that be fun? she said, picking up her comb and tugging it painfully through the snarls in Saffi's hair. In the mirror her eyes were resolute and bright, the skin around her mouth taut and pale.

Aunt Loretta always said that as far as babies went, it was her turn next. Who could doubt her? At her house she had a nursery prepared, the walls papered with kittens tangled up in balls of yarn. There were drawers full of handmade baby clothes and a bassinet with a silk coverlet and when Saffi visited she was allowed to lay her doll in it. Aunt Loretta patted the doll's tummy and said, What a fine baby you have there, and for a moment it truly did seem there was a real baby asleep in the bassinet, snoring and fat as a little cabbage.

On the drive home, Saffi's mother would say what a shame, what a shame, but not everyone could have they wanted. She shifted gears with a brisk movement of her wrist. "You can have a perfectly fulfilled life without children, they say. Sometimes I almost wish ..." She glanced at herself in the rear-view mirror, running a finger along the edge of her lip. "Well," she said. "I wish Loretta luck, that's all." Saffi understood that her mother didn't want Aunt Loretta to have a baby or anything else; she was afraid Aunt Loretta would use up all the available good luck, the small quantity of it there was in this world, thus stealing something irreplaceable from Saffi's mother. But knowing this didn't make Saffi love her mother less. If anything, it made her love her more, but from a little further off, like the time her daddy took her to watch Uncle Vernon's team playing baseball and they sat so high up in the bleachers her daddy said they needed high-powered binoculars to figure out who in the hell was on the pitcher's mound.

"You can make your life turn out any way you want," Saffi's mother said. "You can realize your dreams through persistence and hard work combined with just a smidgeon of good fortune. Just a smidgeon. That's all I ask."

She drove so fast, barely slowing at stop signs, that a police ghost car pulled her over and the officer gave her a ticket and Saffi's mother said, "Not again!" Then she told the police officer he had such a nice smile it was almost worth it. Son of a bitch, she muttered, letting the ticket fall to the floor of the car, where it got ripped in half when Saffi trod on it getting out. She knew she should have talked to the police officer. He was right there beside her mother's car. She could have said, Wait, I know where he is, I know where he's hiding, please listen, but she'd remained in her seat, glued to the upholstery, the heat making her sweaty and numb. She hated herself; stupid, stupid Saffi, what's the matter, *cat got your tongue?*

"We are all autonomous beings," her mother said, her hands on the steering wheel. "We all have free will. It's just a matter of getting a few lucky breaks, that's all."

Within a very few years, as it turned out, Aunt Loretta and Uncle Vernon were the parents of twin boys, and then less than two years later they had a baby girl, so Saffi had three cousins to love and help care for, but she never did get the brother or sister her mother had promised her. Life didn't work out as expected, not then, or, it seemed, at any other time. In 1968, when Saffi was eleven, her father was forced to quit work after developing chronic lower back pain, diagnosed variously as a herniated disc, sciatica, an acute inflammation at the juncture of the sacrum and the iliac, perhaps treatable with cortisone injections, perhaps not. Her father said it was all the same to him, he was fed up with the whole deal. He stayed at home, he watched TV and stared out the window at the rain, drumming his fingers on the glass, a prisoner, he said. Saffi's mother would come home from work and grab his prescription drugs up off the kitchen table and say in disgust, "Beer and painkillers? Not that I care. You're not a child, Danny Shaughnessy, are you? You can do what you damned well like."

Her father moved out of the house. He stayed at a dubious-looking motel on the island highway and collected sick pay until it ran out, and then he packed up and announced he was moving to Ontario. He said he was no good to anyone and Saffi's mother said she wasn't about to argue the point. His hair was prematurely grey; he walked with the slightest stoop, alarmingly noticeable to Saffi, if not to him. Take me with you, she had pleaded. Things went wrong all around her and she was helpless to prevent it. She wanted a normal, happy life, like other girls her age. Couldn't her daddy see that? She beat her fists against his chest and he caught her hands in his, still muscular, fit in spite of the injury to his back, and he said, "Hold on there, little girl, that's enough of that." Saffi swore she'd never speak to him again if he left and he said, "Well, Sugar, if that's how you feel." But she did speak to him. She kept in touch. Several years later, in Ontario, he got married for a second time, to someone called Liz, and then in the 1980s he went back to school and became a photocopier technician.

"What did you say your job was again?" Saffi would tease him on the phone. "Could you repeat that? Could you just run that by me again?" She made him laugh. He said she must have inherited his sick sense of humour.

"Daddy," she said. "I wish I could see you. I really miss you."

He mumbled something and then recovered and said, in his new brusque yet genial voice, the voice of a man in business, with business contacts and a little windowless office of his own, that she would always be his girl. Of course she would. "I know that," she said. "I know."

But the summer she was seven, a little girl in a sundress, her hair in pigtails, she didn't believe anything would change in her life. She wouldn't allow it. "I am not moving to any new house," she said, kicking at the table legs. She sat there crayoning the pictures in her colouring book black and purple. She gave the sun a mad face. Outside there was Arthur Daisy's house with its dark cellar and a bird-boy trapped in it. He had claws and a head full of feathers. If she stayed close nothing bad would happen to him, nothing bad; he would sleep and wake and sleep again and one day he'd fly up into the air, blinking at the light. Shoo, she'd say to him, and he'd fly off like a ladybug.

July 1964, there were dogs at the old potato farm, straining at their leashes, anxious to be let go, to pick up a scent and run with it along the banks of the Millstone River. Or who knows, maybe the dogs dreamed of steak dinners and only pretended to sniff the ground. In any event, they didn't seem to have much luck tracking anything down.

It was a day of brilliant sun eclipsed at intervals by dark clouds. And there was Arthur Dawsley, a man in his late sixties, a bachelor or perhaps a widower, a man seemingly without family of his own, a volunteer member of the search party, after all, in spite of his age. He was given a clipboard and a pencil and told to keep track of the other volunteers. At the end of the day his shoulders drooped a little with fatigue. He wasn't much help, really, more of a diversion, chatting to the police officers, reminiscing about a time when it was safe to leave your doors unlocked at night, you could forget your wallet in a public place and pick it up later, the bills still folded inside. People said that, they got nostalgic for a vanished code of ethics or morality; wishful thinking, in Arthur Dawsley's opinion. He was a likeable old guy, or maybe not so likeable, maybe more of a nuisance, full of questions and bright ideas, not that they were of any real value.

Not everyone appreciated him. A young cop by the name of Alex Walters gave him a hollow, exasperated stare and considered asking him why he was so darned curious and where he'd been, exactly, on the afternoon young Eugene Dexter was last seen, wearing a blue cotton jacket and carrying two Marvel comics, all of which had been recovered from the bottom of the field. Or were the comics found near the three-speed bicycle, red with gold and black decals, the kind of bicycle Alex Waters dreamed of buying for his own infant son some day? He'd have to check the report again to be sure. Questioning Arthur Dawsley was just a thought that came to him, a result of his increasing sense of fatigue and irritation, more than anything, although for a moment the thought felt right, felt germane, almost woke him up, then got pushed to the back of his mind.

What kind of a boy had he been? What kind of boy, before he was lost? It was said he was in the habit of wandering around on his own, that he had a passion for collecting butterflies and tadpoles, that he'd been a good student who had, at the assembly on the last day of school, received an award for academic achievement and a trophy for sportsmanship, his name inscribed for posterity on a little silver plaque. He was well-liked, mischievous, yet thoughtful, a little withdrawn at times, unexpectedly serious, old for his years, some said. For weeks, for months, there had been posters stapled to telephone poles, pictures of the missing boy, his fair hair sticking up a little in front, a wide smile, his teeth milk white and slightly protuberant, a small dimple at the corner of his mouth. An ordinary boy. His parents' only son. How was it possible he was there one day and gone the next? And how was it possible that not one but two boys had vanished within a few weeks of each other, as if they'd never existed, or as if they had existed merely to be each other's shadow image, a sad confirmation.

There were no answers, it seemed. It was a genuine and terrible mystery that infected the town like a virus and then suddenly cleared up, leaving as an after-effect an epidemic of amnesia. Not even the land appeared to remember: each spring the old potato farm erupted in a vigorous new crop of tufted grasses and coarse-leafed weeds drenched in dew, lopsided with spit-bug saliva. Tiny grey moths and butterflies patterned like curtains rose up in clouds. Birds nested in the trees. Children played there, running through the long grass, switching each other across the shins with willow branches. On the other side of the Millstone River the marsh got set aside as a park and bird sanctuary and Saffi walked there almost every day when her own children were young and even she didn't always remember. The field she glimpsed on the far side of the river did not seem like the same field. That was, it did and did not look the same. For one thing, the town had grown up around it, crowding at its outermost boundaries. Some of the alders and hawthorns near the river had been cut down. But it remained just a field, innocent, mild, apart.

For each separate person the Earth came into being. It began its existence anew and surprised everyone with its beauty. So Saffi believed. The loss of any individual, any single life, must, therefore, dull the perception of beauty. Wasn't that true? Loss was something you fought. But if it happened you got over it. What choice did you have? You recovered and went on. Wasn't that what the therapists meant, when they used the word "healing"? Wasn't that the promise implicit in therapy, and, for that matter, in religion? *And all the fine maidens will not go to clay!*

What did Saffi know? What had she seen and forgotten, or not forgotten, but remembered, shakily, in fragments that, once re-assembled, would make up a picture she could scarcely bear to contemplate? For a time she'd suffered with some kind of anxiety disorder, quite incapacitating and disagreeable. She no longer took medication; she had no need of it. But what a struggle! It was difficult to pinpoint a cause for the spells of depression and exhaustion and what she could only think of as an unnameable dread, a nearly living presence that did, at times, choose to haunt her. She'd gone through a hard time when she was first married, when the children were babies, but she'd recovered, hadn't she? She just didn't have the luxury of understanding every little thing that had happened in her life. How many people did? Memory was so imperfect. The habit of reticence, of keeping secrets, was, on the other hand, easily perfected; it was powerful and compelling, irresistible.

She was a vigilant parent. She couldn't help it. If she lost sight of her kids, even for the briefest time, she felt a bleak, enervating moment of inevitability and it was as if she herself had vanished, as if the world was simply gone, all its substance and splendour disintegrating into nothing. She wouldn't allow it. Just as her Aunt Loretta had taught her to love and respect nature, to study and give names to all things — trees, grasses, wildflowers, all growing things — Saffi passed on to her children what she laughingly called *my arcane secrets*. Because wasn't there something arcane and essentially troubling in wild plants — their brief tenure on Earth, their straggling, indiscriminate growth and contradictory natures, both healing and destructive, the small stink of decay at the heart of each flower like a reproach or accusation?

She taught her children to be observant, to see the wonderful, unexpected architecture of an ant's nest glistening like molten lava in the sun. Listen to the crickets, she said. Look at the mallard ducks, how they swim in pairs, peaceably. Look at the dragonflies, filled with light, primitive, unsteady, like ancient aircraft. Even: Look at this robin's egg, shattered, vacant, useless. Look at this dead raccoon, its paws stiff as hooks. Go ahead, look, she said. It won't hurt you to look.

She had a recurring dream, only it was more the memory of a dream that recurred, rather than the dream itself. In the dream she got up from her bed and went outside. She crawled through the hedge and crouched there in its shelter. She could see Arthur Daisy by his shed, the door swinging open, and inside the shed it seemed there was a greater darkness than the dark of night. There was Arthur Daisy, striking with his shovel at the ground, which had baked hard as clay after a long drought interrupted only by that one downpour the day the search party went out with the dogs and all the other useless things they took, sticks to beat down the grass and maps and walkie-talkie radios. All of them searching in the wrong place. Saffi was the only one who knew. But who would listen to her? *What was true and what was something else, a made-up story?*

It happened on the seventh day of the seventh month; Saffi was seven years old. She saw the sevens in a line, affronted, braced like sailors, their little tongues of flame licking at the air. They linked up and made a barbed-wire fence no one could get through. They made a prison house no one could enter.

A mist was rising over the yard. In the mist was a turtledove. The bird-boy wasn't lost anymore. He wasn't a boy waiting near a river-bank for a shape to appear comic and deceptive and dangerous as a troll. He was indeed a turtledove, soaring higher and higher, giving the night a sort of radiance that came from within, his soul or spirit shining out. In the dream Saffi spoke to herself kindly, saying, Hush, hush, it's all right. It will be all right. And the only sound that came to her from the soundless well of her dream was the ringing of a shovel against the unyielding earth.

HOME SCHOOLING

It BEGAN WITH THREE SISTERS who lived in a cottage beside the sea. Except the cottage wasn't beside the sea, it was some distance away, and it wasn't a cottage, it was an old farmhouse, and the farm was no longer a farm, it was a boarding school. Then something happened, a tragic, unforeseeable accident. One night a boy called Randal walked out of his dormitory and was found some hours later in the salt marsh. He had drowned. Less than three years after it had opened, the school closed. On a cold April day parents began arriving to collect their children. At first they refused to speak to the school's principal, Harold Dorland. Annabel and Sophie saw their father trying to placate the parents. They heard him pleading for understanding, a little consideration, a little time. He was waved angrily away. The parents mentioned their lawyers. They accused Harold of incompetence, misconduct, negligence. Harold reeled. A cold wind stirred the trees; rain began to fall. The parents got in their cars with their children and drove to the wharf, where they caught the ferry back to Vancouver Island. And then the school reverted to a farm on which very little farming ever got done.

Sometimes, in the weeks that followed, Annabel and Sophie looked in the windows of the deserted dormitories, at the cots stripped bare, locker doors hanging open, nothing inside but dust and cobwebs and mouse turds. Annabel missed the children. She missed their laughter, their silly jokes, their earnestness and ineffable patience. Just children, and yet how patient they'd been with Harold's pedagogy, which he insisted wasn't pedagogy, but a flamboyant careless engagement with life's unevenness and unpredictability and wildness. Wildness tamed, that was, lined-up and biddable, waiting for further instruction before ripping itself loose and going on a rampage.

"Everything this family does is doomed," Sophie said. In her opinion, the school would have failed even if Randal hadn't drowned. Anyway, he'd only done it to get Nori's attention and sympathy, she said, and for that she'd never forgive him. Sophie could say anything and get away with it, because she was Sophie, with her precise, delicate beauty and her formidable musical talent. Annabel might at times almost hate her sister, but she also loved her. They were, after all, marooned together on this stupid island with no television or movies and they couldn't afford new clothes and, since they were small, they'd been taught at home by Harold and Nori and had only ever had each other for company. Poor darlings, Sophie liked to say, of her and Annabel. She meant it.

Harold's school was, or had been, called Miramonte. When they first came here Annabel had discovered the name carved into a rock near the front gates. When she'd shown it to Harold, he'd said how interesting: the apartment building where he'd lived in San Jose, the auspicious year he'd met their mother, was called the Miramonte. He'd considered the coincidence a good omen. He'd called to Nori, who had been up near the house hanging laundry out on a clothes-line, to come and see. She'd picked Mika up and walked down the driveway to where Harold and Annabel were standing. "I remember that apartment," she'd said. She'd handed Mika to Harold and had drawn a finger lightly over the carved letters, then wiped her hand on her jeans. "It isn't a name I'd pick," she'd said, her voice cool.

"What would you pick?" Harold had asked. Nori had said she didn't have time to think about it. She'd taken Mika from Harold — Mika was still a baby, less than a year old, when they came to the island — and trudged back up the drive to the waiting basket of cold, wet laundry. Harold had brushed dust and grass seed off the rock. The name shone out at him, a light in darkness, Annabel could see, although in truth the letters were weathered, malformed, with a dark greenish tincture, like verdigris on copper.

Annabelle saw first the woman's hands, bruised and scratched from her work. Then she saw her laced-up shoes, blunt at the toes, with rundown heels and draggled laces. The woman's unruly reddish hair tumbled from under a rain-spotted, wide-brimmed hat. She crouched near the rock. I gave our home this name, she seemed to say. Another time, the woman stood in the field near the forest, not alone, but with a companion. Annabel saw them and they saw her, she knew they did. Their names were Jane and Fredericka. Their story went something like this: in the early 1930s they came to the island and purchased five acres of low-lying land on Mariner Road, where they built a house, the same house Annabel lived in now. Jane, it was said, had been escaping a jealous husband — and a child, according to some versions of the story — and Fredericka, who was called Freddy, had given up a promising career in the civil service to be with Jane. On the island they could walk arm in arm along the beach, go skinny-dipping, hold hands outdoors, run through the grass with their hair streaming in the wind, their faces flushed with exertion and laughter. They could do as they pleased, with no one to give them curious looks, not that they would have cared.

Jane shot wild ducks and quail. Freddy dug clams at low tide and kept chickens and acquired an amphibious car that she navigated across the channel to town when she needed to stock up on supplies. Annabel knew these things about Fredericka and Jane because Patrick had told her. When he was six years old, Jane and Freddy would let him feed their chickens and play with the newborn kittens in a cardboard box on the back porch. They'd invited him to their house and fed him treacly oatmeal cookies that stuck to his teeth. They poured glasses of homemade blackberry cordial, sunlight reflected like clotted cream in its murky depths. Iron pots the size of cauldrons simmering on the stove, a mousetrap in a corner, a Westminster clock that chimed the quarter hours.

Patrick was Annabel's best friend — and more than her friend — but she didn't tell him Jane and Fredericka appeared to her at Miramonte. They belonged to her. If she spoke of them, she was afraid they'd vanish, they'd turn into air. She thought of *Macbeth*: "The earth hath bubbles, as the water has,/And these are of them."

Jane was tall and thin. She wore breeches and a wide-brimmed straw hat to shade her face and went around with a shotgun tucked under her arm. Freddy wore a chambray shirt and a voluminous khaki skirt. Her eyes had a hectic, unfocused lustre; dry leaves were tangled in her lank ropes of hair. At night, when Annabel was on her way to meet Patrick, Freddy and Jane followed her as far as the road.

"We hope you know what you're doing," Freddy said.

"Remember," Jane said, "the joy of love endures but a single moment, while the pain of love lasts a whole life long. That's something to think about, isn't it?"

Nori used to play "Plaisir d'Amour" on the piano. She played it for the boy who'd drowned in the salt marsh. The salt marsh was out of bounds, the only place on the island forbidden to Annabel and Sophie. Until Randal's accident, Harold had believed nothing should be proscribed. Not the dark, cold forests of fir and cedar and hemlock, or the stands of alder and cascara and small-leafed bitter cheery. Not the salt marsh with its weird vegetation: skunk cabbages, bulrushes, rotting trees incubating fleshy, tumour-like funguses with names like Dead Man's Fingers, Witches' Butter, and False Chanterelle. In the spring their inky spores gave the air a baleful hue, along with a faintly noxious chemical odour carried by the wind as far as the house, where it made everyone feel sadder and more on edge than they already were. Her parents were scarcely on speaking terms. Her father did nothing about putting up a secure fence, a requirement, according to the government inspector, if he wanted to reopen the school. Instead, her father sat at his desk in the school staring at nothing. He stayed up late at night going over bank statements. Annabel's mother tried to make one chicken last for three meals. Sophie wrote obsessively in her journal and practised her violin, standing on an overturned washtub in the front yard. Mika sucked her thumb and clung to her mother all day.

What could Annabel do? She had her own life. *Your eyes kissed mine, I saw the love in them shine.*

While her parents and her sisters slept and moonlight sparkled on the sea and bats and nighthawks and owls were on the wing and racoons went waddling down to the beach with their kittenish young, she climbed out of her bedroom window, inched her way along the sloping porch roof and jumped to the ground.

Blue Heron Road cut off from Mariner Road at a sharp angle and then meandered through the trees down to the sea, where an abandoned house stood in a clearing above the beach. This was where Annabel and Patrick met. Tonight, Patrick was late. Annabel waited. She walked around the house and then she pushed open the back door and went inside. It was a plain little house, with four rooms downstairs and four rooms upstairs. The glass was missing in almost all the windows. Wallpaper hung in strips that stirred spookily in the wind. The plaster and lathe walls were stained with water and mould. The linoleum was cracked. In the kitchen the cupboard doors were gone, the hearth tiles ripped up, bricks from the chimney pried from the mortar and left scattered around the floor. Somewhere, something made a hollow, tinny sound. The house breathed in and out, like a living thing. Shadows crept along the walls. Annabel couldn't stay in there alone. She ran back outside and sat on the steps, her heart thudding. She thought, What if, in the dark, Patrick had ridden his ten-speed off the road? What if he'd hit his head on a rock? Or what if he was rowing the skiff around the point and it had capsized? Or say his mother had made him stay at home? What if he'd fallen asleep? He needed more sleep than she did. He could fall asleep anywhere. Not her. She never got tired.

To calm herself she went through the Dewey Decimal Classification System in her head; by the time she got to the 500s — natural sciences and mathematics — Patrick was there. He took her hand and they went into the house. They had this little ritual, walking into each of the rooms. They liked to pick which one they'd sleep in and where they'd put their furniture if they lived here. The truth was, they had slept in nearly all the rooms. It had taken them eight nights to accomplish this.

Annabel took off her clothes, putting them in a little pile on the counter, beside a stained sink with a rusty pump handle to draw water up from the well, but either the well had dried up permanently or the pump didn't work. Patrick pulled his T-shirt over his head. He took off his jeans and socks. He and Annabel put their shoes side by side on the floor. A place for everything, and everything in its place, Patrick said. His skin gleamed like marble in the moonlight. He took Annabel's hand. They climbed the stairs. Sometimes they didn't make it as far as the second floor. Sometimes they got only as far as the landing, where Annabel ordered Patrick to remain perfectly still. She began kissing his face and shoulders and chest. She traced his ribs with her mouth. She pressed her face to his heart and felt the lovely unstoppable beat of it. And then he wrapped his hands in her hair, her long hair, and together, one creature, of one flesh and disposition, they sank to the floor.

They left the house at nearly two in the morning. Patrick wheeled his bike up the lane to the road. Annabel kept looking back at the house, starkly outlined against the starry sky. The house was a small planet with its own field of gravity, its own infallible laws of time and motion. Once they got beyond its reach, things changed. Patrick changed. When he and Annabel were in each other's arms, he'd tell her he was going to buy the house, tear it down and construct a new one in its place. Wherever they went in the world, they'd always find their way home. When they got old, they'd live here happily, with their memories. Annabel believed him. Everything he said seemed possible and sensible. He was nineteen. He was studying to be a scientist, which presented a problem, he said, since science wasn't something he could do on this island. He spoke like this when they were walking away from the house. Buying the house was a crazy dream, he said. He didn't mean to end up like his parents, operating a little marina and general store no one frequented on an island so small it took less than two hours to walk around it at low tide.

When they got to Marina Road, Annabel said, "Don't go." She didn't know if she meant don't go now or don't go ever.

"Annabel, I have to get some sleep," he said. It was either very, very late, or very early, one or the other, he said, and at six in the morning he had to open the gas pumps at the marina.

"But I'll see you tomorrow?"

"I don't know," Patrick said. "I don't think I can get away. Not tomorrow. Maybe not the night after, either."

"What do you mean, you can't get away?" Annabel said.

"You're wearing me out," Patrick said, laughing.

Annabel kissed him and bit lightly at his neck. "See," she said. "You're not worn out, you liar."

"Annabel," he said. "Don't. I've got to go."

"Tomorrow night? Promise?"

"I can't. I can't promise."

"You can," she said. "You have to."

She watched him pedalling down the road until all she could see of him in the moonlight was his hair and his T-shirt. Then he turned a corner and she couldn't see him at all. In the ditches on either side of the road frogs were croaking their sad froggy lament. She walked to Miramonte and detoured over to the schoolhouse. She tried the door, but it was locked, so she sat on the doorstep. She remembered how, when she and Sophie had been the school's first two pupils, the only pupils, Harold would stand in the schoolhouse door and ring a cast-iron bell he'd found at a junk store in Portland, Oregon. Sophie and Annabel had walked out of the house and down the path with their books and pens and gym shoes, as if they were real students going to a real school. It was all pretense and they knew it. They went along with it. Harold taught them mathematics and history and read *Hamlet* to them, and *Macbeth*. He took all the parts. He stormed around, shaking his fist and declaiming. *Out, out, brief candle.* The truth of the world is in poetry, he said. He read to them from William Wordsworth. He assigned essays and put algebra problems up on the chalkboard. While Annabel and Sophie worked, he read Wittgenstein, Rudolph Steiner, A. S. Neil, and John Holt, who, as Harold liked to point out, had also taught fifth grade for a number of years at private schools, just as Harold had.

Annabel had rested her head on her hand and tapped her fingers against her skull. Her skull was a vessel for her brain and her brain was a pale tuber. One day it would send forth its green shoots. Harold provided the sunlight and the nutrients and she was the raw material. She and Sophie both. With their music and drawing, their photographic memories and aptitude for making sense of the obscure and unreasonable, which was not an underutilized gift when you had Harold for a father.

Annabel saw someone running across the grass. For a moment she thought of Jane and Freddy; she thought of the boy who had drowned. In this place a shadow could be anything: a deer, a dog on the loose, an owl, a spirit. But it was Sophie. She was wearing a sweater over her nightgown. She didn't see Annabel. She flew into the night like one of those creatures that belongs to it: a bat, a nightingale, a firefly; not that they had nightingales or fireflies on the island. Sophie ran to the gate and then out to the road, taking the same route Annabel had taken a few hours ago on her way to meet Patrick. The frogs sang. The trees stirred in a light wind. Where was Sophie going? Later, Annabel would think: Why didn't I run after her? Why didn't I catch up to her and make her tell me what she was up to? Instead, she went back to the house and climbed onto the porch roof and into the window. Just before dawn she heard Sophie creeping up the stairs and getting into bed. Later, when Annabel went into the kitchen, Sophie was already at the stove, stirring a pot of oatmeal. Harold was sitting at the table, his head in his hands. Nori was at the counter, sprinkling yeast into water and sifting flour for bread. Mika sat on the floor playing with her doll. Harold rubbed his eyes with the heel of his palms.

"Has anyone seen Patrick lately?" he said.

Annabel saw Sophie flinch. She held the spoon over the stove, oatmeal dripping onto the element. "I saw him at the marina," Sophie said. "I was talking to his mom. Patrick was down on the wharf, talking to a guy on a boat." Her voice was steady. She held her hair back with one hand. "I made too much oatmeal," she said. "I hope people are hungry."

"I miss Patrick," Harold said. "I enjoyed our conversations. He isn't avoiding me, is he, because of what happened? Perhaps he blames me."

"He doesn't blame you," Annabel said. "He's not avoiding you." Not for the reasons you think, anyway, she thought.

"Well, if you happen to see him, invite him over for coffee or something," Harold said. "Tell him I'd like to see him."

"I will," Sophie said. "I will tell him, if I see him."

Annabel and Sophie, seventeen and fifteen years old, stood in front of the old mirror in the upstairs hall. Two Japanese girls who had never seen Japan. Olive skin, finely arched eyebrows, long black hair. They looked like twins; they even had identical shadows beneath their eyes, from lack of sleep. They were fine-boned and slender. Annabel was half an inch taller than Sophie. When they were little, strangers used to stare at them, Nori said. Strangers followed her down the street when she was pushing them in their strollers. Nori was afraid to take her eyes off them, in case they were stolen from her.

Annabel looked more Japanese than Sophie did. Even Nori said so. Annabel resembled her grandfather, the famous orchestra conductor. She wasn't musically gifted, not like her grandfather or Nori and Sophie, but she adored music. She heard music in her head at night, before she slept, and also words, beautiful words she tried to hold onto as they flew past, like bright, errant birds. Annabel drew a comb through Sophie's hair. Then she braided it and wrapped an elastic band around the braid. In the mirror she could see the wall behind her. A ladder-back chair stood beneath a painting of windswept moors in some unknown country. She could see the window she climbed through to get onto the sloped roof over the porch. The window had a cracked pane where, in her haste, she'd struck it with her foot. No one had noticed. Her parents were too worried about other things to worry about her.

Annabel could hear Nori downstairs on the phone, talking to Annabel's grandmother. She was saying it was unlikely the school would reopen in the fall. No, she said, she really didn't know what they were going to do. If she could borrow a small amount of money, just to get them through the next few months, she said. A small amount. Anything would help. "I hate to ask," she said. "You know that. But at this moment, I don't know what else I can do."

Annabel saw Sophie looking at her in the mirror. She gave a small shrug, almost a shiver. When she walked away, over to the window, Annabel had the dizzying sensation she'd peeled away from herself and become two separate individuals. She waited another minute, until her mother had finished on the telephone, and then she went downstairs. Nori was sitting in a rocking chair near the open French doors. Mika was sitting at her feet playing with her cloth doll. Harold was standing with his hand on the doorframe. He was wearing his work clothes, the plaid shirt he put on to do chores. He didn't seem to see Annabel at the foot of the stairs. He must have overheard the telephone call, because he was saying, "How could you ask your mother for money, without discussing it with me first? How do you think I feel, when you go begging to your parents?"

"I was not begging," Nori said.

"Yes, you were. I heard you. You know what your parents think of me. How gratifying for them to have their suspicions confirmed."

"I'm not listening to this," Nori said. "I have better things to do than listen to your paranoia."

"Is that what it is? I'm paranoid?"

"It's just a loan," Nori said. "We need the money. It would help pay for a fence."

If they built the fence, Nori pointed out, their problems would be solved; they could reopen the school. Harold said a chain link fence would be an atrocity. It would make Miramonte look like any institution, any school. He wanted the children to feel as if they were at home, not in jail.

"If the school can't be as I envision it, then there is no school," he said.

"Without the school, how are we going to live?" Nori said. "How are we going to feed our children?"

"I don't have an answer for you," Harold said. "I just need time to think. If you'll just let me think." He pressed his hands to his eyes. Then he turned and went outside.

Nori bowed her head. Her braided hair hung down her back like a rope just barely able to anchor her to earth. She was wearing jeans and one of her hand-knitted Icelandic sweaters. She picked up Mika's doll and gave it a little shake, rearranging its yarn curls. She tied its sash and handed it back to Mika. Annabel went into the kitchen and toasted a slice of bread. While she'd slept, an idea had come to her. She and Patrick could live together while he went to school. She could work and study at the same time. They'd have this simple, uncomplicated life, learning and growing together. She thought of Wittgenstein, one of her father's heroes, who'd given away his inheritance in order to teach at a progressive primary school in Austria. Like Harold, he'd believed in intelligence. Like Harold, he hadn't believed in wealth. But a certain amount of wealth was essential. What could be worse than being poor? All her life so far her family had been poor, or at least they'd never had enough of anything. Her future would be different.

Mika came into the kitchen. She dragged a stool over to the sink and turned on the tap, letting the water trickle into her palm. "What are you doing?" Annabel said. "We have to save water. The well is getting low." She turned off the tap. It dripped into the sink. There were shadows under Mika's eyes, as if she, too, were lying awake at night worrying about money. "Baby bags," Annabel said, running her fingers lightly over Mika's face. She looked like Harold. She had a light scattering of freckles across the bridge of her nose. Her hair was light brown and naturally curly. It needed brushing.

"How about if I make a chocolate cake?" Annabel said. Mika nodded. She hardly ever spoke. She spoke less than Sophie did. Harold said Mika's thoughts were too deep for words. Annabel opened a cupboard door and got out a mixing bowl. She handed a wooden spoon to Mika. "You can stir," she said. What could be more normal than baking a chocolate cake? If she could find the necessary ingredients, everything would turn out all right, not just with the cake, but also with Harold and Nori, with the school, with her and Patrick.

She assembled two cups of unbleached white flour, six brown eggs, a can of powdered cocoa. She used the last of the butter and a full cup of sugar. She mixed powdered milk with water. She looked out the window. Harold was out near the barn, just standing there, his hands in his pockets, scanning the sky as if for signs of inclement weather, ominous clouds, a supplementary inrush of bad luck. But it was a fine, clear day. Here they were, teetering on the absolute edge of disaster, and yet the world was as beautiful as ever, the trees like spires, a few white clouds like silk sails racing across the sun.

Annabel slid two cake pans into the oven. She wiped chocolate batter from Mika's mouth. Nori walked into the kitchen. She looked at the empty egg carton on the counter. "You used up the eggs?" she said. "You used the butter?"

"It's okay," Annabel said. "If the cake turns out, our bad luck will turn to good luck."

"You know that for a fact, do you?" Nori said.

Through the window Annabel could see Harold furiously scything grass beside the footpath to the barn.

"In Japan," Nori said. "Well, let me begin this way. When I was seven years old, my father took me to Japan. My mother stayed at home, in Toronto, because my Japanese grandparents had no interest in meeting my father's Norwegian wife. I missed her. I was lonely and frightened. One day, at dusk, my grandmother gave me a lighted paper lantern. It was August. It was the Festival of Obon. We put my lantern in a river, where it became one of a flotilla of lanterns. My grandmother said the lanterns guided the spirits into their own world, where they'd be happier than if they were lost in our world, hanging around outside the kitchen door, waiting for scraps to eat.

"I got the idea my soul was in the lantern. When I couldn't distinguish my lantern from among all the others, I thought it meant I'd never see my mother again, that one of us was going to vanish, which shows what an odd child I could be, I suppose."

Abruptly Nori picked up a basket of clean laundry and carried it upstairs. Annabel heard her talking to Sophie. She heard Sophie laugh. Mika got down from the kitchen stool and followed her mother. Sophie came downstairs and went outside.

When the cake had finished baking, Annabel put it on the table to cool. Then she picked up her sunhat and went outside, intending to look for Sophie. When she couldn't see her, she kept walking until she got to the north end of the island. On one side of the road, driveways led down through the forest to summer cottages beside the sea. Once, many years ago, a famous Hollywood actress had owned one of these cottages. This, too, was a true story that Patrick told Annabel. His grandmother had been invited to a party at the actress's house. She wasn't his grandmother then, of course. Her name was Ruth, and she'd been scarcely older than Annabel. At the party she'd drunk a lot of whiskey for the first, and probably last, time in her life. She'd passed out on the sofa. The actress had covered her with a satin robe trimmed with downy marabou feathers. The actress, who possessed a heroic capacity for whiskey, was sympathetic. In films, she could still play the ingénue. She looked even younger and more beautiful on celluloid than she did in real life. So the legend went.

The island was full of dead people. Every inch of it, it seemed to Annabel. Harold was always advising her to scrutinize the flora and fauna, and she did; she drew it and diagrammed it right down to the cells, the chloroplasts and the mitochondria and the endoplasmic reticulum, all the complex inner workings, but it was the strangeness of the human landscape that caught her attention. She pictured the actress riding off the ferry in a limousine driven by a chauffeur. The limousine would be loaded down with crates of food, tins of smoked oysters and caviar, suitcases stuffed with the actress's splendid wardrobe. Annabel thought of Jane and Freddy watching from their garden as the limousine raced along Mariner Road, raising a cloud of dust. Perhaps the actress sent them an invitation for dinner. Annabel saw the three women clearly, sitting on a veranda at the cottage, gazing at the sea. It was a calm evening, arbutus trees framing a pale sky, the horizon lightly tinged with pink, the Coast Mountains blue as the sea. Freddy, Jane, and Ruth, who must have been there at the same time, couldn't take their eyes off the actress. They had never seen anyone like her. The actress smiled, perfectly aware of the effect she was having. She was a wayward, selfish creature, with her whiskey, her money, and her men. Everyone coveted her, men and women; she knew it. She lit a cigarette. She hummed along to a record on the gramophone.

Most people love music in one form or another, Nori believed. She was a classical pianist. She loved jazz. She liked rock and roll, and folk songs. She was happiest playing the piano, but she also liked teaching music. Randal had been the most promising pupil she'd ever had. He'd known instinctively that music was another language, an authentic human language: a purer means of communicating what was in the mind and in the heart. Beneath Randal's skinny and often not very clean fingers, thirty-second notes cascaded like icy rain striking glass, a whole note maintained its integrity for the entire length of its being in the world, and then, like the beak of a songbird, closed and was heard no longer. But the vitality and beauty of the music must have weakened Randal. Nori should have known this. She knew he tired easily. He wasn't a strong child. But more than that, the perfection of his playing seemed to frighten him. He would tremble and shut his eyes and sway as if about to topple over. She yearned to place her hand on his forehead, to hold him tight. Instead she said, All right, time to take a break.

Randal was ten years old, but he had seemed younger to Nori. He was a very quiet boy. He found it hard to make friends with the other kids. Every day he begged Nori to phone his mother. "Please," he said, "tell her to come and get me."

Nori phoned Randal's mother and said, "Your son misses you. To be honest, I've never seen such a severe case of homesickness. Perhaps you should come and take him home." Randal's mother was always leaving on a trip — to New York City, to Dallas, to Riyadh. She was an executive with a petroleum importing company. Randal's father was a movie producer. Randal lived with his mother. She said, "The thing is, if I give in, he'll never learn. He has to learn, doesn't he? That's why I sent him to you." She had another, older son, who was, she said, almost ridiculously independent and self-assured.

"I hate to say it," Randal's mother said, "but Randal can be manipulative at times. You have to be firm with him, in my opinion."

Her older son had learned to read the way fish learn to swim, Randal's mother told Nori. Randal could barely read a word.

"Frankly, I don't understand it," his mother kept saying. "Because Randal is a really bright kid. He talked at ten months. He started playing the piano at two years of age. Look at the way he sight-reads music. So why can't he read words?" Harold and Nori were her absolute last hope, she said. That was why Randal couldn't come home. He had to stay where he was and learn how to read, now, before it was too late for him.

For a while Nori slept on a cot in the boys' dormitory, so that she could be near Randal. Before the boys went to sleep she read to them from *Treasure Island* and *The Odyssey* and *The Last of the*

Mohicans. She left a light on at the end of the room where Randal slept. But Randal crept out of bed and came and stood beside Nori's bed. He complained of stomach pains, headache. He shivered convulsively. His hands were like ice. She taught him to knit. She put her arms around him, her hands over his holding the knitting needles. Together, they knitted a scarf. This had started a craze for knitting among the other students. For a while, everyone went around wrapped in scarves of different colours. As they'd hurried down the path from the dormitories to the school, they'd looked to Nori like autumn leaves swept up in a windstorm.

No one at Miramonte was allowed to say anything mean to anyone, but Nori had caught some of the children taunting Randal. They called him a crybaby and a mommy's boy and told him to grow up and act his age. She was furious. She'd said, "What do you mean: act his age? We are all the age we are, no older and no younger. Isn't that so?"

She'd made hot chocolate in blue stoneware mugs for her and Randal. They drank it at the kitchen table, so that Randal couldn't see the piano or start playing scales under the table, on his arm. She told him about her childhood. She told him about the hours she'd had to spend practising. Always other children were outdoors playing. Not her. She'd wanted to be two children: one at the piano doing her Czerny studies, while the other played hopscotch on the street outside. Her parents were strict. Her father was a renowned orchestra conductor. Her mother was an opera singer. Her mother's parents were from Norway. Her father was born in the city of Osaka, the third son of a professor at Kansai University.

Nori told Randal she'd met Harold at the Flint Center for the Performing Arts, in Cupertino, California. Harold had somehow got past the security guards to her dressing room door. He didn't have flowers to give her, or anything. He'd stared at her in a disconcerting manner. One minute he seemed shy, then brash. She didn't know what to make of him. He said he'd been overwhelmed, captivated by her inspired interpretation of Schumann. She'd had the feeling he didn't know all that much about Schumann. Later, when they were seeing more of each other, he'd confessed it was her waist-length black hair and her Nordic blue eyes that had truly enthralled him.

A miracle, she'd said, that you could see the colour of my eyes from where you were seated.

That night she'd worn her favourite dress, burgundy chiffon, with a full skirt, a wide satin sash tied around her eighteen-inch waist. "I was twenty years old, ten years older than you are," she told Randal. She laughed. She said she'd known right away that this man was going to mean something important to her. What she hadn't known was that he was going to change her life irrevocably. She hadn't known she'd have to give up her career completely and move to this isolated island, where, even though the house was practically in a swamp, the well ran dry in the summer.

"How could I have known?" she said to Randal. "No one knows their life in advance. It's the same with music. Even when you've practised a piece a million times and committed it to memory, you can only really only know one note at a time. Your heart has enough room for one note at a time, doesn't it? One note and then another."

Sometimes, when she was at the piano, she believed he was right there beside her, itching to push her hands aside, so he could place his own on the keyboard. "You have a remarkable gift," she had told Randal. "You just need to learn the one thing that really matters, which is how to survive such a gift."

Randal had been a beautiful child. His hair was a rich chestnut brown, his eyes hazel, more green than blue, flecked with gold, long-lashed, dreamy. She'd tried to keep him safe, but she couldn't watch all the children every minute of the day and night, could she? She remembered a thin froth of cocoa and milk on his upper lip. His hands lay motionless on the kitchen table, quiescent, his fingers raw from biting at his nails. He was a skinny, undersized, unhappy boy, but he had also been, Nori now understood, very strong, full of power. When he died he took everything with him: their chance at happiness, their future, their luck.

The first year they lived on the island, Harold had paid Patrick to tutor Annabel and Sophie in chess. Annabel remembered the first day he came to the house. This was in the summer, when Patrick was home from university. When he knocked on the door, she got there ahead of Sophie. She let him in. In the kitchen the three of them sat at the table. Patrick set up the chessboard. His hands trembled slightly.

"Anyone can learn to play chess," he'd said. "But it takes a lot of dedication, more than most people have. You have to block out all distractions and concentrate like crazy on the board. You need an understanding of strategy in order to win. Not many players learn to win with any consistency. Not many get that far."

"What about you, Patrick?" Sophie had said. "Do you win with consistency?"

He'd blushed, tossed his hair out of his eyes. "Yes," he said. "Mostly I do win."

After two weeks of lessons, Sophie said she was going to marry Patrick when she grew up.

"Oh, is that so?" Annabel said coolly. "Patrick doesn't even like you. He thinks you're a stupid little kid. I'm older than you. I'm the one he likes."

"You don't act older, dearest sister. You act like a moron. 'Oh, Patrick, that was my queen. I can't play without my darling queen.'"

"Shut up, shut up," Annabel hissed at her. She pinched Sophie's arm and Sophie yanked at her hair.

Patrick was slender, not tall, with light brown hair and brown eyes. Annabel had written a poem about him, in which she'd talked about his little monkey hands hovering over the chessboard. She'd meant dextrous, judicious, skilled, or something like that. She'd read the poem to Sophie.

"That stinks," Sophie had said. "It has no rhythm. It's sentimental. And monkey hands. What kind of monkey? A howler monkey, or a marmoset? Dead monkey, live monkey? Monkey soup? Monkey brains? I think in a poem you have to be a little more precise than that."

"You don't know anything about poetry," Annabel said. "You have no imagination whatsoever."

Sophie lunged at her. She grabbed the poem and tore it up. "Monkey hands," she sang. "Let me feel your monkey hands on mine, you little ape."

"Go ahead, tear it up," Annabel said. "I memorized it, you little shit."

"You memorized it?" Sophie said. "What a supreme waste of time."

"I hate you," Annabel said.

"I hate you," Sophie said.

Now it seemed to Annabel that she and Sophie had both chosen Patrick. They had identified him as their likeliest means of rescue. Was that true? She didn't know. When she got back from her walk she was tired and hot, but she went straight upstairs to Sophie's bedroom and began looking for her sister's journal. If she couldn't ask Sophie outright, she could perhaps get at the truth by stealth. She pulled open dresser drawers. She looked under the mattress, in the closet. The journal was missing. Sophie must have hidden it outside, in the chicken coop, in the barn, in a hole in the ground. Maybe it was better not to find it. Did Annabel really want to read her sister's private thoughts?

She thought of Sophie running across the field in the dark, a flash of white like a flame or a falling star. She thought of Freddy and Jane and the actress, that vision of two susceptible individuals yearning toward a third. Whenever there were three, one was going to get left out. She, too, seemed to be in a fever of paranoia. Some things you knew before you could possibly know them.

Nori was in the kitchen, cutting the cake Annabel had made. She cut a single slice and placed it carefully on a gold-rimmed china plate. She licked a crumb off her finger. "Too bad we don't have any icing sugar," she said. She garnished the plate with a sprig of cherries from a tree near the barn.

"Come with me," Nori said. Annabel followed her into the living room, where Nori assembled on the old Welsh dresser two candles in brass candlesticks, Mika's wooden boat that had belonged to Nori when Nori was a child, a Japanese doll in an embroidered blue kimono, a battered copy of *The Wind in the Willows*, the plate of chocolate cake, a glass of milk.

Nori gave her handiwork a critical look. "Ideally," she said, "there should be red and white lanterns hanging from the roof of the house and in the trees. And there should be bonfires on the hillsides. In Osaka there were bonfires."

A small fire would do, she said. It would serve to guide lost spirits to the house. Once they got here, the cake would comfort and sustain them.

"Is this about Randal?" Sophie said. She had just come in. Her cheeks were flushed. Her eyes were bright. Annabel kept looking at her.

"It might be," Nori said. "I think it is, yes."

"I didn't know you believed in stuff like this," Sophie said.

"I don't know if I do," Nori said. "Fire for light, food for comfort, toys for — I don't know, for amusement, I guess."

"Well, I have some news," Sophie said. "I have a job."

Even before Sophie spoke, Annabel knew, or believed she did. If she'd found Sophie's journal, this was what she would have learned: Sophie was always ahead of her. Sophie already knew how life worked, where to find the secret doors, what passwords to utter to get what she wanted. Sophie had a job. She danced around the room, her hair flowing around her like a scarf. She said she was starting work at the marina tomorrow. Patrick's mother had hired her. She would wait on tables, wash dishes, scoop ice cream. She'd do everything, pretty much. She would be paid minimum wage, plus tips, she said.

"You can have what I earn," Sophie was saying to Nori. "You can have every single cent I make. It'll help, won't it?"

Before going into the house on the beach, Annabel showed Patrick where to find the Summer Triangle. She started to tell him a tale Nori had told her, about a peasant boy who walked across the River of Heaven to reach his lover, a princess. He and the princess were so in love they neglected their duties, weaving silk into cloth and caring for a herd of cattle. This made God so angry he tore them apart and flung them to opposite ends of the sky. Now every year the peasant boy, in the form of the star Altair, had to retrace his journey across the River of Heaven to find the princess, the bright star Vega. And even then they were allowed only the briefest interlude in which to find happiness.

"Just like us," Annabel said.

"Well, being a star is never easy," said Patrick.

The house smelled to Annabel like an apple slowly rotting from the inside. She and Patrick stood there in the darkness. There was no moon. The stars were shining with such brilliance. Annabel was wearing a long blue skirt and an embroidered blouse, gifts from her grandparents in Toronto. She'd brushed her hair until it gleamed.

"I have an idea, Patrick," she said. "When you go back to school next month, I'll go with you. I'll get a job and you can go to school. We can find somewhere cheap to live. I've thought about everything. I know it will work. I want to be with you."

Patrick was quiet. "Annabel," he said. "I'm nineteen years old. And you're seventeen. What are you talking about?"

She moved away a little. "You think I'm too young?" she said. "After what we've been doing practically every night this summer, now you think I'm too young?"

She had an urge to accuse Patrick, right now, this minute, of seeing Sophie, her younger sister, Sophie. She wanted to tell him that if he dared touch Sophie, she would kill him, not because she was jealous, but because she loved her sister. What was she to do? She loved her sister, but she loved Patrick more. "Why didn't you tell me your mother wanted someone to work at the marina? Why did you let her give the job to Sophie?"

"You're mad because my mother hired Sophie? I didn't know she was going to. Neither did she, I think. Sophie just happened to turn up when my mom was complaining about how she gets tennis elbow from scooping ice cream. She gets eczema from washing dishes. It's not a plot or anything. Anyway, the job would bore you, believe me, Annabel."

"I never get bored," Annabel said. If I got bored, she wanted to say, do you think I'd meet you here in this empty old house night after night? "I really didn't come here to discuss your mother's tennis elbow," she said. "I wanted to know what you think about my plan, us living together, now, this fall."

"I think it's too soon for plans like that, Annabel."

She walked through the kitchen door into what must have been a living room. A family lived here, once. A woman sat by the window, reading a book, or sewing. A man lit a fire in the fireplace. There might have been a radio playing. There might have been a child asleep upstairs. It gave her a strange feeling, to think of normal life going on in a house that was slowly dissolving into the soil, its rotten-apple smell mingling with the salt air. She heard a little cacophony — rustling sounds, rats, maybe, but incessant, like the wind, or grains of sand drifting across the floor. "Listen," she said, holding up a hand.

"What is it?" Patrick said. He was standing in the doorway, as if afraid to get any closer. She went to him, leaned her head against his shoulder. If you leave, I will die, she said, inaudibly. Without you I would be nothing. The words made her feel bereft. She wasn't sure if she'd spoken aloud or not. She didn't even know if she meant what she'd said.

"Did you touch my sister?" she said. She wanted to punch him. "Did you make her fall in love with you?"

"No," Patrick said. "No, I didn't."

"Did you bring her here? Tell me the truth."

"All right, yes, I met Sophie here once or twice. Yes, we talked. It was a game. You know what Sophie's like. She thought it was fun, exciting. I would never hurt Sophie. How could you think I would? Sophie is just a child."

"Sophie is almost exactly the same age I was last summer. You remember last summer, don't you Patrick?" She hit him on the arm.

"Ouch," he said.

"That didn't hurt," she said. "If you think that hurt, you just wait. I'll find out the truth, you know I will. Anyway, why use Sophie's age as an excuse? Why not say what you really mean?"

"Because you're twisting everything I say," Patrick said. "I don't want to fall out with you, Annabel. I don't want to lose you."

"Oh, Patrick," she said wearily. Even in the dark, she saw the truth curled in his eyes like a snail and felt an urge to extract it with an ice pick. It was so cold in the house she could see her breath. She heard waves racing in along the shore. She thought: Imagine the house is a ship at sea, and the wind is singing in the rafters, or the sails. On deck, three passengers: Freddy and Jane and the famous actress, a triad, like the bright stars in the Summer Triangle. Freddy and Jane look just as she imagined they would. They're having a little party, with drinks and trays of delicacies, smoked oysters and caviar. Jane wears a hat that shows off her perfect profile, her aquiline nose, her delicate chin. Freddy sits with her knees apart, her canvas skirt a hammock in which she rests her plump hands. "Let me get this straight, Annabel," Freddy says. "Every night Patrick says he can't see you, Sophie sneaks out at midnight and doesn't return home until dawn."

"Compelling evidence, but circumstantial," says the famous actress.

"Oh, my poor darlings," Jane says. "That's the thing, isn't it? *Chagrin d'amour dure toute la vie.*"

Nori built a small fire on the gravel path in front of the house. She fed it with twigs she'd gathered from under the trees. She threw a dead cedar branch on it. Just a small branch, but it burned quickly. Sparks flew into the air and set new fires in the grass. Nori kept turning around and there was another fire, and another. Flames raced along the ground right up to the porch steps. It happened so quickly, she couldn't do anything. She picked up a stick and prodded at the flames, trying to put the fire out. She saw Mika's shocked face, her wide eyes. "Get out of the way," she shouted at Mika. "Go," she said, giving her a little push. She ran into the house and coaxed a trickle of water from the tap into a glass, then ran outside to throw the water on the flames. What was she doing? How could she extinguish the fires with half a glass of water?

Sophie and Annabel were running around with buckets. Annabel said they should take water buckets to the salt marsh. Sophie said they should smother the fire with blankets.

"Quiet," Nori said. "Stop running around. Let me think." Clearly she wasn't using her head. She tried to remember her original intention. She remembered that distant August night, when her grandmother had taken her to put a lighted candle in a river that resembled the Milky Way, all those fallen stars. She'd wanted to summon a feeling of reverence, the same childish wonder and fear she had felt then. Instead, here was this ridiculous out-of-control fire mounting the steps of the house like an automated toy.

She almost laughed when she saw Harold's face as he drove up to the house in the truck. He leaped out and ran to the side of the house, where the garden hose was lying on the ground.

"There isn't enough water," Nori called.

Harold threw the hose down. He ran over to the shed and got a shovel. He shovelled dirt onto the flames. "I presume it wasn't your intention to burn down our home?" he said.

"No, no," she said. "It was supposed to be just a little fire." She measured a tiny space with her fingers. She and Harold stared at each other. The smell of bitter ashes seemed to originate in them, in their hearts. Resentment and discontent left smouldering too long, Nori thought. Yet Harold couldn't keep from smiling. She found this, too, ominous. He took an envelope from his shirt pocket. He waved it in her face. "This," he said, "is a letter from a man in Calgary. He wants a prospectus. He wants to enroll his son and his daughter for the fall term."

"You can't have a school with two pupils," Nori said.

"We would have five pupils. We already have Annabel and Sophie and Mika. It's a start, isn't it?"

Couchin. She remembered: *couchin* was Japanese for paper lantern.

That night in March, nearly twenty years ago, in Cupertino. If Harold had arrived at her second floor dressing room door on any other evening, she might have been impervious to his charms, his good looks. But earlier that day she'd made an important decision. She'd decided she was a good pianist — she had performed Schumann's *Arabesque in C Major, Opus 18* and Schubert's *Wanderer Fantasy* nearly flawlessly that night — but she wasn't good enough. Or she didn't have enough ambition. Did she want to spend her life in hotel rooms, suffering debilitating bouts of nerves before every performance? Did she want to be judged by strangers? Worse, did she want to perform with her parents in the audience, listening and jotting down a list of her mistakes — a messily executed arpeggio, an overly controlled passage that would have benefited from more spontaneity?

That night, for luck, she was wearing a gift from her father, a diamond heart on a platinum chain, and this was the luck it had brought her: this handsome, crazy man who looked at her as if she were a saint, an angel, a rare butterfly he could ensnare, not understanding that the butterfly would die in captivity. She hadn't exactly died, though, had she? In fact, she'd flourished, she had to admit. She'd turned out to be Harold's perfect co-conspirator. She'd agreed to marry him even though she knew he was an underpaid, over-qualified teacher at a private school in San Jose. He was thirty-five; she was twenty. She had never tried very hard to dissuade him from his dreams of having his own school. She'd agreed to home-school their children. She'd agreed to move from San Jose to Berkeley, then to Portland, to Seattle, to Victoria, and then here, to this remote island.

She had loved Randal. She thought of the scarf he'd knitted, its flame-like colours, the way he'd carried it everywhere with him. The scarf was the first thing Harold had found, when he'd gone in search of Randal that terrible morning.

If she could help Randal to find his way home. Come into the house, she wanted to say. Here is some cake. Here is a doll for company, a boat to play with. Here is the piano, waiting for you. Here is the music.

"Mom, what were you doing? You almost burned the house down," Sophie said. She stared at the smouldering ashes on the porch steps. She was shaking. Nori put her arm around her and guided her into the house. "It's okay," she said. "It was just a little wildfire, nothing serious. You'll be fine, Sophie." She went into the house. Even in the kitchen she could smell the smoke. It was bitter, yet strangely bracing. She'd made something happen, and out of that small action, something else would happen. She made tea and served it with the remains of Annabel's chocolate cake. Her plans had gone awry, but still, this was a small celebration, in honour perhaps of some small triumph she couldn't yet identify.

Harold talked about giving the schoolhouse a fresh coat of paint. He intended to caulk the windows and replace the weather-stripping, render everything ship-shape, he said, before September. He'd hired some local people to begin work on the fence. Nori was mending sheets, sewing pillowcases. Two more pupils had regis-tered, and then another two. Annabel and Sophie had swept and dusted in the dormitories. Of course, it was just a beginning. In some ways the school remained a dream, Harold said. He knew that. It was makeshift, provisional, like one of those airy constructs that formed in cumulonimbus clouds just before a thunderstorm: a castle, a sailing ship, an entire continent, and then a moment later there was nothing but sky. He paused. "Well, anyway, we'll hope for the best, and see what transpires," he said.

Annabel sat near the fireplace, across the room from Patrick, listening to him and Harold talking. Her mind wandered, and then she would catch a few words about artificial intelligence, or genetic sequencing, or the merits of homeopathy. At one point Harold got up and threw a few charred sticks of wood on the fire, remnants from Nori's bonfire. Nori had gone upstairs to put Mika to bed and when she came back she went to the piano. It was a Heintzman upright, its walnut case a dusky, bruised-looking purple, like the skin of an Italian plum. Sophie came into the living room in a robe patterned with peonies. She'd washed her hair and wrapped a towel around her head. Her eyes glittered in the firelight. Annabel thought she looked like one of the dolls her grandfather had brought back from Japan for her and Sophie.

"Are you ready?" Nori said. Sophie nodded. She picked up her violin and positioned it beneath her chin. At the piano, Nori flexed her fingers. She let her hands hover above the keys a moment and then allowed them to descend. Patrick leaned forward, entranced, or seemingly so. Being in the same room with Patrick made Annabel feel a little fretful and uneasy and tender, all at the same time. She wanted to go to him and take his hand and kiss him, startle him. She saw that he couldn't quite meet her gaze. He kept sneaking surreptitious looks at Sophie, whose slender form swayed as she tuned her violin.

Annabel looked into the fire for a moment, to recover her composure. When she looked up again, Harold had closed his eyes. His hands were clasped across his chest. He looked old, suddenly, to Annabel, and tired. The music rose and fell. It filled Annabel's heart. Clever Patrick, she thought. In life as in a game of chess he knew better than to betray his thoughts to his opponent. All her pawns lay in a little wounded heap. She wouldn't capitulate. She hadn't lost. She thought of Patrick in this house with Jane and Freddy. They took comfort in the solemn dark-eyed little boy, in his beauty. They brought him kittens and told him stories. They fed him treacle cookies. They loved him just as Nori had loved Randal. Love was necessary to life, but it was rare; it was a rare element, and she didn't know, she hadn't worked out a strategy yet to cope with that fact.

The music was so pure and graceful it hurt Annabel. It made her catch her breath. She couldn't stay in the room any longer. She got up to go into the kitchen, to put the kettle on for tea. At the door, she looked back at her people, her family. For a moment she believed Nori's fire had in fact burned their house to the ground, and they had gathered mistakenly in its luminous afterimage, unable, or unwilling, to see how tenuous their situation was, how fragile and beautiful and transparent they had become.

FAMILY IN BLACK

IN HER BEADED TULLE DRESS, flowers scattered in her hair, Nadia's mother, Sherry, looked like the miller's daughter in *Rumpelstiltskin*, just as she began to believe she really could turn straw into gold. She was dancing with her new husband, Nolan Ganz, an imperious little man who'd made a lot of money as a logging contractor on Vancouver Island. He had deep lines on either side of his mouth and large, heavy-lidded eyes that were watchful without giving anything away. Nadia thought he was very ugly and severe. Yet here he was letting his hand slide down Sherry's back to rest possessively on her hip. He put his mouth close to her ear and said something that made her laugh. Her laughter was high and bright, sharp as a flung sword.

At the reception a man called Maurice danced with Nadia. Maybe he felt sorry for her, sitting alone at the littered banquet table. Or maybe Sherry had asked him to be nice to her shy daughter. When she said she didn't really know how to slow dance, he said she was doing fabulously. His silver hair was long and tied back. His grey eyes were mild and kind and intelligent. One side of his face was badly scarred, and he kept that side turned away. He told her he'd been in a car accident, back in the 1970s, when he was a student at Osgoode Hall. It was his car, he said, but his girlfriend had been driving; luckily, her injuries were minor, but the accident had ended their relationship. For twenty years he was a trial lawyer and that, he said, about summed up his life: socializing with other lawyers, defending some pretty lame-brained mendacious individuals, making money out of it and spending the money. Then he'd quit the law and moved to Victoria, where he'd opened a little bookstore on Fort Street, near Richmond. He'd always had a fondness for books, he said; the way their spines lined up on a shelf; the prickly sense of expectation and dread in just taking one down and opening it. He'd hoped to withdraw from society, like Bartleby, yet he'd ended up in the thick of it. Words on a page were the words of life, after all. And people browsing in a bookstore liked to chat. They liked to get his opinion before making a commitment. Or they used to, he said, back in those halcyon days. Still, he was doing all right.

When the music ended, Nadia walked with Maurice over to a wall of windows that looked out on the beach and the marina, where yachts were tied up for the winter. Berthed, she should say. Nolan Ganz's boat was there. Last summer Sherry had sailed with Nolan to Desolation Sound. This was after she'd left Jonah and Nadia, but it wasn't the first time she'd gone away. In the spring she'd stayed at a hotel for a week, to be alone and think. Nadia had imagined her mother lying on the bed in her room, listening to sad songs, staring up at shadows as lush and dark as birds in their winter plumage. When she came home, she brought the shadows with her. She had seemed to shrink into them, her eyes burning with fervour. She made tea and put out a plate of cookies she'd picked up at her parents' bakery, in the village. She told Nadia and Jonah, in a soft, not unsteady voice, that Nolan would be picking her up in the morning. "Well," she said. "That's about it, I guess." Jonah flinched. He walked out of the room, his shoulders back and his head up, an unnaturally formal posture for Jonah, Nadia had thought. She couldn't bear to see her parents in such pain. Until that moment, she'd thought people reached a certain age and became immutable, like gold or lead. She'd thought they didn't change, but they did.

Maurice was saying he couldn't call himself a friend of the groom, since Nolan didn't have any friends, as such. He had alliances; he had a sphere of influence, like a country on a war footing. "Nadia, I shouldn't be talking to you like this," he said. A waiter came by with a tray of drinks. Maurice took a glass of beer. Nadia helped herself to white wine in a plastic wine glass. The waiter beamed at her. He gave her a look. He was tall and thin, his wrists bony and clean, scoured-looking. His waiter's jacket had a patchy greenish sheen and his tightly curled hair looked wet, as if he'd just emerged from the sea.

"Thanks," she said. He nodded and smiled again. She sipped her wine. She was thinking of possibly getting drunk.

"Nadia," Maurice was saying. "Nadia, the truth is, Nolan and I go back a long way. My sister, Marjory, was married to Nolan — not unhappily, as far as I know. Poor Marjory died a long time ago. She left two young sons, James and Simon. James lives in Australia and Simon lives in Florida, where he's an attorney. He's a good kid. I'm very fond of my nephews." He smiled at Nadia. "After Marjory, there was Eleanor. Nolan was married to Eleanor for four years and then she drowned in a tragic boating accident. It should never have happened. It was a stupid accident. Anyway, then came Samantha. Of course, you know Samantha's daughter, Marni, don't you? The bridesmaids: Nadia and Marni," he said, in an amused tone. "You both look very sweet, by the way, in those Russian princess getups."

He took a quick, nervous step aside, as wedding guests who'd gone out to the deck for some fresh air or a smoke began drifting back in. The disc jockey played Jonah's favourite song, "American Pie." Nadia loved the part about driving the Chevy to the levee, but the levee was dry. It made her think of the island in summer, when the creeks dried up and the mud cracked like an old clay pot and the rocks in the creek beds were bleached white as bone.

She sipped her wine. She felt cold in her silk dress. It had a little chiffon cape trimmed with fake fur that kept slipping off her shoulders.

Sherry came over, a glass of champagne in her hand, and said how pleased she was to see Maurice. "He's family," she said to Nadia, adjusting Nadia's cape. "I mean it," Sherry said. "He really is. You should call him Uncle Maurice. Uncle Maury."

"Oh, please," Maurice said. The unscarred side of his face was flushed. His scars made Nadia think of the curdled foam the sea left on the sand after a storm.

"Darling, have you seen Marni?" Sherry said, shouting to be heard over the music. "We have to find her, *tout suite*, to say good-bye." She smiled at Maurice. "Nolan and I have a plane to catch," she said.

"Well," Maurice said. His expression at that moment made Nadia see him as a trial lawyer, coaxing some witness to sound honest and believable, which no one ever was, she was starting to think. She almost wished she could rest her head on this man Maurice's shoulder. She wished someone would bring her a glass of water. Or anything. A life raft. A new life.

Jonah was waiting for Nadia at the far end of the yacht club's parking lot. He was leaning against his car. At the opposite end of the parking lot Marni's mother, Samantha, was sitting in her car, waiting for Marni.

Sherry hugged Nadia and kissed her. She said, "Imagine me, in Paris." She promised to bring Nadia something back. And Marni, too, of course, she said. She put her gloved hands on Marni's shoulders and drew her close and thanked her for being such a beautiful bridesmaid. With a small smile Marni stepped out of Sherry's grasp. Her hair was a dark tangle around her pale face. Her bare arms were all gooseflesh. "Marni, where's your coat?" Sherry said.

"I lost it," Marni said.

"What do you mean, you lost it?" Nolan said.

"Someone stole it," Marni said.

"Don't be an idiot," Nolan said. He wanted to go back inside and look for the coat, but Sherry said they didn't have time. "You know what airports are like," she said. She took Nolan's arm. She was wearing a dark blue coat and a fur hat. Nolan wore an overcoat that flapped around his ankles. As Sherry climbed into the waiting limousine, he gave her a slap on the butt.

Nadia glanced over at Maurice. He was standing on the steps of the yacht club, turning his collar up. It was raining and there was a wind. You're doing fabulously, he'd said. Well, he was wrong. She was doing awful. She watched as the limousine drove off. It got smaller and blacker, like a beetle, and then with a roar folded itself into the dusk. Nadia gathered up her skirt and ran over to Jonah. They got into the car. Jonah said, well, how was it, and she said fine. She could see he was upset. Last week he'd told her he'd rather die than see this day. Then he said, Don't listen to me, Nadia.

I shouldn't talk to you like this, Maurice had said, minutes ago. Did they think she cared to listen? She didn't. She'd had champagne and wine and way too much tiramisu; her head ached, she felt woozy, numb. She wasn't drunk, though. She couldn't even get that right, it seemed. In the car she fell asleep and when she woke they were already at the ferry terminal, rain pounding on the car, and Jonah was paying for their tickets.

Jonah was a wood carver and an artist. He'd built their house the year Nadia was born. It was a small house. It was halfway up a mountain and looked out over pastures and forests and, in the distance, the Strait of Georgia. The house had arched doorways and little clerestory windows — as Jonah called them — that let in sunlight and the shadows of trees. The walls were white; the ceilings were pine boards. The floors were wide fir planks. A woodstove stood on a raised brick hearth, its chimney poking up through the roof. Over the years Jonah had added his carvings to the doors and cupboards and the backs of chairs. Scenes of deer and fawns, and spotted frogs, bug-eyed frolicsome rabbits, blackberry vines, Scotch thistles, fir trees with ponderous branches, stars that seemed to shine like lamps. Nadia liked to trace over the carvings with her fingers. The wood was cool and smooth as stone. When a winter storm knocked out the power and the room was lit with candles, the images came to life. In these carvings, every single thing was happy. It was like living inside someone else's dream. Jonah's dream, quirky and childlike, irrepressible.

She dusted the carvings with a damp cloth. She got at the corners and little hollows where the dust collected. Sherry used to do this. Sherry was everywhere and nowhere in the house. Nadia would think she saw her in a corner of a room. She would hear her walking up the gravel path outside. She would think she heard her at the door. It never was Sherry, though. It was just her memory of Sherry.

Nadia went over the carvings again with a clean, dry cloth. It took her a long time and made her shoulders ache. It was like a ceremony, her way of saying she'd stay here, she'd be on Jonah's side. This would be the home she'd come back to, whenever she went away. She loved her mother and she would forgive her, a little at a time, as much as she could manage.

She remembered the morning of Sherry's wedding day, how she'd found her way through the house, down the long halls, past closed doors, to the kitchen. Nolan Ganz had been sitting at the breakfast table. When Nadia walked in, Nolan had rustled his newspaper impatiently. Sherry had refilled his coffee cup, her hand on his shoulder. The fridge had been full of wedding bouquets that gave off a dank syrupy fragrance every time someone opened the door for the milk. Nadia had tried to eat a piece of toast. She had tried to drink the coffee Sherry poured for her. Marni had scraped her chair noisily across the slate tiles so that she could sit near the window and yank a comb through her freshly washed hair. When Sherry had spoken to her, Marni had responded with a blank stare that had made Nadia angry. As for Nadia, Marni had acted as if she were a bug on the floor. She hadn't even glanced at Nadia when they walked together down the church aisle in their matching Russian princess dresses, as Maurice had called them. He, at least, had been kind. But how kind was it, really, to give her a rundown of the bridegroom's previous brides, two of whom were dead?

Nadia had repeated Maurice's story to Jonah and he'd said Nolan Ganz's personal mythology was of no interest to him whatsoever. Nolan was a scoundrel, Jonah said, but he wasn't going to fall into the trap of hating him. Anger just rebounded, in the end, he said, and smacked you in the heart.

"We'll do fine," he said. "We'll adapt." He said this to cheer himself up, Nadia thought. She worried about him. Jonah the bone rack, subsisting on black coffee and raw nuts and dried fruit he took to his workshop in a bowl and ate while he painted or carved. He'd grown a beard as blond and ratty-looking as his hair. He bought a five-year-old Volkswagen Cabrio, parked his pickup behind the workshop, and drove around the island in his new car with the top down on the coldest days, a Norwegian-knit toque on his head. He picked Nadia up after school so she didn't have to wait for the bus. In the village they shopped for fruit and vegetables, bread and cheese. They went to the library, where Nadia did her homework while Jonah read newspapers and chatted with the new library clerk, Laurel, who wore sweaters that looked just like Jonah's toque.

When she revealed she'd knitted his toque, which he'd bought at a craft co-op a few doors down from the library, he acted like a miracle had occurred. "You're kidding," he said. "That's amazing. How's that for synchronicity?" He kept touching his toque. Nadia wanted to walk out, but how could she leave Jonah alone with Laurel, who couldn't take her eyes off him. She waived his fines. She handed him his books in both her hands. "What's up with her?" Nadia asked when they got outside. "Not a thing, as far as I know," Jonah said cheerfully.

They went to a café on the waterfront, close enough to a shipwright's that the smell of varnish and copper sulphate paint seriously infiltrated the smell of pizza and hamburgers. Jonah and Nadia sat near a window that looked out at the street and the pool hall. Above the pool hall there was an apartment where Jonah and Sherry had lived when they were first married. When they were young and happy, Jonah said. Nadia knew what would come next: Jonah's story of how he and Sherry had met when they were only sixteen years old, yet they'd known at once there'd never be anyone else for either of them. A moment like that was a contract, a covenant, Jonah said. It was something to be honoured. Even at sixteen he'd known that much.

He took off his toque and raked his fingers through his hair. He stirred his coffee. Island kids were wild, he said. At least, when he was a kid they were. He and Sherry were surely the wildest, in their day. They drove at insane speeds on the narrow island roads and hiked up Cufra Mountain, the only real mountain on the island, to spend the night in the woods. They'd drink and smoke dope — not that he was necessarily advocating dope — and stare in rapture at the stars. He'd hide behind a tree and leap out yodelling like a fool and Sherry would pretend to be scared, but she wasn't, she'd known it was him. Their friends called them the golden couple. They got married the year after high school, in Jonah's parents' backyard, cherry blossoms drifting onto the grass, both of them in white, equally tall and blond and righteous. What tender idiots, he had to say.

He said he wanted Nadia to know he'd always be there for her. Nothing had changed, as far as that went. However, he had to be realistic. As if he didn't have enough work, he'd just taken on a commission for double entry doors for a vacation home a Microsoft engineer in Seattle was having built on the island. The doors were a massive undertaking, a good six months' worth of work. One thing, a project like that gave him plenty of time to think, which allowed an interesting retrograde view of every mistake he'd ever made, every wrong turn and ill-considered action. And there were so many.

"Don't be like me," he said to Nadia.

"I'll try," she said, but he didn't get the irony.

The café was warm. People were talking, a juke box was playing, dishes clattering. There was the hollow thunk of waves against the building's foundation. She felt happy, spooning up her soup, ripping little pieces off her bread roll. She didn't want to leave. When she and Jonah got outside, it was dark. The library was closed. Music was blasting out of the pool hall. Blinds were pulled down over the windows of the rooms where Jonah and Sherry had once lived. The air was damp, the streetlights haloed in mist. She loved the smell of the sea. She loved the island in darkness, stars burning coldly above the sleeping forests. Or in rain; she loved it then, too.

On the way home, Nadia imagined Sherry would be waiting in the house. She'd be curled up in a chair near the woodstove. When she heard the car, she'd run to meet Nadia and Jonah at the door. Nadia always imagined this, but it never happened. When they got home the house was cold and dark and empty. She had to make herself walk in. She put the groceries away. Jonah threw himself in a chair and stared defiantly at his reflection in the window.

"Here's what I hate," he said. "I hate that I'm turning into such a relativist. Nothing seems all that wrong to me anymore. The love of my life marries her own worst enemy and she's happy as a pig in shit, and I think, well, good for her. Good for Sherry. She's got the life she thinks she wants. She's got the six-burner kitchen range, the trips to Europe, the sessions with the Reiki master, her own car. Meanwhile, Nolan Ganz goes on clear-cutting mountain slopes and silting up streams, burning slash, polluting the air for miles around, and I can't condemn him, can I, because I work in wood and the wood comes from somewhere, doesn't it? So, you know. What can you do? Adapt or die. Isn't that how it goes?"

At first, they were outraged, thinking the logging was taking place on their land. Jonah went outside. Nadia went with him. This happened on a morning in April, more than two years ago.

The sun, rising over the Coast Mountains, illuminated the forest, where the underbrush was just leafing out and the trilliums were in bloom. The air smelled of loam and pine needles and diesel fumes. As Nadia stood there with Jonah a Douglas fir fell with a crack like knuckles striking bone. The earth shook. Dust and alder pollen swirled upward in a cloud. Jonah was so pale Nadia thought he was going to pass out. Sherry said he should go back to the house before he made himself ill.

Sherry and Nadia got in the truck. Sherry hesitated a moment before starting the engine. She waved at Jonah before she put the truck in gear, but he didn't see her. He just stood there, braced against the noise, the incursion.

After Sherry dropped Nadia off at school, she drove into the village, to the bakery and coffee shop her parents owned. One of their employees had gone to Mexico for two weeks and Sherry was helping out. Soon she had a regular customer. Every morning at ten a man came in and sat at the same corner table and read the *National Post*. He always ordered coffee and a cinnamon bun, warmed in the microwave. He asked Sherry her name. She hesitated and then told him. He nodded. He took off his glasses. He said his name was Nolan Ganz. Of course Sherry already knew his name, because by this time he was a topic of conversation on the island. People either vilified him for clear-cutting on Cufra Mountain, or praised him for giving a boost to the island's economy. There was no middle ground. Sherry, however, pretended ignorance. She'd asked him if he was visiting the island.

"In a way," he said, folding his newspaper.

Had she lived here long, he asked. She started to say since she was sixteen, then lied and said all her life. She was, she said later, thinking of Jonah.

"All your life?" Nolan Ganz said. "Well, that can't amount to a whole lot of time."

He was nice enough, Sherry said to Nadia and Jonah. He was charming, in a way. Not that she was impressed.

One morning, as she refilled his coffee cup, she pointed out that he was logging right up to her property line, which meant her trees were going to die, too. "A forest is a fragile ecosystem," she told him. He said, thanks, he didn't need a lecture on forestry.

Was he aware, she said, that he'd displaced a population of red-tailed hawks during nesting season? They were flying around her house screeching like lost souls, she said, and it was breaking her heart.

"I don't want you to have a broken heart, Sherry," he said.

"I'm sure you don't," she said, taken aback. He wasn't a young man; she guessed he was close to the same age as her dad, late fifties, early sixties.

"It rains here all the time, Sherry," Nolan Ganz said. "The trees grow like weeds. A forest regenerates in no time. That's why it's called a renewable resource."

"I know what renewable resources are," Sherry said. "And I know what conservation means. I know what respect means, and responsibility."

He had stared at her and she had stared at him.

Sherry acted out this encounter for Nadia and Jonah, in the kitchen, when the logging had finally ceased for the night and it was quiet.

"There I was," she said, "in my jeans and plaid shirt, and there he was, in his fancy suede jacket and leather boots." For Nadia and Jonah she played herself, wagging a finger at her adversary, and she played Nolan Ganz, first mildly diverted and amused and then laughing out loud. Nadia and Jonah watched, mesmerized. Jonah said it was quite a *tableau vivant*, but even then, at that early stage, he'd sounded to Nadia a little dazed and mistrustful.

Sherry brought Nadia a present back from her trip to Paris, a blouse in a sheer, cobwebby fabric that caught at Nadia's fingers. Gingerly she smoothed it over her knees. She and Sherry were sitting on a log on the beach near the ferry dock. Sherry had left her car on the other side and walked over. It was a mild, spring-like day at the end of January. The wind must have been from the west, because the air had that rotten-egg smell from the pulp mill across the water.

Sherry said she wished she could stay longer, but she and Nolan were dining out with friends and Nolan hated to arrive anywhere late. She kept glancing at her watch. "Do you like it?" she said, of the blouse. "I wasn't sure. It's got that dull finish, and with the black, and the little collar, it's kind of sombre. But playful. Do you think?"

"It's great," Nadia said. "I do like it. Thank you so much."

Sherry said Nadia should wear it with the cuffs turned back. She leaned close to show her. "In France," Sherry said, "women have such style. They wear skirts and darling little shoes just to go grocery shopping. Here, everything's two years out of date before it gets to the stores."

They sat with their feet on the pebble beach and watched the tide coming in. Gulls swooped and landed on pilings near the wharf and took off again.

Sherry held tight to Nadia's hand. She asked if Nadia and Jonah were eating properly. Was Nadia doing okay at school? "I've never had to worry about you, Nadia," she said. "You've always been such a sweet, good, self-reliant child."

Nadia would come and stay with her and Nolan, Sherry said; they'd have a fun family time. They'd plan this for the spring, she said, when she and Nolan got back from Cancun, where they were going for a week. Less than a week — five, six days. Sherry didn't especially want to go, not so soon after the European trip. She needed a holiday from holidays. "I should tell you," she said. "Marni is coming with us. You don't mind, do you? There'll be other times. We'll have the whole summer together, won't we?"

Nadia wanted to say, I am not going to fit into your new life like — a pet dog or cat.

She watched the sun slip behind a mountain, a brief flare of gold low in the sky. A cold breath came off the sea. She saw the ferry glide into the bay, its lights rippling on the water. Sherry shot her arm out and looked at her watch. "I have to go," she said. "This has been too short, hasn't it?" She was shivering. They both were. They climbed back up to the road.

Nadia knew none of them was the same, after what had happened, but Sherry seemed the most changed. Her eyes glittered, her hair hung in sleek polished-looking curtains on either side of her face. Nervously she touched her earrings, her hair, as if to reassure herself of her presence here, in this place, at this time. Then she smiled and kissed Nadia. She said, "I miss you, baby. I love you." She walked backwards a few steps, tripped, caught herself, laughed. She turned and walked down to the ferry. Nadia held onto the bag with the blouse in it. Her heart felt pinched and empty and painfully full at the same time.

She flagged down a car that had driven off the ferry. The driver was a neighbour, who said he'd drop her off at her house, no problem. That was how she'd got here in the first place: she'd begged a ride from a kid at school. Jonah didn't have to know. He didn't have to know anything about this meeting between her and Sherry. By the time she got home it was just after five. She and Jonah went to her grandparents' house for dinner and afterwards watched a video and it was, in that way, much like any other day.

When Nadia stayed with Sherry, she slept in the guest room across the hall from Marni's old room, which was filled with her dolls and stuffed toys, her figure skates and sports ribbons. Sometimes Nadia and Marni were there at the same time, sometimes not.

The sun woke Nadia early. It came through the window and heated the dust in the pale blue carpet and made the room smell like Jonah's toque when he'd worn it out in the rain for days. She lay in bed, listening to traffic on the street outside. Her shoes were on the floor in the closet. Her hairbrush and lipstick were on the dressing table. Yet she felt like a guest in the house. When she woke up, she had to take a moment to orient herself.

She heard someone walk past in the hall. Sherry, talking quietly to Nolan. Then their voices faded away. At last she got up, pulled on jeans and a T-shirt, and went into the hall. She opened a door by mistake, or perhaps not by mistake, but because she wanted to know what was in there. There was a big desk and an armchair with a reading light behind it and a bookcase and two filing cabinets. On the wall over the desk there was a portrait of a woman in a frothy sea-green gown that left her shoulders bare. Her pale gold hair was a mass of carelessly upswept curls. Her hands were loosely clasped in her lap. Her rings sparkled. The portrait was in a frame that was a darker gold than the woman's hair. The drawer pulls on the desk and the oak filing cabinets were gold; sunlight pooled on the wood floor, which had the kind of shiny plastic finish Jonah deplored. The overall effect was costly, yet counterfeit and vaguely hostile, in a useless way, like barbed wire around a duck pond. Nadia pulled the door shut with a small click.

She knew the room was Nolan Ganz's study. She knew she wasn't supposed to go in there. She could irritate her stepfather — if that was what he was, she never knew how to think of him — just by keeping the fridge door open too long, or sitting in what would invariably turn out to be his favourite chair. One minute he'd be joking with Sherry and the next he'd be ranting that he wanted a shower and someone had used up all the hot water, or else someone was talking while he tried to watch the news. He never spoke directly to Nadia, apart from asking her what subjects she liked at school and what she planned to do after she graduated. He advised her to make plans and stick to them, rather than letting things happen holus bolus.

With Sherry and Marni he was almost boisterous, comical. He controlled them with the force of his personality, Nadia thought.

She refused to let herself think of Sherry and Nolan in bed, but sometimes these images came into her mind: her mother and him in each other's arms, the things they did. Anyway, she didn't believe her mother loved Nolan Ganz. How could she? Sherry was young and pretty; he was old and ridiculous, with his narrow shoulders and short muscular neck and big, clumsy hands and staring, dark eyes. Sometimes she watched him. He'd be standing in the kitchen or out in the yard, his arms folded over his chest and Nadia would be aware of his strength. His strength was innate, she thought. He didn't have to work at it. If he got near a radio, it would crackle with electricity. He'd walk out of a room and back in, just to demonstrate this phenomenon. When he played tennis with Marni, he played to win. When he went fishing, he caught the biggest, feistiest salmon in the sea. Everything had to be the best, the rarest and most esteemed. He bragged that his son, Simon, was the most promising young attorney in his firm. James was one of the top realtors in Sydney, Australia. You aimed high, he said, you never fell short. He adored Marni. They were like the only father-daughter team on earth, to listen to him. Nolan sent Marni to private school. He wanted her to study medicine. Given the chance, he said, he would have been a surgeon, but, tough luck, he was a moron at science.

But then, he said, he hadn't had the advantage of a good education. Poverty was a crucible, he said, an evolutionary pressure cooker. You lived, you died. He was born just outside of Dresden in 1944. His mother passed away three days after his birth. He never knew his father. Think about it, he said to Marni.

Nadia was sitting across the table from Marni. Sherry kept jumping up to get things from the kitchen. Nolan told her to relax. "Enjoy your dinner," he said. As soon as she sat down he asked if there was, by any chance, any of that peach chutney left. Sherry said she'd take a look. "I could have done that," he called after her.

He wiped his mouth on his napkin. He talked about how, in 1952, an aunt and uncle had sent for him from Canada, where they'd lived since just after the war. They were *Volksdeutsche*, ethnic Germans displaced from their little home in Moravia, which he, of course, had never seen. In fact, he'd never entirely believed he was related to them. They were fair-haired and slight, stooped, anxious, while he was dark and, at least back then, sturdy, full of rude good health, as they used to say. His aunt and uncle sent him to school; he quit in grade ten. Mr. Know-It-All. He went to work in the woods with his uncle. He'd hated working in the bush. He'd hated being out in the wind and rain. The rain really pissed him off. He dreamed of dry clothes, clean, warm socks. He was just a kid, a lonely, angry kid. He wanted to do something with his life, but he didn't know what.

He talked. He buttered a roll.

"It's like I told her," he said. He pointed his knife at Nadia and she straightened in her chair.

"Nadia," he said. "It's like I told Nadia. Don't put off making plans. Get your ducks in a row, I said. I've told you the same thing, Marni, haven't I?"

"I don't know," Marni said. "Get your ducks in a row? Is that what you said?" She laughed. She propped her chin on her hand. Her eyes flickered in Nadia's direction. She had her father's dark, watchful eyes. She'd learned to keep her thoughts to herself, Nadia could tell. In this house, where people played real-life musical chairs and someone was always getting shunted out of the game, it was good to hold back, Nadia thought. It was good to have that reserve. She put a finger lightly, absently, to her lips, took it away.

"If you really want to know," Sherry said, "I'll tell you. Eleanor was out sailing and the boom caught the back of her head. Perhaps she lost consciousness or was simply knocked off balance and somehow slipped into the water."

Eleanor was a good sailor, Sherry said. She knew the sea. Perhaps she'd let her thoughts stray; a minor lapse, yet it had proved catastrophic. Nolan dived in after her, of course. It was dusk; a marine fog was rolling in, erasing landmarks, anything he might have used to orient himself. He stayed in the water, searching, but he started to go hypothermic and had to give up. Eleanor wasn't found for weeks, and then Nolan had to identify the body. There he was, with two young sons who'd lost their mother and their stepmother. He blamed himself, Sherry said. He had a kind of breakdown. Maurice flew out from Toronto to look after the boys. He took care of everything, Sherry said, and Nolan still said he could never repay him.

"At first, to be honest, I thought Maurice hated me," Sherry said. "I thought he wanted to protect Nolan from me. Or to protect Nolan from his own romantic nature or something. Maurice is hard to read. He can be, if he wants, and I think he does. I think he likes being enigmatic. Nolan says so."

In a way, Sherry said, what Nolan and Maurice gave each other was continuity, a sense of family. Maurice was an uncle to Nolan's sons, after all, and family mattered to Nolan. "I know Nolan can be brusque, but at heart he's very kind, very tender." Sherry paused, as if searching for words sufficient to the challenge of describing Nolan Ganz.

She was polishing spoons on a tea towel and handing them to Nadia, who placed them on the table beside the cereal bowls. Sherry had taken some pink and yellow roses out of a vase in the dining room, cut off the stems, and put them in a shallow bowl of water on the breakfast table. She stood back and studied the effect. "It's all new and strange, isn't it?" she said. "To me, it is. You come into someone's life and it's like catching the second act of a play. You pick it up as you go along. Finally, it starts to make sense to you. You hope it does, anyway."

Nadia was thinking of the third act of this hypothetical play. Could Sherry see that far ahead, she wondered? And if she could, would it still make sense to her?

Nadia argued with Sherry over some paltry thing, like Sherry telling her she should change out of her jeans for dinner, as if anyone did that anymore. "Keep you elbows off the table," Sherry would say. "Don't talk with your mouth full." Or she'd say Nadia should be more polite and respectful when speaking to Nolan. "But I never speak to him," Nadia said.

"Yes, I mean that, too," Sherry said. "That's another thing. You're very welcome here, Nadia. We both love having you here. This is your home, too. We're a family, aren't we? You and me and Nolan and Marni."

Sherry looked at Nadia, her eyes brimming. She always asked Nadia how Jonah was doing. Nadia said Jonah was seeing Laurel, from the library, and Sherry said she was pleased to hear it. "She's just a friend," Nadia said. "Jonah goes on hikes with her and sometimes she comes to the house for dinner. It's not serious, or anything." Sherry said, well, she was glad Jonah was getting along okay.

"He misses you a lot," Nadia said.

"Nadia, I miss him, too," Sherry said. "My memories of Jonah are precious to me, of course they are. I'm very fond of Jonah. But I have to tell you, nothing is going to change, Sweetheart. You know that, don't you?"

On the boulevard outside the house there was an immense pine tree that looked to Nadia like it could, if it chose, give anyone passing by a whack on the head with its twisted-up branches, like the tree in the Harry Potter movie, which she and Marni actually sat through at a matinee while Sherry was shopping. She loved this old tree, partly because Nolan Ganz said it got pitch on his driveway and his car's tires picked it up and in the fall its dried-up needles littered the lawn and burned the grass. It was one tree he couldn't cut down, which was why Nadia worshipped it. Its bark was silvery, thick, and spongy as cork. Its shadows were an inky violet, cleansing on the skin as water. What she liked to do was put her hands on a low branch of the tree and let herself slump forward, her spine bowed, weightless, drifting. Her hands picked up a kind of energy the tree had, right at its core, and through her this power got transferred out into the world. Once, she'd been walking back from a swim at the public beach three blocks away, and she saw someone standing under her tree. He wore sunglasses, baggy shorts, a sleeveless T-shirt. He had a handkerchief tied over his hair, gold earrings in his ears: very cool. She thought he glanced at her as she walked past. Later, she wished she'd said something, asked him if he needed directions or anything. She should have; she should have spoken. Once she got inside the yard, the laurel hedge and the old pine tree hid him from her sight; she couldn't tell when or if he left.

Sherry wanted a book on rhododendrons. She and Nadia drove to Maurice's bookstore, which was in a small shopping centre near a busy three-way intersection, not far from the Royal Jubilee Hospital. On one side there was a flower shop and on the other a pharmacy.

Inside the store it was noisy from the traffic and a construction site on the opposite corner. On the counter an electric fan ruffled a pile of papers. A woman stood behind the counter. She was talking on the phone, her back turned to the store, and she didn't look at Sherry and Nadia. Sherry went to find the gardening books and Maurice came from the back of the store and intercepted her. "How good to see you," he said, kissing Sherry on one side of her face and then the other. "And you, Nadia. You've changed. I forget how quickly young people grow up these days."

He found Sherry a book on rhododendrons.

"Does it say anything about black spots on the leaves?" Sherry said. "We've got that, on some of our rhododendrons. I'd hate to see those big old plants dying. If they are dying." She sat in a child's chair at a child's table and opened the book. She slid her bare feet out of her sandals and crossed her ankles. She leaned forward, an elbow on the table. Maurice sat beside her on one of the little chairs.

Nadia browsed through the books. She heard Maurice say that if they hadn't had lunch yet, he'd like to take them to a place he knew, a little Mexican restaurant.

"I'm parked in a fifteen-minute zone," Sherry said.

"We'll take your car," Maurice said. He stood up. He slid the little chair under the little table. He picked up the book Sherry had been looking at and closed it and put it on the counter. He arranged with the clerk, whose name was Shannon, for her to take her lunch break when he got back. He sat in the back of the car, leaning forward, his hand on the driver's seat, directing Sherry. His fingers touched the ends of her hair. Nadia saw this. Only the unscarred side of his face was visible to her. He had put on dark glasses. He wore a white linen suit.

When they got back from the restaurant, Nadia picked up a book and opened it, not with any sense of anticipation and dread, or however Maurice had described it at Sherry's wedding. She flipped through the pages while she waited for Sherry to pay for her book on rhododendrons. "Let me know if you find it helpful," Maurice said as he put the book into a bag. "If not, you can exchange it." Then he said, "What's that you've got there, Nadia?" He came over and took the book from her. He said it was famous and had been made into a movie more than once.

"Excellent summer reading," he said. "Take it. It's on the house. You are a reader, aren't you? A reader who's somehow missed this celebrated novel. Let me know what you think."

Last night I dreamt I went to Manderley again. So began *Rebecca*, the book Maurice had given Nadia. Rebecca had died aboard her sailboat. At least, it had seemed so, but it turned out her husband had murdered her and put her body on the boat, which he then sank. In his haste, however, it seemed he didn't take the boat far enough out to sea to evade detection and eventually he was caught. *When I killed her, she was smiling, still.* Rebecca's husband, Maxim de Winter, confessed to his new wife, the novel's unnamed narrator, that yes, he had murdered Rebecca. He didn't think of himself as a murderer though: he thought he'd been provoked, because Rebecca had been unfaithful to him. In spite of everything, the murder and the fear and the uncertainty, *Rebecca* was a love story. The punishment came in the form of love everlasting.

The book seemed to Nadia a pallid, half-swooning vision of some former time. Yet it was also, she could see, a faint, imperfect echo of Sherry's life here in this house. Was that why Maurice had wanted her to read it? Did he want her to notice the similarities between Rebecca and Eleanor? Did Maurice really believe Nolan had murdered Eleanor and would now do the same to Sherry? Was Nolan capable of murder?

Killing began in the mind and moved outward until it found its object, Nadia thought. The one who killed was the hunter and the other was ... nothing.

Had Maurice moved here because he believed Nolan had been

responsible, in some way, for Eleanor's death? Had he dedicated his life to watching Nolan, so that the same thing didn't happen again?

Nadia had only a few pages left in the book. She took it with her into the kitchen and got an apple out of the fridge and sat at the table. She started to read and she heard Marni at the front door, talking to someone. Marni walked into the kitchen with the guy Nadia had seen on the sidewalk a few days earlier, beneath the big old pine tree.

"This is Gavin," Marni said, very casually.

Nadia smiled at Gavin. He gave her the same high-voltage smile she remembered from the wedding. Could it be? No, it couldn't. Yet it was: Gavin was the waiter from the wedding.

She said, "Were you ... do I know you?" He said, yes, she did know him. "Quite a coincidence, isn't it?"

"Not really," Marni said. "It's not a coincidence at all." She opened a can of pop and handed it to Gavin. Then she opened one for herself. She and Gavin sat down at the table with Nadia. Marni told her how, the day of the wedding, after her dad and Sherry had driven away, she'd gone back into the hall to look for her coat. Gavin had helped her. Of course, the coat wasn't there. She'd known it wouldn't be, some creep had definitely walked off with it. So Gavin had loaned her his jacket.

"Anything to cover up that atrocious dress," Marni said, laughing. She and Gavin had exchanged e-mail addresses and phone numbers. They met when she returned his jacket. After that, they got together whenever they could, either here, in town, or in Vancouver. She hated secrets, she said; she wanted Gavin to meet her dad and Sherry, properly meet them, not like at the wedding.

"Gavin is studying environmental science," Marni said.

"And film animation," Gavin said.

"Yes, but mainly environmental science," Marni said. "Where's Sherry? What are we having for dinner? Are we having a barbecue? It's too hot to eat, anyway, isn't it?"

Marni reached for Nadia's book. She said she'd read *Rebecca* when she was about twelve. She preferred *Jane Eyre*. Weren't they kind of the same book?

"'Reader, I married him,'" she said, scornfully. "That was in *Jane Eyre*, wasn't it? The fire, the maimed hero. It was all kind of the same." She handed the book back. She put her elbows on the table and leaned her face close to Gavin's, their foreheads touching. Nadia saw her tender, complicit smile and looked away. The window was open, but no air came in. The back of her neck prickled. Each day was hotter than the previous one. She thought of how Gavin had appeared to her at the wedding, like a kind of merman: he was in the sea and then he walked out of the sea and became mortal. She liked Gavin. She wished she'd talked to him instead of to Maurice. She could have pretended she'd lost her coat, too.

The summer after she finished school, Nadia worked at her grandparents' bakery. She hoarded the money she earned. She got her driver's licence and sometimes drove Jonah's beloved car over to Sherry's, where she'd stay for a day or two at a time, rarely longer. On the island she got to witness Jonah and Laurel's on-again-off-again romance, while at Sherry's house she had the drama of Marni and Gavin, which had eclipsed the drama of Sherry and Nolan.

One day she arrived at Sherry's just in time for a crisis. Sherry met her at the door and told her Marni had just informed her father she was going with Gavin to Belize, where his ecology class was going to study the environmental effects of logging in protected forest preserves. "Can you imagine how impressed Nolan is?" Sherry said. "Anyway, go ahead. Go on in and join the fray."

In the living room Nolan was sunk into his chair, his hands resting on the arms. He glowered at Nadia and Sherry like a large disgruntled baby. Sherry went over and patted his arm. Gavin was sitting on a hassock, his legs stretched out in front of him, his hands in the pockets of his shorts. Marni sat in a chair behind him, her hand draped over his shoulder. Sherry said she was going to make coffee. Nadia said she'd help. She took a step toward the door. "Stay," Nolan said, snapping his fingers at her. Nadia sat down.

"We can't stay Daddy," Marni said. "Gavin and I have to leave. We're going to a movie."

Nolan thumped his fist on the arm of the chair. He said Marni wasn't going anywhere. She couldn't just walk in here and make a pronouncement like that and then take off. Nor could she go to some foreign country without his permission, for God's sake. There were things to discuss. For one thing, she had her education to think of.

"Oh, Daddy," Marni said. "This will be an education."

"Actually, Mr. Ganz, it's going to be really cool work," Gavin said. "We'll be right up there, in the rainforest, on these canopy walkways strung between the trees, up with the bats and the birds, taking samples."

"Samples of what?" Nolan said.

"I don't know yet. Samples. Leaves and bird droppings and stuff, I guess. Insects." Gavin sat up. He looked uneasily in Nadia's direction, as if for assistance.

"We're going to miss this movie," Marni said. "I have one day in which I can see this movie and I'm going to miss it."

"Shut up," Nolan said. "You're acting like a spoiled brat."

"You made me into one," Marni said.

"That can be changed," Nolan said. "You can try living without my help if you like. You can go and be a hippie with Gavin in the jungle, if that's what you want."

"A hippie?" Marni said. "Oh, Daddy. That's so cute."

"Look at Nadia," Nolan said, waving a hand in her direction. "Nadia doesn't have everything handed to her on a silver plate. She's got a job. She works. She looks after herself. She's a credit to her mother."

"She works for her grandparents," Marni said. "That's not exactly a job."

"Marni, you are not going to Belize," Nolan said. "And that's my last word on the subject."

"I'll be nineteen by then, Daddy," Marni said. "Nineteen-year-olds are fighting in a war at this minute. I can do whatever I want. Why can't you be happy for me? Belize is a beautiful country. Gavin will be doing important research."

"Not another word from you," Nolan said, shaking a finger.

"My mother said I can go," Marni said. "She's given her permission."

"Marni, I'm warning you," Nolan said. He closed his eyes and put his hand to his forehead. Sherry came in with the coffee. Nolan said he'd have coffee later. He needed a breath of fresh air, he said. He stood up and went to the door. He turned and said, "Marni, don't go anywhere. I want you to stay here for supper. I don't want you to leave while you're angry with me. Do you hear me?"

In Gavin's opinion there was no hope. He mentioned this at dinner, in a conversational tone. Nadia had to hand it to him: he seemed perfectly relaxed, while she still felt nervous eating at the same table as her stepfather, invariably dropping her fork on the floor or spilling water on the tablecloth. Tonight they were having lobster and shrimp and salad. Nadia helped herself to some salad and passed the bowl to Nolan. Even with the napkin he'd tucked into his collar bunched up around his neck he managed to look formidable. Nadia was surprised Gavin had the nerve to argue with him. Gavin said scientists knew for sure that if greenhouse gases weren't reduced right now — this year, this decade — the world was doomed. "I can give you stuff to read," he said to Nolan. "It'll really open your eyes. We all have to come together and act now, if we want to avert catastrophe."

"I am not unfamiliar with catastrophe," Nolan said. He asked Sherry to pass him the bread rolls. "Every generation thinks the earth is coming to an end," he said, splitting a roll apart and reaching for the butter dish. "That's the nature of human life. We are born knowing death is inevitable. That's what separates us from the animals."

"This will be a catastrophic event, Mr. Ganz. This will be outside of human history. That's the hard thing to understand, but it's true. There won't be anyone left even to think the word 'catastrophe.'"

"If this is what you sincerely believe, why do you bother to keep breathing?" Nolan said.

"Daddy," Marni said. "Please. We're trying to eat. Don't argue with Gavin right now."

"I'm not arguing," Nolan said. "I would just like Gavin to answer my question."

"Well, Mr. Ganz, the answer is that right now there's still a little time. I guess that's why I keep breathing." Gavin smiled. "I guess I do have a little hope."

Marni leaned her head briefly on Gavin's shoulder. She smiled at Nolan. "That's why we're going to Belize," she said. "We're going to do something while there's still time."

"I would like everyone to please change the subject," Sherry said. "Please. We can talk later. Right now I would like a little more wine, Nolan."

They were in the living room, with all the windows open. They'd tried sitting outside on the patio, but it was a muggy, humid evening and they'd got chased inside by mosquitoes. Nadia sat in a chair in the corner and when Sherry came in she took a chair nearby. Marni and Gavin were on the far side of the room, on the sofa, holding hands.

One night, Nolan was saying, when he was out at his company's operations in the Nitinat Valley, his crew had left him behind. It wasn't intentional, he hastened to add. One of the fallers had injured his hand, not too badly, but they were taking him to a doctor. The rest of the crew had decided to leave a few hours early and go along, while the crummy was there. It was Friday. They were heading into a weekend of warm baths and dry socks. Who could blame them for being in a hurry?

Nolan had driven off in a truck to pick up some equipment, a couple of chainsaws, axes, ropes. Before he went, he mentioned to someone what he was doing and had said he wouldn't be long. Maybe he spoke too casually. Maybe he wasn't clear enough. Whatever, he got several miles down a cut-line when his truck's engine stalled on him. The truck was an International Harvester model, with a six-volt electrical system notorious for failing to start up again if the engine stalled, which it had a tendency to do. It was late October and the nights got cold fast. He thought about walking back, but he was sure his men would have left. He decided he might as well stay with the truck. He had a thermos of coffee and half a sandwich. He was dressed warmly. As night fell, though, it began to snow. He tried the engine. No luck.

Why worry? he thought. He was where he was.

The hours went by slowly. He got out of the truck and stamped his feet, trying to get warm. He walked around in a tight little circle, staying close to the truck. He brushed the snow off his hair and his face. Something, a small sound, alerted him. He looked up and there, not twenty feet away, was a mule deer, a magnificent buck with a full set of antlers. Its eyes glittered. Its ears twitched. Good, he'd thought: a creature to share his lonely vigil. Well, all right, his first thought was, too bad he didn't have his rifle. Not that this would have qualified as hunting: the deer was like a statue. Then he began to think how strange, to see a deer in the night. It began to seem like a bad omen. His situation was kind of grim. He knew that even if he got the truck started, the snow might have made the rudimentary road out impassable. If they sent a search party, would anyone think to look in this spot? He doubted it, at that moment. The effect of the snow falling was hypnotic, mesmerizing.

He was about to clap his hands or shout, to scare the deer away. Then he saw that he and the deer were not alone in the clearing. Two people stood beneath the snowy branches of a Douglas fir. He knew who they were. His mother and father. They were as real as he was. As real as anyone in this room, Nolan said. His mother wore a coat with a velvet collar, a snug waist, a little flared skirt, like this. Nolan spread his hands. His father, now, had a big warm scarf wrapped around his neck. His head was bare. It was night, but Nolan saw the two in colour. His mother's blue velvet collar, her brown gloves. His father's close-cropped brown hair. His heart was full of love for them. You didn't forget, he said. His mother, very polite, asked him how he was, her voice soft and clear. He told her he was doing well. He said he had two little boys. He had a nice home, a business. They stood there, in the winter's cold blue-white. This, he thought, was what he had always dreamed of: to be even for one moment with his parents. When they vanished, as suddenly as they'd appeared, he felt bereft. He watched as the deer picked its way through the snow to the edge of the forest and then bounded into the trees. He went and sat in the truck and after a moment he cranked the ignition and — guess what? — the engine fired up at once. He had known it would. He drove back to the camp without incident. He stumbled into the dark, empty bunkhouse. He lit a kerosene lamp. He ate his one-half of a sandwich and tried to drink the coffee, which had gone cold and tasted disgusting — but he drank it anyway, because, after all, he was alive and he knew who he was. He knew who he was. That was, to him, an amazing thing.

Nadia felt as if she'd been there, too, in the snowy clearing. She suspected that Nolan at least partly intended the story as reprimand to Gavin, an irresistible lesson on how to convey a convincing and authentic message, which was, in this case, that Nolan Ganz understood life better than Gavin did. Gavin looked, for a moment, stunned. Nolan clasped his hands over his midriff and grinned insolently at him. Nadia would have felt sorry for Gavin, if he weren't lounging in that blatant way against Marni's bare legs. She stared at him, secretly. She did like his straight nose, his rather large and stubborn chin, the luxuriance of his hair. Gavin could, she thought, be underestimated.

"Why, Nolan, what a beautiful story," Sherry said. "Is it true?"

"Of course it is," Nolan said. "I honour the truth, Sherry, you know that."

Car lights shone in the window. A car door slammed and a moment later the doorbell rang. No one else got up, so Nadia went into the hall and opened the door. Maurice walked in. He was wearing a white open-necked shirt and beige pants and Birkenstocks.

"I was driving around," he said. "It's too damned hot to do anything else. Do you know how depressing that is, driving around at night alone?"

"Come in," Nadia said, stupidly, because he was already in the hall. "Everyone's in the living room."

He leaned against the far wall, beside a table with a Tiffany lamp on it. He folded his arms. "How is Nadia?" he said.

"I'm fine. Thank you," she said. Maurice had brought the scent of sun-warmed pine needles in with him, from the tree beside the driveway. As she'd opened the door, she'd glimpsed the tree's bulk against the night sky. It seemed to have inched closer, as if drawn to Nolan's voice.

"Nolan was telling us a story," she said to Maurice.

"Well, I am here to rescue you," he said.

The light in the hall was dim, the lamp set low. The hall was wide, almost as large as a room. On the other side of the wall behind Maurice was the room with Eleanor's portrait. In the warm night the gold of her hair and the gold of the frame would pulse weakly, like a decaying element. Nadia had seen a cloud chamber once, on a school field trip. She remembered the delicate tracings of cosmic particles, like a malfunctioning Etch-a-Sketch. Or the mind, the way the mind worked, stray thoughts.

Maurice pushed himself away from the wall. He came over to her. "Nadia, you are lovely," he said. "Already you've attained a very fine control over your life, haven't you? That's not a bad thing." He brushed her face very lightly, very slowly, with the back of his hand. A tremor passed through her. She breathed very quietly. She wanted to touch his scarred face. She wanted to know what the scars felt like, what they would feel like to him. She felt as if something inside him, in his mind, had burned them into his skin.

Marni and Gavin came into the hall. Maurice had moved away from Nadia a second earlier. He went and kissed Marni. He shook hands with Gavin. Marni took a set of keys from a bowl on the hall table, as if plucking a grape. "I'm taking your car, Sherry," she called. "Is that okay?"

Sherry called back. "Drive carefully."

Marni grimaced. She and Gavin left. Nadia noticed they didn't invite her along. She followed Maurice into the living room. He said what an uncomfortably humid night it was and Sherry said, yes, indeed. "August can be like this," she said. Maurice said there would be a storm. Nadia thought perhaps there already had been a storm and this was its aftermath. She thought of the ending of *Rebecca*, the sun rising, the air filled with the bitterest of ashes.

In the morning Nadia went back to the island. She didn't see Sherry and Nolan again until just before classes started in September, after she'd spent a day at the university campus, paying the balance of her housing fees, searching the bookstore for her textbooks. When she got to Sherry and Nolan's, they were in the backyard, where Nolan was cooking salmon steaks on the barbecue. He greeted her affectionately. He even gave her an awkward, moist kiss on the cheek. She kissed the air beside his face. She had brought flowers for Sherry, and Sherry went into the kitchen to put them in water. When she came back to the patio, she told Nadia how nice she looked. Nadia laughed, because they were all wearing black. She was wearing the blouse Sherry had brought her back from France.

Sherry was wearing a black shift. Nolan was wearing a black golf shirt with khaki shorts. How suitable, Nadia thought: the family in black. She thought that she, like Nolan, had at last learned who she was. Not that the knowledge was all that edifying, but still it was there. This was her family. This was one part of it, anyway. Jonah and Laurel. Marjory. Eleanor. Samantha, of course. The sons, James and Simon. A broken, patchily reassembled family in the early years of a century no one had yet learned to trust or had any reason to trust. Gavin was right, Nadia thought. She, too, believed history had moved beyond human control. She hoped not. But everyone she knew agreed something was wrong: the summers too hot, the clouds strange, the sun too intense. She thought of the red-tailed hawks evicted from their forest, their panicked shadows passing over her, as ominous and misplaced as Nolan's deer in the snowy night. It wasn't easy to achieve a balance. She remembered, at the wedding, listening to "American Pie." She remembered the part about music saving the immortal soul. Could it be done, the song had asked.

She thought of Sherry at the wedding in her beautiful dress, flowers in her hair. If only, Nadia thought, it really was possible to spin straw into gold. She would give the gold away. She would dress in black exclusively, as a sign, a sign of her seriousness and devotion to an elusive dream. She'd give everyone gold from a vast, inexhaustible storehouse. She'd do it out of love, like the miller's daughter.

SAND AND FROST

Only once that semester did Lydia feel happy, and that was when it snowed and everything got quiet and acquired a sense of gravitas and beauty that made her think it must have been like this in the nineteenth century or at an enclosed monastery somewhere, where no one spoke or raised their eyes and all thoughts remained secret and hidden. But the snow quickly turned to incessant rain, and many little things began to go wrong. She lost her only pair of gloves. She woke at night, thinking she heard her grandmother's voice. During the day, as well, she heard the same voice, always goading her, telling her: Lydia, this is what happened in our family, we have this shame we can't get rid of. In her direct, bossy tone, she blamed the unspeakable event in their family's past for Lydia's present unhappiness. What can you expect? she said. It was their heritage. It was in their genes. Which Lydia did not, frankly, disbelieve. Something made her different. She was twenty years old. She was the recipient of a small scholarship. She had no friends, apart from Declan, another outcast. The only other people she ever spoke to were her parents, when she called home on Saturday mornings from the pay phone at the end of the hall. They didn't want to hear that she was lonely or hated the food or couldn't concentrate on her work. They said, Ah, student life! Her father said she must refrain from burning her candle at both ends, as Elinor Wylie advised.

You mean Edna St. Vincent Millay, Lydia said.

Oh, my, yes, of course, her father said. St. Vincent Millay it is! Something about oh my friends, oh my foes, and the candle giving a lovely light as it burns. Isn't that it? Lydia, how I envy your supple young mind! Oh, dear, he said, he had a call on the other line, from a parishioner. Take care, my love, he shouted, and then he was gone.

Her father was an Anglican priest. Her mother was a secretary at the same elementary school Lydia had gone to. She sent Lydia parcels of cookies and sweaters she'd knitted in strange nubbly wool. In the communal washroom on the third floor of the residence, girls whose names Lydia didn't know, their shoulders pink and moist from the shower, would pluck at her sleeves and say, Oh, cute sweater, when what they really meant was: That sweater is ugly as hell! In the steamed-up mirror Lydia could see for herself: the sweaters made her breasts look heavy, her waist thick, nothing like as supple as her mind was supposed to be. Even her hands looked pudgy, like her mother's stodgy dumplings in a stew pot. In class she kept her coat on and tucked her hands inside her sleeves. She tried to concentrate on Dr. Julian Schelling's lecture on Matthew Arnold, how the poet had considered the English church a civilizing influence, how he'd insisted the Bible should be approached as if it were an epic poem, full of blood and lust and infamy.

The way Julian pronounced those words — *blood, lust, infamy* — sent a delicious chill down her spine. It seemed he'd discovered, through osmosis or divination, the precise, startling details of her unspeakable family history. But he didn't glance once in her direction. His voice was low, indistinct. Or maybe she just couldn't hear over the grandmother's lament: *We deserved better, Lydia. We deserved to live, all of us.*

After class, she followed Julian as far as the car park. That morning he'd assigned "Stanzas on the Grand Chartreuse," by Matthew Arnold. *Wandering between two worlds, one dead, / The other powerless to be born.* She loved the poem and also the poet — his tender, abstemious mouth and lavish, frizzy sideburns — but mostly she loved the professor, his elegant, fawn-coloured leather jacket, the complicated knotting of his scarf. He set his briefcase down to unlock his car and when he turned to pick it up he must have seen her, but he gave no sign. Long after he'd gone she stood there, watching two black squirrels skittering around in the bushes beside the path. Her breath, visible on the still air, looked like small cartoonish pleas for help.

In December Lydia went home. She took the bus out to Horseshoe Bay, where she walked onto the ferry. There was a storm. The sky was black. A woman with three small children came and sat on the bench facing her. The two smaller children kept crying, or grizzling, as Lydia's grandmother would have said, and their mother, who had long curly hair and very large pale eyes, tried to mollify them with cans of pop and gummy bears. The oldest, a little girl of about five, planted herself in front of Lydia, keeping her balance in spite of the ship's fractiousness. She was wearing patent leather shoes with ankle straps, a short, flared skirt, like a figure skater. She looked like her mother, but with small, shrewd eyes. She began a long unvoiced indictment of Lydia's primary failings, admittedly legion: her introversion, her possessiveness, which concealed a gaping maw of insecurity, her willingness to live exclusively in the milieu of disgruntled dreams. Lydia knew the little girl wasn't real. She was a vision, a device of the gods, put on earth to destroy the last shreds of Lydia's self-esteem.

The ship juddered and veered sideways. Navigation in a storm. What could be more invigorating, more receptive to risk? The little girl showed off for Lydia, standing on one leg, arms out. Lydia prayed for shipwreck. She wanted to grab the little girl's tatty unwashed hair and drag her down with her, down into the cold, uncharted recesses of the Georgia Strait.

In the end the ferry docked safely and Lydia took a taxi to her parents' home, arriving just as the rain let up and a few tinselly winter stars glittered overhead. Her parents were in the living room. On a side table there was an advent wreath, with one candle that had been lit and extinguished. Her father drowsed in his reclining chair, a tattered paperback copy of *Christian Believing* by Hans Küng open on his chest, while Lydia's mother knitted, her feet up on a hassock. The grandmother sat upright, ankles crossed. She was and was not the grandmother who had haunted Lydia's sleep. She got up and took Lydia's hand and said, Darling, darling girl, what a surprise!

Lydia's mother went into the kitchen and made a cold roast beef sandwich with Dijon mustard, a favourite of Lydia's, usually, but she was too wrought up to eat. She put the sandwich in the fridge, beside a triple-layer chocolate cake destined, no doubt, for a church bake sale or a Parish Council meeting. She stuck a finger in the icing and licked it clean, sugar flooding her brain like anaesthesia designed for a low-functioning, panicky lab rat. Her mother, in the living room, was saying things like: But it's the end of the term, she should be studying. I'm going to have a serious little word with her, right now.

Sit down, June, Lydia's father said.

Leave her be, the grandmother said. Just leave the child alone.

The grandmother had fine white hair she combed out and let lie flat against her head. Her bedroom slippers were threaded with gold, like ancient dancing shoes. Her name was Pauline. In the morning she came to Lydia's bedroom door. Since you're here, she said, you might as well get up and make us a cup of tea.

Lydia got up. She got up, but her body remained on the bed, palms open like a mendicant. The trueness of it, the accusatory blankness, the blunt refusal to wish for more, more of everything: poetry, love, a real life. In the kitchen she filled the kettle and put it on the stove. Her parents left for work early, in separate cars. Her father ate breakfast at a café, where, he said, roughly the same people assembled at the same hour, every morning, like an unusually faithful and receptive congregation. Later, these same people made brief, luminous appearances in his sermons, which possessed the easeful veracity of parables: there was a blind man with a small brown dog; there was a retired pilot who'd developed a fear of heights; there was a woman who sang Janis Joplin songs to herself, in a rich and emphatic voice: *the blues ain't nothin' but a good man feelin' bad.* Her father loved the parade of life, the mishmash. Not Lydia. Even around the grandmother she felt shy. She thought regretfully of the campus silent beneath snow, the earth's soft wintry breathing. She thought of Julian. How lonely he'd seemed, and yet how self-sufficient and contained, as if he needed no one.

Her grandmother spread marmalade to the four corners of her toast. She sipped her tea. She said, We will take this one day at a time, Lydia.

How strange, Lydia thought, that each person was made up of innumerable past selves and these selves were hidden and unreachable. She could barely remember being three years old; she had no memory of her own infancy, and the grandmother across the table from her seemed completely unrelated to the grandmother she remembered from her childhood or even from a few years ago.

Somewhere there must exist, still, the Pauline who'd walked innocently toward a house in which a terrible crime had assembled its mysterious, transgressive elements. Pauline's mother and her sister and brother, what remained of them, had been in that house. Her father, the Reverend Elliot Saunders, had one day come home with a gun and had picked them off one by one, and then he'd gone outside and shot himself. When it was finished, no one but Pauline survived.

An old tragedy, but persistent, the sole narrative at the heart of Lydia's family. It made them what they were: good people, meek people.

That day, on her way home from the bank where she worked, Pauline had thought she glimpsed her father up ahead of her on the road. He was there, then he was gone. It was a Wednesday in October, a clear, cold day. She remembered birches ghostly against dark firs, leaves like gold coins strewn across the road. A sense of urgency gripped her and she'd started to run, but she got a stitch in her side and had to slow down. What came next? The truth was, she saw only so much. Outside her house a little knot of people had gathered. They stood around her and wouldn't let her pass. The police constable staggered out of the house and was sick on the ground. He wiped his mouth on his uniform sleeve. He ordered the others to take Pauline home with them and keep her there. Later he'd gone to see her, and had talked to her about what had happened and about how she felt. She'd said, Constable Morgan, I have no idea how I feel. He had smiled and told her to call him Henry. He became a good friend to her, she told Lydia. His sister, Jane, who was a professional photographer, with a studio of her own in Victoria, had been staying with Henry for a few weeks. The two of them had taken Pauline for meals at the hotel dining room. They'd made a trip out to the house for her, and brought back a few things she'd asked for: her sweater, her toothbrush, her mother's Bible.

Lydia remembered her own grandfather saying it could happen in the best of families, the *crime passionnel*, although in fact it didn't, not usually. His advice was: never turn your back on a Saunders. His little joke caused Lydia's parents to recoil. Lydia had recognized her grandfather's audaciousness as a bulwark, a reverse charm. She remembered him clearly: a tall man, gaunt, with unruly silver hair. In the 1940s, he'd studied architecture with Frank Lloyd Wright at Taliesin West, in the Arizona desert, and something of that had stayed with him: an expansiveness, a warmth, a dry humour. When he'd died, after suffering a stroke, his widow had mourned like a vice-regent. She couldn't be left alone; she couldn't sleep. She sold her house in West Vancouver, the handsome, sprawling house with windows but no interior walls, or as few as possible, nothing to impede the line of sight. She'd moved in with Lydia's parents and then pronounced the rectory unliveable, an architectural nightmare with no view, nothing to look out at, unless you counted the asphalt in the church parking lot. She'd found a house more to her taste and had purchased it and turned the title over to Lydia's parents, and that was where they lived.

Lydia had been twelve when her grandfather died. She'd adored him. He'd given her a dollar every time she saw him. He'd told her about working with Frank Lloyd Wright under a canopy of canvas, the desert sun rising in a conflagration, stark shadows of Saguaro cactus like pen strokes on the sand, mountains of folded silk, rose, and coral. One spring he took Pauline on a driving holiday through the American southwest, with a side trip to Scottsdale, Arizona, where he'd introduced her to the famous architect. They'd hit it off at once. They'd talked for hours, although neither was aware of the other's history, the chain of violent death and sudden inexplicable fires, although Frank Lloyd Wright, like one of those bright little desert lizards, had a knack for slithering out from under catastrophe. He was a visionary and a capitalist; he looked at the mountains and stars and did things with them, turned them to account. He didn't let anything interfere with what he wanted out of life. Neither had Pauline. Nor should anyone, Lydia, her grandfather had said, touching a finger lightly to her nose. On Sunday afternoons, he took her to Queen Elizabeth Park and showed her a view of the gardens from a dizzying height, emerald lawns, spires of evergreens, etiolated broad-leafed shrubberies, winding arterial paths, a human world of beauty, harmonious, tamed, and yet still Lydia felt the delicious threat of letting go and falling.

Every day Lydia and her grandmother were alone in Lydia's parents' house on the east coast of Vancouver Island, where the air was fragrant, moist, palpable, somehow, and the mountains of the Coast Range were respectably distant, like a scene in an old travel brochure. In the afternoons Lydia read to the grandmother from a murder mystery, an unsuitable diversion, Lydia would have thought, considering her grandmother's history. And yet she could see how necessary death was to the story; how it moved things forward, how it had to happen the way it did, in ordinary rooms, in landscapes blurred with gentle mists. Without violent death, it seemed, there would be no genuine passion, only ill-tempered, unfulfilled individuals, full of anomie, grating on each other's nerves.

She thought of her Victorian Poets professor, Julian Schelling. There'd been a rumour he'd been married or living with a woman who'd killed herself with sleeping pills and a plastic bag over her head. There were rumours that Dr. Schelling was convinced it had been a case of murder, not suicide, and that someone was out to get him, as well. His paranoia, if that was what it was, had escalated to the point where, when a student gave him a box of chocolates, he'd put it on the floor outside his office and called the police, demanding they send in the bomb squad. Lydia only partly believed this. In her mind she saw Julian clearly. He had a way of tossing his hair and keeping his eyes focussed on the ground, as if crossing an engorged river on a rope. How she'd loved the defiant way he'd read from "The Grande Chartreuse": *Take me, cowled forms, and fence me round / Till I possess my soul again.* She knew she could be the steadfast presence he needed, the ameliorating influence. *Take me, cowled form and fence me round!* she'd wanted to misquote teasingly.

The worst thing — or second worst thing — she'd done was to phone his extension repeatedly, hanging up if he answered in person. On two occasions she'd lingered near his office until he'd emerged and walked past her in his quick, tense way. The moment was full of potential and then it was gone. Then, when she was turning in an assignment, she'd found in his mailbox a list of faculty addresses and home phone numbers. She'd copied Julian's address on a scrap of paper. No one witnessed this. The next day she took a bus out to Jericho Beach and quickly located Dr. Schelling's house, which was old and painted blue, with lots of small, shining windows casting unimpeachable, darting glances up at the sky. She walked around the block and discovered a narrow lane behind his house, with garages, walled gardens, hedges on either side. A small black-and-white cat jumped down from a fence and came and rubbed around her ankles, purring and butting her with its head. A car turned into the lane. She moved aside, but the driver, who she could see was Julian, had to stop for the cat. Here kitty, Lydia coaxed. She pretended the cat belonged to her. Bad cat, she admonished, clapping her hands. Shoo, she said. Shoo. The cat stalked off, its tail held high.

Julian pulled into his driveway. She heard him shutting his car door and running up a flight of stairs and then a house door banged shut. She walked quickly up and down the lane, to calm herself. It was a mild October day, but the lane seemed to have become colder, more arboreal. The trees cast their shade extravagantly on the ground, where it pooled in inky glacial streambeds she could slip into and drown, like Ophelia. She thought of the professor's erstwhile wife or lover. Had she died in this house? Lydia would bet she had. She could feel the death, the cold injudicious engine of its arrival and then the follow-through, the trajectory, which, once set in motion, could not be averted. She could sense the whole event, as if it were just taking place.

She sat on the grass, her back against the fence. She was hungry. She remembered being a child, too engrossed in a game of pretence to make it home in time for dinner and reluctant to get there, anyway, because often at her house there were parishioners or visiting clergy as guests. They had to join hands around the table and say grace all in one voice. Lydia's grandmother refrained from prayer. She inspected her fingernails or picked lint from her clothes, going assiduously after the last speck, then delicately spearing a broccoli floret with her fork, taking her time, taking her time, like someone abstracted by the work of getting over a debilitating, irreproachable malaise.

Lydia heard a door open. She got up and took a look around the fence and saw Julian coming down the stairs of his house carrying a small child in one arm and in the other the kind of bag used for diapers and bottles. She couldn't tell if the child was a boy or a girl. It was dressed in pants and a little hooded jacket. She drew back. Of all the secrets she might have uncovered concerning Julian, the dire and the beautiful, astonishing secrets, this was the one she'd least expected. She felt betrayed, as if she'd been displaced in Julian's affections, even though she knew he had no feelings for her yet. She wanted to shout: A child! A child! Why didn't you tell me!

By the time she got back to the campus, the cafeteria had closed and she had to go to bed hungry. In the morning she woke up hungry and the imposed fast seemed like a deserved penance. She knew she had to stop following Julian. She knew she was being irrational and obsessive. But, if anything, her infatuation deepened. She dreamt of herself and Julian and the child as a small family. She thought of the stories she would read to the child, evenings when the child slept and she and Julian talked quietly and listened to music on a fantastic audio system. The black and white cat would live with them. It would sleep in Lydia's arms.

The oak tree outside her dorm room window misted over and disintegrated. She clutched at her desk to keep from being sucked into the empty space where the tree had stood. She was a vast empty space. She tried to work on an essay, but language was not serving her well; it fled on horseback, galloping off like a band of high-spirited mercenaries who had all the power, all the power and glory, forever.

She met Declan in the line-up at the cafeteria. They sat at the same table and talked about how gross the food was and how not worth it their courses were. Declan was a pale boy with a mass of curly brown hair and a beard that glinted like copper filaments. He touched things and gave off blue sparks. He was nineteen. He wanted to be a filmmaker, but as far as she could see his chief activities consisted of lying around in his room and drinking beer. They both drank a lot of beer. Declan showed her one of his projects: a portfolio of black and white photographs of people standing around on a beach, singly or in groups, dressed in dark flowing garments that contrasted in an interesting way with the grainy drift and sub-sidence of sand. In his photographs, he said, human forms were analogous to celestial bodies in a void, the space between humming with weird energy.

Declan said she made him think of Maria, the real one, the good Maria, in Fritz Lang's *Metropolis*, which was a real trip. That woebegone little bunny face, he said. He pinched her chin. I love that face, he said.

Can you feel that? he said. Can you feel that energy? He brought his hand closer to hers, until their fingers were suggestively entwined. Tell me if you can feel this, he said, pressing her hand firmly to his crotch. How's that for energy? he said, getting a little carried away, snorting with laughter, until, overcome with his own high spirits, he had to release her hand. Lydia said she didn't think they were that kind of friends and Declan hooted and rolled around on the floor. Not *that* kind of friends! he repeated. Jesus, no. Not us!

She smiled tolerantly. Declan was good at acting older than his age most of the time, but when the mask slipped he was his true, young self: younger than young, a boy whose skin broke out and who frittered his student loans away on leather pants and cannabis and called home every day to talk to his mom. She knew these things about him. But she was willing to put up with him, because he was her absolute equal in wasting time, in falling short, in under-achieving, in screwing up. The appealing thing was, he had no idea this was so. In his mind he was already a sought-after filmmaker, nothing left to do but kick aside the fetters of youth and inexperi-ence and penury.

Lydia ended up sleeping with Declan, more out of loneliness and horniness than anything. The truth was, she considered him less a boyfriend than a sort of human antechamber — or did she mean decompression chamber? — between her yearning for dear, mysteri-ous Dr. Schelling and a more tenable, less febrile way of being.

Declan said she wasn't like anyone else he knew. Is that a compliment or an insult? she'd wanted to know. He'd just laughed his bored, ugly little laugh. In May he was going to Ireland with his parents. He said he might never come back. He might get a job there, making documentaries or something.

I could come with you, she said. I could fly over and meet you there. Yeah, maybe, he said. She was sitting on the floor beside him. Classes had been cancelled due to a snowstorm. Declan was going through his portfolio of photographs, complaining that this one needed cropping, that one was overexposed. They were crap, basically.

No, they're good, Lydia said. She pointed at a photograph in which a lone figure stood tensely, indecisively, on the sand. Who's that, she said, and he said how should he know? But you took it, you must know, she said. It's one of the professors, isn't it?

What are you talking about? Declan said. Leave it alone, you're getting fingerprints on it.

She knew the figure in the photograph was Julian. Robed like a monk. His face concealed, but not from her. Not from her.

Could you move, Declan said. Could you just please quit crushing me?

He kept sending her down to the vending machine in the lobby for munchies and pop. She ran back up the stairs, trying to rid herself of a nearly intolerable excess of energy. It was the snow, the unnatural silence, the disagreeable, yet poignant, smell of wet boots and micro-waved popcorn and the cavernous pulse of rap music coming from behind closed doors.

In the hall she stopped to look out a window. The wintry scene made her think of the time she and her parents and her grandmother had travelled to the small town in the West Kootenays where the grandmother had lived as a girl and where her family was buried. Lydia's father said the trip would be healing — therapeutic — for all of them. *Yes, it's true, we are the direct descendants of a homicidal maniac, and, yes, there are noticeably few of us, a scant few survivors, most of our family having been massacred in a fit of pique, but still, we're good people, are we not; resilient and well-intentioned, and above all very, very likeable.*

Lydia, who'd been fifteen, had sat in the back, with the grandmother. She'd felt sorry for her, because she was used to being the wife of an architect and going to Maui on vacation and suddenly there she was, a widow, trapped in a cold car hurtling through a frozen landscape.

The road through the mountains was a sheet of ice and a wind was picking up, flinging pellets of snow against the windshield.

Lydia's father said it might be wiser to turn back, though that might be just as risky. We don't have to do this, he said. I'm afraid this may not be the best thing for you, mother, he said.

What's the problem, don't you believe in redemption anymore, Phillip? she said. She leaned forward and prodded Lydia's father, telling him to turn up the heat, she wasn't as well insulated as some.

By the time they reached their destination the clouds had thinned; the sun cast a pale glow on the mountains, while the town itself was in deep shadow. There was a Shell station, a coffee shop, a Sears Catalogue outlet, a Rod and Gun Club in a brick building that had once been the bank where Lydia's grandmother said she'd worked. The house where she'd lived was further out, in the foothills. She said she couldn't remember how you got there.

Let me think, she said. Let me get my bearings.

The next day they drove out to a little graveyard beside the highway. Lydia's grandmother was wrapped in a fur coat. At that time, she'd worn her hair crisply waved, tinted pale blond. Her mouth was painted a savage plum colour. On her hands she wore all her rings, all the diamond and sapphire rings the besotted architect had given her on anniversaries and birthdays and for no reason at all, except that he adored her.

Lydia's mother went and sat by herself on a headstone with a thermos of coffee. Lydia's father began a little prayer. It meandered around, touching on this and that, the weather, the road conditions, then segued to the exigencies of real life in a troubled world. Words like mercy, grace, forgiveness, scrabbled at the icy air, fleeting and insubstantial, but sharp of beak, like small, startled birds.

Around the graves marched Lydia's grandmother, setting her feet purposefully in the snow, leaving a trail that never deviated, and to Lydia it seemed she was hauling a rope after her, she was a sailor winding a rope around the graves like an anchor, and Lydia had wanted to say: *let go, let go.* But she knew the grandmother wouldn't let go, and neither would anyone in her family.

Wandering in two worlds, one dead, / The other powerless to be born. One was the world of faith, in the poem, and it was — dead? Only poetry was real, Matthew Arnold had proclaimed. Poetry was the mind, the true mind, without any garbage getting in the way. Religion was illusion, but it had its own poetry; that at least was true, according to Matthew Arnold, and Lydia believed him. Julian reading poetry in class — that was real to her, that was all possible worlds, the dead, the powerless, the one here and now with its hours and days, its light and dark, its sand and frost.

She trudged back to Declan's room and handed him the Pepsi and taco chips. To get his attention, more than anything, she told him what had happened in her family. The story came out briefer than she'd thought, and crueller. Now, thanks to her, Declan would have it in his head always. He'd tell his mother and his mother would say, Couldn't you find someone normal to be friends with?

Well, little Lydia, Declan said at last, tugging at his beard. Are you making that up? He said it reminded him of Keyser Soze in *The Usual Suspects*, when he kills the wife and kid before anyone else can get to them, a kind of pre-emptive strike.

Yeah, very astute, Lydia said. It hurts to be in love. She put on her coat. You don't have to go, Declan said. He stood up and smoothed her hair away from her face and said she felt feverish. She said she was fine. In fact, she felt very alone and a little disembodied. She went outside, but, instead of going back to her room, she stamped around in the snow. Alone, she felt happier. She scooped up snow and tasted it, freezing her mouth. Everywhere the night sky shone with light reflected off the snow.

She saw, or thought she saw, someone running toward her. At first she thought it was Declan. Whoever it was, he was wearing a bulky, hooded jacket, kicking up plumes of snow as he ran clumsily, powerfully, with intent. As he got closer he put out an arm and pushed her, hard. She lost her balance and fell backwards. Her assailant, or whatever, kept running. All she could think was: why her? Why did it always have to be her? It took her a long time to feel angry, to feel anything at all, besides empty and sad and pissed off, mostly with herself. She got up and looked around, afraid someone had seen. She brushed weakly at the snow clotted to her coat. She limped a little, as if she'd been injured, but she was really okay, except she'd lost her gloves. She went back to her room and picked up the clothes she'd left lying around on her floor, stuffing everything into plastic garbage bags. Half-completed assignments, practically unused notebooks, her journal, she put in another bag and both bags went down the garbage chute in the hall. Everything she did felt rational and necessary and full of grace. She had no ego. She had no substance. She'd dropped biology after the first week, because it was just too hard, too hard to open the mind to the harsh reality of life, but she remembered hearing that the human genome contained not eighty thousand or a hundred thousand genes, as expected, but a measly twenty thousand. Everyone pretty much the same, a thin soup made of the most humdrum ingredients: potatoes, a carrot, maybe, at best a rutabaga or some egg noodles. A soup always on the simmer, self-interested, inflated, anxiously waiting to be pronounced uniquely nourishing and flavourful. So it seemed, to her.

She remembered how hard she'd tried as a child to please her mother, to make her laugh at her feeble jokes (Knock, knock. Who's there? Lydia. Lydia who? Lid of your garbage can, that's who!), but her mother had already heard all the jokes at school. She'd laugh politely and get on with what she was doing — knitting, sweeping the floor, reading a magazine. When the grandmother came to live with them, there'd been a brief competition for Lydia's affection, a little minor tugging and pulling, which had made Lydia feel pliant and expendable, like a misshaped dough doll. In those days the grandmother still drove and on Saturdays she and Lydia would go to a restaurant, where the grandmother flirted with the waiters and let Lydia taste her wine. At home, the grandmother had badgered Lydia's mother into serving dinner by candlelight, on gold-rimmed china, at the old elm dining table imported from the grandmother's house in West Vancouver. Lydia's grandmother would cosy up to Lydia, inching her chair closer, so that she could say in a perfectly audible whisper: This is an interesting variation on beef bourguignon, I must say. Why didn't I ever think of leaving the gristle on the stewing beef?

In the evenings, Lydia remembered, her mother would lock herself in her bedroom, saying she had a headache, and, for a time, she'd ostentatiously swallowed a small white pill every morning at breakfast, for her nerves.

Julian had told the class how close he'd once come to visiting the Grand Chartreuse. Not the monastery itself, which was unavailable to visitors, but the famous *Musée de la Grande Chartreuse*, where all nine hundred years of the monastery's history were documented: the struggles against oppression, the devastating destruction by fire on something like eight separate occasions, the subsequent reconstructions. He'd been staying at a hotel in St.-Laurent-du-Pont, the very village mentioned by Matthew Arnold in the poem. But Julian's travelling companion came down with one of those minor tourist's maladies, nothing serious, although she'd taken it seriously enough. She'd demanded a doctor. She'd wanted the sun to be less oppressive and the people in the next room to be quieter. An argument ensued, over their itinerary and the cost of everything. One thing led to another, Julian said. They'd ended up cutting short their vacation. He didn't see the museum or the Grande Chartreuse. He'd missed what might well have been his only chance to fulfill a dream, to see what he'd yearned with all his heart to see. He stopped. He looked shocked, as if he'd said far more than he'd intended, and it was true, he'd never spoken so openly in class before. Of course his travelling companion must have been the woman who had died, the mother of his child. And, as if he knew Lydia knew, he turned and stared bitterly at her. He dismissed the class. He strode quickly out into the hall, where she caught up to him.

She wanted to tell him how alike they were, how brave in their willingness to confront the inexplicable, terrible events at the very centre of their lives, or his life, anyway. In her case, it was just the after-effects that were harmful, and even then it was an optional kind of harm, like a frightening book you could pick up and put down at will, the kind of book her grandmother liked, perhaps for that very reason. Julian gave her a look of such fear and distaste she couldn't speak. His eyes were watchful — lupine, was that the word? And the wolf was trapped, or thought it was. But it wasn't her. He didn't need to be afraid of her.

He started to walk away and, unthinking, she caught at his sleeve and he swung around, his teeth gleaming wolfishly in the darkness — it seemed suddenly dark, as if they were in an enclosure in a wood, the chill vault of the sky immeasurably far off. She thought of the lane behind his house, the shadows there. She thought of that dark, anonymous figure pushing her over in the snow. But this was not that figure. This was Julian. He put his face close to hers. You, he said. He hissed at her that if she had something to say, she could see him during his office hours. Yes, she said, yes, she was sorry. Sorry, she repeated, but he was gone.

Lydia went to the Ash Wednesday service at her father's church, where she knelt at the altar to have her forehead smudged with ash: *a sign of our mortality and penitence.* It was a little silvery cicatrix, a third eye, tracking, tracking. It saw everything. Behind the altar the assistant-priest wafted here and there in her beautiful embroidered surplice, her hair in spiky little tufts around her head. Her name was Iris. That week she came to Lydia's house for dinner. She'd been a financial adviser or a stockbroker or something, and now she was a newly ordained priest and also a vegetarian, something Lydia's mother hadn't known until they sat down to a dinner of roast beef and Yorkshire pudding. Iris ran her fingers nervously through her spiky hair. She was having a hard time, she said to Lydia's father as she took a tiny spoonful of mashed potatoes, a very hard time, reconciling her spirituality with the exigencies of daily parish life. Oh, my, she said, putting down her fork. All those personalities, the neediness, the bickering about this prayer book versus that one, a sung liturgy versus a spoken liturgy, kneeling versus standing. It was all so political, and she just wasn't a very political person.

How *do* you cope? she said to Lydia's father.

You'll adjust, he said. He went to place his hand on hers, then took it away. He assured Iris that in time she'd acquire a thicker skin. Iris gave him a grateful look.

Lydia's grandmother pointed her fork at Iris. You're mistaken if you think religion is harmless, she said. It's not just lambs and choirs and candlelight, you know. You should read Julian Huxley, Iris, you really should. Not Aldous, but Julian, the famous biologist. Of course, religion has given us better architecture than biology has, I'll grant you. And better music. But biology is truer, in my opinion, and a whole lot more useful. Did Phillip tell you my father was a preacher, too? You must pry the story out of him some day. I was deeply hurt when my only child became a preacher. His father and I had hoped he'd go into architecture or engineering.

She smiled. Tell me, Iris, do you have children?

No, said Iris in a small voice.

Mother, please, Lydia's father said. He took a deep, uneven breath. To Lydia's mother he said, perhaps Iris would like a little more water.

No, thank you, said Iris. Then: Yes, that would be nice.

Lydia's mother pushed back her chair and got up and went into the kitchen. She walked as if she were aboard a ship. Lydia, too, felt the unsteadiness, like weather balloons launched in unpredictable currents. And indeed that evening it began to snow heavily. Highly unusual, Lydia's father said, so close to spring. Later, when Iris was leaving, he walked her down the driveway to her car.

Phillip is clearing the snow off her windshield with his sleeve, Lydia's mother reported, parting the curtains a little. He's opening her door for her, she said. He's going to slip and fall, if he doesn't watch out. He should have a coat on. She sat down heavily and opened the newspaper and then folded it up and put it on the table beside her. When Lydia's father came in, stamping his feet on the rug, Lydia thought there was going to be an argument, a confrontation. Even Lydia and her grandmother would be in for it. The walls would shimmer and dissolve, the room would fill up with lost souls: her great-grandfather, the woman from the café singing her Janis Joplin songs, Declan, Julian, his child in his arms. At last, at last, stillness would be shattered, molecules would arrange themselves into new forms, new shapes, perhaps permanently. Her grandmother must have thought this a possibility, too. She sat up straighter in her chair. She moistened her lips. She looked first at her son and then at Lydia's mother.

Lydia remained where she was, near the door to the kitchen. She felt in herself something triumphant and flailing, needy, yet replete, satisfied, because these were her people, this was her family. Many small things would happen in her life. There would be an accretion of small events. It would, she imagined, be like climbing steps that were slightly too shallow and numerous, and reaching a high place where she could look down, and it would be beautiful and scary, and she'd want to let go, she would have that chance; it would be hers to make.

She missed Declan. He'd sent her a single postcard from Dublin. *Cool country,* he wrote, *beautiful and weird: like you.*

In the spring Lydia's father's long-awaited, long-deferred appointment as archdeacon was at last confirmed. Her parents had to sell their house and prepare to move to another diocese. Lydia's mother had to leave her job. At the same time, Lydia's grandmother suffered a small stroke, possibly a series of small strokes. She was in the hospital and then, instead of moving into the new rectory in Victoria with Lydia's parents, she went into a nursing home run by the church, where, Lydia's mother said, she'd get the care she needed.

Lydia visited her grandmother almost every day. Pauline would be waiting for her in the hall, leaning on her walker, which she called Our Lady of the Sorrows. She showed Lydia the things she'd made in art therapy class, scoffing at her attempts to glue beads to fabric and braid strips of felt into whatever. What folly, she said, making angry little dabs with the glue stick. The nursing home was like prison, she said, or, worse, kindergarten. At night she got up and walked the halls, causing the night staff to mistake her for a ghost. *Boo!* she'd say, fluttering her hands. The director of the nursing home mentioned this behaviour to Lydia's father. His mother frightened the other residents, she said, with quite sensational accounts of mass murder, shootings, infernos. It was not unusual for people of that age to invent such stories.

She's quite a character, Lydia's father had said weakly.

We are all going there eventually, the nurse said. We are all going to that strange place. Lydia's father was delighted with this. He repeated it to Lydia several times when they happened to meet at the nursing home. They were waiting in the main hall for Lydia's grandmother to wake from a nap. Along the opposite wall each closed door had on it a photograph of the room's occupant. Behind Lydia was a wall of glass that looked out onto a fenced area with a security gate and an empty fish pond covered with netting.

Years ago, Lydia's father said, when he was a kid, his mother had been a notorious insomniac. Nothing could cure her, not pills or warm milky drinks or meditation, all of which were tried. She'd be up until dawn, reading or playing cards, listening to music. Often his father stayed awake, keeping her company. They would waltz around the room in their nightclothes. He'd wake up and watch them from behind a door, alarmed and intrigued by what he saw. By day his mother was a dynamic, energetic person — of whom he was a little frightened, to be honest — but at night she was fragile, agitated. No doubt she should have received help, trauma counselling, Lydia's father said. Once, briefly, she'd consulted a psychiatrist, he believed. But there was a lot she'd suppressed.

When I was about fifteen, Lydia's father said, my dad told me he'd done some detective work in the town where Pauline had lived. He'd talked to a few long-time residents. He'd read old newspaper accounts. To his surprise he'd discovered my mother's version of events was not the only one. Not the factual one. For one thing, the bank where Pauline worked closed early on Wednesdays. She was at home when her father arrived. From what the police constable deduced, Pauline's father must have shot her sister and Pauline caught her in her arms, or she collapsed against Pauline, and they fell together to the floor. One particularly lurid newspaper account had the young constable saying there was so much blood he'd had to peel Pauline's hair and dress off the floor.

Lydia tried to look out the window, but the sun got in her eyes.

A woman in a pink nylon smock came by with a teacart. She handed Lydia's father a cup of tea. He stared at it, bemused, although in life, in his professional life, women were always handing him cups of tea, he should be used to it by now, Lydia thought. His eyes shone with humility and fear. Fear that someone, somewhere, might fail to see him for what he was: a good man, a genuinely good and kindly man, devoid of malice or discontent or any other sin. And Lydia had to be the same. If not, everything would unravel and stop making sense; the world would get as cold and dangerous as it really was; there would be an abyss and people would fall into it and they would be crushed. And she knew this. It was what her grandmother kept telling her.

Beside her, her father smiled warmly at a small, hunched woman in a wheelchair, who tilted her head back and gave him a cold, ferocious stare. His smile wavered. Oh dear, Lydia, he said. What a conversation we seem to be having. Then he quoted:

What voice can my invention find to say
So soft, precise, and scrupulous a word
You shall not take it for another sword?

Now that's definitely Elinor Wylie, he said. I'm sure of it. He went and knocked softly at Lydia's grandmother's door. He pushed it open and looked in. Ah, she's awake, he said.

Sometimes Pauline pretended to be asleep, but really her mind was working at a great rate and then it would shut off, she'd cease to exist; it was like a preamble to non-existence. When she was young, she and her brother and sister would play quietly for hours on the back porch, keeping out of their father's way. Through the window they could see him with his Bible open on the kitchen table, scribbling his annotations. Their mother would be going back and forth from the counter to the stove. There would be this little sizzle in the air, kerosene lamps, wood sparks from the fire, a state of flux and indeterminacy that nevertheless gave a small light. Pauline remembered their first house burning to the ground. They'd camped in a tent. They'd cooked over an open fire and bathed in a river. Her father had said fire was a brand and what it marked was marked forever.

She wanted to know: could it be as simple as that? Pure bad luck, poison in the well water? Her father called himself a preacher; he'd never been ordained, but he had a little church and a staunch following. He used to practice his sermons outdoors, preaching to the trees and the wind. When Pauline was small she'd hidden in the long grass and spied on him. She'd stare up at the sky and try to imagine God looking down on the world and all the people like grains of sand, separate but the same. Or not the same: distinct, but too small to be differentiated one from the other. That was what being God would feel like, she'd thought: sand and grit under your fingernails, the beginning of a fever.

The house had two windows like eyes. There was a lean-to and a stack of firewood infested with deer mice and there was a cat to catch the mice. Her father made a pet of it and fed it table scraps and it lost interest in mice.

She remembered the police constable, Henry Morgan, and his beautiful dark-haired sister, Jane. She remembered Jane's camera, a George Eastman field-view camera, with black fabric bellows and a mahogany case. How Pauline had coveted that camera, which to her had represented everything she desired: freedom, independence, art, a life of her own. She remembered that, on the day Henry and Jane drove her out to her house, the camera had been beside her in the car, its eye sealed up, its brass hinges gleaming. Henry said, Take your time, Pauline. If you need anything, give a shout. They let her go inside, while they waited on the steps.

She'd walked from room to room. The house had been cleaned, but still, she could tell. In the kitchen she stood at the window. Snow falling, wind in the chimney, a truck or car going past on the road. She imagined her father in the room, putting a bowl of food on the floor for his cat, straightening a chair, tentatively moving her brother's exercise book, left open on the table, as if he were searching for something he'd misplaced. She imagined turning and their eyes meeting and then she'd look away. She went outside and the icy air came at her tenderly, as if it had the utmost regard for her plight. She saw the cat near the fence. She asked Henry Morgan to please catch it for her. He ran, his long black coat billowing out, but the cat disappeared into the trees and she never saw it again. Henry and Jane took her back to the boarding house. Henry walked her to the door. Is there anyone we can get to stay with you? he'd asked. No. There is no one, she'd said.

One night Henry and Jane came to her door. Pauline had been asleep. Jane's face was rosy from the cold, her hair in little damp tendrils. Henry removed his coat and pulled back the blankets and lay beside Pauline. He lifted her nightgown and began to make love to her, not roughly, but as if it were a duty, one of the lesser-known police duties he was compelled to undertake from time to time. He took her hand from her eyes. She was ashamed of her thinness, her ribs visible, the pallor of her skin. Jane sat on the bed and gently stroked Pauline's arm and eased the tangles from her hair. Where Jane and Henry touched her, Pauline became new, restored, transcendent. She thought: I am like them. In fact, she was like anyone; she was human, she was herself. She remembered how she used to write down her father's sermons as he dictated them to her, about how some would get victory over the beast, the image of the beast, and how they would stand on a sea of glass and their breasts would be *girded with golden girdles*. She could hear a dog barking, a shout, everything distant and safe, going on as it was meant to.

Before dawn, Jane and Henry left. Pauline got up and went to the window and scraped at the frost with her thumbnail, at the tiny, crystalline grains, which felt like sand but melted away in her fingers, and she understood — she thought she understood — that transience was a property also of things unseen, such as grief, sorrow, love. Loss was terrible, phantasmagorical and yet plain, unadorned, serviceable. It could, presumably, be survived.

That day she packed her few personal belongings into an old cloth valise that had belonged to her mother. She went to the bank where she'd worked and withdrew her savings, just enough for a one-way ticket to Vancouver. Once she was on the train she felt calm, yet eager, full of anticipation, and she was content just to sit quietly and watch as the miles went by and snow fell without cessation in the dark forests.

Lydia, kneeling at the altar at her father's church, began to think of Julian. Almost in a trance she pictured him going into his house, at that very moment. Someone would have been there, caring for the child, and that person would leave, and Julian would go to a window with the child in his arms and look out at the rain and the dark sky. He'd remember, for no particular reason, Lydia creeping around in the lane behind his house and he'd try to work out what could have possessed her to behave like that — what had been in that girl's peculiar little mind? Lydia imagined that she went to his house again and he saw her and let her in. They would stand there in each other's arms, silent in their shared knowledge of what could happen in the world and indeed did happen, continually, without respite: acts of passion and bile, regret and love. At the same time, she'd see how ordinary the room was, a book open on the table, a coffee cup. A place of shelter. Yet there would be in that house the memory of tragedy, of loss. It would linger in the air, she would breathe it in. She'd have a sense, also, of the child's presence, the child deeply asleep in its crib in another room, dreaming something quite contrary to Lydia's dream, something necessary to its own survival.

FELT SKIES

WHEN I WENT BACK to the town where my mother, Bethany, and I had once lived, I wasn't surprised to see our house was gone. The lot was a dump. But I was happy to see that some of Bethany's garden remained: the hardier trees and shrubs, a hedge of western red cedar, unkempt, but grown impressively tall and lush. I remembered how Bethany would dig trees out of wild land and cart them home in the trunk of our car. She'd go around to nurseries and persuade the owners to give her their ailing or misshapen specimens, which she'd then plant and coax back to health. Where the sun was hottest, she'd planted heather, lavender, and roses. She liked everything about roses: the fabulous colours and intricate, perfectly arranged petals, the fragrance, the serrated leaves like little arrows, even the hurtful, distressingly numerous thorns.

The reason I was here wasn't important. I just was. It was a perfect spring day. I was standing near a trio of tulips, satiny-black, fat as goblets, blooming with surprising vigour near what remained of the house foundations.

When we'd lived here, I'd just finished school and had got a job at the local radio station. I had no real training, but I could write grammatically and type with some accuracy. My manner on the telephone was, I believed, helpful without being effusive. But then, I was never very talkative, which made Simon remark, in a baffled, suspicious tone, "You write poetry, don't you? You must have some thoughts inside that head of yours." It was true; I did. But I was used to being solitary and keeping my thoughts to myself and until Simon began to goad me I hadn't known this was a flaw.

Bethany called Simon a bad influence, and I suppose he was. I remembered driving home from some party with Simon and he'd be so woozy from drink he'd have to hang on hard to the steering wheel for balance. His tolerance, he'd said, wasn't as good as it had been. Simon was forty-seven, although I had the presence of mind to subtract a few years when Bethany pressed for details. Far from being a detriment, Simon's age made him seem a romantic figure to me. He had the dusty, tattered appearance of a traveller from some vast, arid country fraught with danger. His hazel eyes were flecked with grains of light, as if he were continually focusing on some new thing. His person was weighted down with well-thumbed note-books, ballpoint pens, a small tape recorder. He talked to me about serious things, world politics, economics, the books he'd read. He even looked at my poems and told me which ones he liked and which ones, in his opinion, didn't work all that well.

I pictured our house the way it had been in those days: small and plain, rundown, and me inside it, nineteen years old, slightly hung-over following another debauched night in Simon's company. I remembered getting out of bed at noon and going into the kitchen in my pyjamas to pour myself a cup of coffee. From the window I could see Bethany weeding a border of sweet alyssum and those little dwarf marigolds. It must have been a Sunday, because she wasn't at work. I winced at the light, the radiance of the flowers, which seemed like nothing you'd find in an ordinary garden. Bethany used to make me do some weeding or pruning as punishment for some misdemeanour, like not phoning home to say where I was, or not getting home until nearly dawn. Where's the punishment in that, I'd ask, laughing and holding out my hands for her to see: gardening had already destroyed my fingernails and left dirt permanently embedded around my cuticles. Bethany had said, Fine, if that didn't sound enough like punishment, she'd lock me in my room. She would lock me in and swallow the key, if necessary. I'd laughed and said she wouldn't dare. She said try her and see.

It was hard to keep up to Bethany's high standards. She worked six days a week as a clerk at a building supply store, and after work she kept busy tending the house and the garden. That morning, I remembered, she was in faded denim cut-offs and stubby yellow clogs. She looked about twelve years old. She must have sensed I was watching her, because she'd stood up and shaded her eyes with her hand and called, "Is that you, Rachel?" Through the open window I'd called back, "It's me." Who else would it have been, I'd wondered? I finished my coffee and rinsed out my cup and then tried to comb my hair into some kind of order before she saw me.

I'd met Simon at the radio station. He'd come across the street from the newspaper office to read the news as it came off the Teletype machine in the newsroom and then he'd stay, clutching torn-off sheets of newsprint, he and the station news director arguing about whether Patty Hearst had been kidnapped or had joined the Symbionese Liberation Army of her own free will, and about Watergate and the possibility the American president would be impeached. My desk was nearby, and as I worked I'd imagine Simon being as distracted by my presence as I was by his. No one was supposed to know we were seeing each other, mostly because Simon didn't want to get teased about robbing the cradle, as he put it. I didn't care. I was pleased Simon was interested in me. The first time he'd asked me out was the same day the news director had introduced us, as an afterthought more than anything, as in: Oh, yes, this is our new girl, Rachel.

Simon and I got in the habit of driving over the Malahat to Victoria every Friday, to a theatre Simon was fond of that showed foreign films with subtitles. They were old films, even then. Simon had a way of becoming completely engrossed as the story unfolded on the screen. I would rest my head on the rough tweed of his sports jacket, which smelled of marine engine oil, salt water, and spicy aftershave lotion, and amuse myself dreaming up words that would in some measure describe my state of mind: bemused, ecstatic, well-content. Once, the word "happy" came into my mind just as it appeared on the screen. "Oh, I'm so happy," a young Polish woman was saying to her lover. "I'm so happy," I whispered in Simon's ear, and he patted my hand and said, Please, Rachel, be quiet and let me watch the film.

After the movie, Simon and I liked to stroll around the block in the June twilight to a restaurant he claimed made authentic British-style fish and chips. He told me how, when he was younger, he'd liked nothing better than to stand on a street corner in Durham eating chips straight out of the newspaper wrapping. His first foray into journalism, he said. He was born in the north of England and had lived there until he was thirty, when he and his wife, Rosemary, had immigrated to Canada. They'd divorced years ago. Rosemary still lived in the area, but Simon rarely saw her. He claimed his ex-wife was the most neurotic person he'd ever met, although her neuroses manifested themselves in small, obscure ways that had to do, mostly, with disapproving of whatever he did. For example, he said, when they were married she forbade him to eat fish and chips, partly because she couldn't abide the smell of grease, but mostly because she considered fish and chips to be working-class fare. Going for a beer after work was also working-class, in Rosemary's estimation, and so he hadn't been allowed to do that, either. The worst thing, of course, was his acquiescence. Rosemary had trained him to be as docile as his dog, Mitzy, and Mitzy, he said, was an extremely docile animal.

By the time we drove home over the Malahat it was long past midnight and the road was free of traffic, which gave Simon an opportunity to demonstrate how fast his MG could go. The clean, cold mountain air, perfumed with the scent of dry pine needles, blew my hair around and made my eyes stream with tears, and all I could think was, well, if something happens, it happens; if we crash, we crash. As Simon leaned heavily into a corner, or grappled with the stick shift when he headed into a steep downhill bend, I found myself involuntarily repeating in my head one of the simple prayers Bethany had taught me when I was small. *Matthew, Mark, Luke, and John,/Guard the bed that I lay on.* The words slipped through my mind at about the speed of light, which was approximately how fast Simon's car was travelling. I prayed my childish prayers and laughed too loudly, out of fear.

Simon lived miles out of town in a place called Venice Bay, a community of marinas, houseboats, and summer cottages situated at the end of a narrow unpaved road. Simon's rented cottage perched out over the sea on pilings coated with creosote. It had a deck shaped like the prow of a ship — or perhaps I should say a raft, since it had no railings. The sea, enclosed on three sides by forested land, was green, heavy looking, with iridescent pools of oil on the surface, and the air, thick with insects, had about it a drowsy, golden quality. There was a marina down the road where Simon kept his boat. The boat was a cabin cruiser with a diesel engine. It was an old boat, but it had a galley in good repair and bunks to sleep in. So far, though, we hadn't. We hadn't slept together on his boat or anywhere else. Naturally, Bethany suspected otherwise. Even though she'd had what she called a strict religious upbringing, Bethany had a harder time than most people recognizing the simple truth when she heard it. Of course, I found it hard to believe myself, at times. Was it that

Simon found me too immature, too boring? Or was it the other way around? Was Simon too mature to want to bother with sex? This seemed unlikely, based on what I'd learned from those foreign films, and from books, and even from the behaviour I'd observed at the parties I went to with Simon, where everyone told dirty jokes and some guy was always trying to cop a feel. I couldn't ask my mother for advice, obviously. Who could I ask? I thought of Dr. Bergius. Bring your problems to me, he had advised, running his hand over his crisp Sigmund Freud look-alike beard.

Dr. Bergius was the new owner of the radio station. He arrived four weeks after I started work. One of the first things he said to me was that people always told him he looked like Freud. Isn't it the truth? he'd said, touching a hand to his long, thin face and perfectly barbered silver beard. For all I knew, he did look like Freud. He looked like a lot of different people, a lot of older gentlemen. He sat behind his desk like a train passenger, apprehensive yet anxious to be off. He said he knew he wasn't a great psychoanalyst like Freud — he wasn't any kind of psychoanalyst, come to that. As a medical practitioner, however, his primary concern had always been to listen to his patients' stories, no matter how insignificant or pointless they seemed. He'd been in love with words since he was a boy in Germany and his mother had read to him before he slept. Great books, she had read, like *Robinson Crusoe* — in translation, of course — and also novels and poetry by German writers such as Theodor Storm and Goethe and the incomparable poet Rainer Maria Rilke. Why, even now he remembered perfectly certain of Rilke's lines, such as: *For her he loves and spoils her with felt skies.*

Did I have any idea what those words meant? he'd demanded. Dr. Bergius's intensity frightened me a little, and so did my ignorance. What did the words mean? What did they mean? I pictured Dr. Bergius running frantically around under a low grey sky, his arms raised, while a young woman stood petulantly off to the side.

Well, Dr. Bergius said at last, neither did he know the exact meaning of the words. And yet, didn't I feel, as he did, their wonderful musicality?

On Dr. Bergius's desk, between a black telephone and an onyx pen stand, there was a framed portrait of his late wife, whose name, he told me, was Eva. With her prominent cheekbones and small, shrewd eyes, Eva seemed unnervingly lifelike. When he'd met Eva, he said, he'd been a medical student and she'd been studying what would now be called Home Economics at a girls' academy in Leipzig. She was, he said, a lovely, lovely girl who adored nature, flowers, and animals. That was in 1934, in a very different world, he said, absently tugging at his bow tie.

In spite of his long interest in the subject, Dr. Bergius was a newcomer to the realities of commercial broadcasting. He might as well be honest about this, he said. The station had been on the verge of bankruptcy when he took over, and the situation was still precarious. He was going to need the help of the announcers, news director, music director — not that the station had a music director at present, but that would come, fingers crossed — and the salesmen. And the copywriter. "That's you," he said, beaming.

"Yes," I said, nervously. I didn't want Dr. Bergius questioning me about my qualifications. I'd been hired as a receptionist, but during the transition period, in the days before Dr. Bergius arrived, the previous copywriter had quit, and I'd been offered his job, no questions asked, no experience necessary. I'd inherited a desk in a corner near the coffee room, and an antique Royal typewriter on which to compose copy. I thought I was improving. As far as I could tell, it was all a matter of rhythm and timing, in order to transform the dull, repetitive half-truths of commerce into something that didn't entirely offend the ear. A matter of musicality, as Dr. Bergius had just said of poetry. I thought of mentioning this, but I didn't want to sound pretentious, as if I was trying to come across as more knowledgeable than I was, or worse, trying to compare myself to a famous poet.

At the conclusion of the interview, Dr. Bergius came out from behind his desk and took my hand. He was tall, with the slightest stoop. His bow tie was the same velvety midnight blue as his eyes. No doubt he should have gone into radio years ago, he said, but his mother had wanted a career in medicine for him. Such a devoted mother, how could he have disappointed her? Anyway, medicine had been good to him. He had no regrets.

And now he had his own little radio station. He smiled slightly and opened his office door for me. Before I left, I happened to glance at the window in the wall of Dr. Bergius's office. It looked directly into the control room. One of the announcers, Brent, was at the microphone, reading a piece of my copy. Once, Brent had buzzed me on the intercom and summoned me to the control room. "Never begin with a question," he'd told me. He'd been referring to a piece of copy I'd written for the Star Cinema, on Station Street, the first line of which read: *Are you in the mood for a Wild West adventure?* Anyone listening, Brent had pointed out, would naturally feel like saying, No, damn it, I'm not in the mood. "Starting with a question is a sure sign of a novice," he'd said. He'd put his hand under my chin, forcing me to look at him. "It's all right. Everyone makes mistakes," he'd said. "That's how you learn."

One morning Dr. Bergius came and stood beside my desk. He straightened my pile of yellow newsprint. Then he said, "I met your mother. She was in the grocery store when I was there. To be honest, I thought she was you. You resemble her to a remarkable degree."

"I know," I said. "Everyone says that."

"It's true" said Dr. Bergius, "Let me tell you what happened. I said good morning to your mother, or, as I thought, to you. Then something made me a little unsure. I took a closer look. 'Excuse me,' I said, 'but are you Rachel's mother?' She laughed and said indeed she was. It was very pleasant, meeting unexpectedly in the store like that. Your mother is a very gracious person, Rachel."

"Thank you," I said. I erased a typing mistake, then typed: *Don't miss out! Prices have been slashed — quantities are limited!*

I wouldn't have called Bethany gracious. She was too plainspoken, without guile. However, it was true, we looked alike. We were the kind of mother and daughter people often mistook for sisters. We had the same heart-shaped faces, the same large, pale-grey eyes. Even our feet were the same shape, narrow at the heel and wide across the toes. We both tied our light brown hair back in a ponytail. We borrowed each other's clothes and went shopping together. All the years I was growing up, going to school, sitting at the kitchen table doing homework, Bethany would say, "Thank the Lord I have you, Rachel. I'd be lost without you." What she meant, I thought, was that we had each other. We had each other and no one else. Not long after I was born, my father had disappeared. His name was Gary. I knew nothing about him. When I was younger, I had begged Bethany to tell me what he'd looked like, what kind of person he was, what kind of music he liked, whether or not he smoked, if he went to church, and she would shake her head. Well, I would say, you must remember something. No, I don't, she'd insisted, laughing a little; I have total amnesia.

For years I tried to add the name Gary — its two crisp, hurried syllables — to the list of people I prayed for at night. But what I breathed into the darkness returned to reside stubbornly in my mind. I imagined a father with a different name: Charles, Edward, Rupert. Something substantial, the name of a conscientious, reliable individual. Finally, I gave up. I came to believe there'd only ever been Bethany. Bethany in the moonlight, working magic in the soil, digging and tilling and adding nutrients and then something, some little thing, germinating. Me.

It occurred to me that Gary, wherever he was, whoever he might be — if, indeed, he had ever existed — would be only a little older than Simon. Or even the same age, or younger. Thinking this, I started a game. I imagined that Simon was Gary in disguise. He was biding his time, pretending to be my boyfriend so he could get to know me. He cared about me the way a father would. He planted kisses on the top of my head and took me for Sunday afternoon rides in his car. I came to believe this wasn't a game, but the truth. Then Bethany invited Simon to our house for tea, and there was no sign of recognition between them, only a little animosity on Bethany's side.

She'd made a pot of herbal tea and set the table with her pink raffia placemats. She offered Simon freshly baked oatmeal cookies and raisin scones. Simon talked to Bethany and ignored me. He and my mother were adults together, he seemed to be implying, while I was merely a child. I was jealous. Did Simon find Bethany prettier than I was, livelier, more interesting? Before he left, Bethany had taken him on a tour of her garden, pointing out her successes and her failures, including a clump of dried-out, decaying bog myrtle. Gallantly Simon said he couldn't imagine anything dying on her, and she laughed and cut two of her precious peony blooms for him. They were a deep rose pink, the size of the human heart.

He thanked her, looking slightly dumbfounded, and I said, "Watch out, they're crawling alive with earwigs."

Dr. Bergius straightened my supply of yellow newsprint, then immediately brushed against it with his suit jacket and had to straighten it again. He took his time, then stood back and gave me a long look.

"That's a bad sunburn you have, Rachel," he said.

"I know," I said. I lifted my shoulders a little, defensively, which made me wince. I was wearing a sundress with spaghetti straps. My legs were sunburned, too, but at least they were hidden under my desk.

"Cold compresses," Dr. Bergius said. "Plenty of fluids. Aspirin would help. I have some in my office, if you like."

"It doesn't hurt," I lied. "It looks worse than it is." I did feel ill and feverish, and every part of my body ached and burned. The day before, I'd gone out with Simon in his boat and we'd got stuck for hours on a sandbar in the narrow channel between two small islands. Simon had been sure he could navigate his way through at low tide, but he'd been wrong. He'd tried ramming the engine from reverse into forward, then running out of the cabin to stare down at the murky water. He'd banged his head hard on the lintel over the door, which infuriated him and he started cursing, calling his boat an unseaworthy old tub, threatening to sink it. And you, he said, pointing a finger at me, you'll go down with it, how will you like that? Then he looked away, breathing hard.

The unhappy excursion in the boat had been all Simon's idea, not mine, but I did feel responsible for the way things had turned out. While we waited for the tide to float us free, we sat on the bow of the boat and drank beer and passed a bag of stale potato chips back and forth. On one of the adjacent islands a party was going on, five or ten kids out on the lawn in front of a house, a Rolling Stones song blasting out across the water. I loved the Stones, but it was true the music seemed to get caught in the recalcitrant ocean currents and the burning heat of the sun, becoming oppressive, inescapable. Simon stood, hands on his hips, at the boat's rail and yelled across the water at the kids to shut up, shut the fuck up. Naturally they responded by shouting obscenities in return, parodying Simon's anger, jumping around like apes, beating their chests. I had to smile. I saw the scene through their eyes: the middle-aged man, his naked sparrow's chest, his gut slack over the waistband of khaki shorts. Me in my pink two-piece bathing suit, my ponytail. The adamantine sky. The sinking ship. I was starting to enjoy myself. In my head, I began to compose a poem. I felt myself grow distant from the scene. I viewed Simon objectively, coldly. Then again I allowed myself to look at him with pure affection and warmth. I imagined that he would, in front of our motley teenaged audience, begin to make love to me. I slipped my bathing suit straps off my shoulders and stretched out in front of the cabin window, now somewhat aslant, to sunbathe. I intended to look voluptuous and irresistible, but instead I fell asleep. When I woke thirty minutes or so later, we were underway.

Dr. Bergius repeated his advice, telling me I should rub cold cream on my sunburn; I should have a cool bath and let the water soak into my skin. "Let me bring you a glass of water and an Aspirin," he said, and I said, "No, I'm fine, really." I wished he would go back to his office. He had this sad, far-off look on his face. "Perhaps one day I will have a chance to talk with your mother at greater length," he said. "I must see what I can do."

His interest was unwarranted enough to seem like trespass. He went down the hall, then turned abruptly and walked back to his office and shut the door. I depressed a few typewriter keys softly, without leaving a mark on the page. I liked being a copywriter, even if I wasn't very good at it yet. The stuff I wrote wasn't beautiful, or poetic, or even especially true. I knew it was mostly junk. Even so, if I did manage to write something that seemed okay, even more than okay, brilliant, perfect, I sat there reading to myself over and over the lines of faded type on the cheap yellow paper.

In the back porch of our house Bethany hung bunches of everlasting flowers to dry. In the winter she took the dried flower heads and separated the petals, spreading them out on the kitchen table. Then, using a pair of tweezers, she painstakingly glued each individual petal to a sheet of paper. The petals formed textured designs that represented birds or deer or flowers. Once, she did an evening landscape, a sky of gold and mauve and crimson above a field of russet-browns. She liked it enough to hang it on the kitchen wall.

That summer I took it down and ran my fingers slowly over the rough, prickly surface. I felt within myself a corresponding irritability. Felt skies, I thought.

Since that day in Dr. Bergius's office, I had learned that Rilke's mother had wanted a daughter, not a son. Her disappointment made her spiteful, and she forced Rilke to pretend he was a girl; she took hours to comb his hair into fat, silky ringlets. She pinched his pale cheeks to give them some colour. I thought of Dr. Bergius listening in some long-ago twilight as his mother read to him — a simple, motherly act he'd spent his whole life trying to repay. Then I began to think about Bethany's mother, my grandmother, whose coldness and remove were incomprehensible to me. Bethany had run away from home when she was eighteen, because her parents wouldn't give their permission for her to get married. And then, when things hadn't worked out with the man she'd loved and she got pregnant with me, she'd tried to go home, but her mother refused to see her. Clearly, there were shades, gradations, in the spectrum of parental love that were dangerous, extreme, yet somehow, in the end, tolerable. Bethany said she didn't blame her mother, not any longer: people were what they were, she said. And I suppose I didn't blame my father. Not entirely. I wished I knew, though, what had caused his sudden flight or banishment, because that would tell me something, wouldn't it? Tell me something about myself. Bethany promised one day she'd tell me everything. One day.

But that day never arrived. Bethany was always too busy cultivating and nurturing all those fragile, needy plants. In her garden shed she kept poisons to eradicate disease, fertilizers to encourage growth. She had little sharp scissors and knives to cut out dead or stunted shoots. She was a horticulturist; she was a woodswoman. Her hands were sinewy and tanned and muscular, and looked as if they rightfully belonged to someone else. That summer, the summer of 1974, the summer the American president resigned from office and received a full pardon — an event that came to serve as a kind of neutral marker in my mind — I found her in a far corner of the garden. She was wandering among the great massed shapes of shadow and light in a kind of trance, her eyes shining, her dress stained with grass and dirt. I said her name and she didn't hear me. I went right up to her and put my hands on her shoulders. The air between us became as clear and untroubled as glass. We were our twinned selves, like to like. We were in a dream. It was a good dream, mostly, all the menace and danger kept manageably distant, like a thunderstorm far out at sea.

If I sat on the edge of the raft-shaped deck in front of Simon's house and extended my legs far enough, I could just skim the surface with my toes. This evening the water was dark, turbid, as if the passage of a deep-sea creature had recently stirred up the mud at the bottom. When Simon had nothing better to do, he fished for bullheads from the deck. When he caught one, he removed the hook from its mouth and tossed it back into the water. He stretched out on his stomach and scooped jellyfish out of the water with his hands and let them melt into a silvery puddle on the hot, rough wood planks. "That's cruelty to animals," I told him. Simon laughed. He stood and looked down at me. "You can't be cruel to a jellyfish, Rachel," he said. "Being melted alive is what they were born for. Jellyfish karma."

I believed a jellyfish could experience pain and fear. Everything could, every single thing. I got up and went into Simon's kitchen, where he was stepping over Mitzy to get to the fridge. Mitzy was fourteen years old, which was pretty old for a dog of her size and breed, Simon said. Plus she had a heart condition and cataracts, which caused her to keep bumping into walls. "Look at this. I'm out of bloody dog food," Simon said. He took a slice of cheese out of the fridge, unwrapped it, and threw it on the floor. Mitzy heaved herself up and staggered forward. "Here, here, dummy," Simon said, pointing at the cheese. I knelt on the floor and rubbed the space between Mitzy's ears. The dog stared at me with her milky, sorrowful eyes. I broke the cheese into little pieces and fed them to her. Simon filled Mitzy's water bowl with fresh water and put it on the floor beside the fridge. He poured two glasses of whiskey and handed one to me. Then we went into the living room, where we sat on the couch, which was covered in a blue and green afghan that Mitzy had slept on so much her coarse golden hair was woven right into the wool. Simon put his arm around my shoulder. He took my glass and put it on the floor next to his. Then he kissed me. His mouth tasted of metal, the same metallic smell my hands got from my old typewriter at the radio station. He placed his hands on my shoulders and increased the pressure until I was flat on my back. I didn't try to resist. I was curious, mainly, about what would happen next. I was listening to Maria Muldaur on the radio singing Simon's favourite song, "Midnight at the Oasis," about moonlight and shadows and sending camels off to bed and I'll be a belly dancer and you can be a sheik, and at the same time I was thinking of the foreign films Simon and I went to see in Victoria. Here it was, at last, I thought: the seduction scene. It was and at the same time it wasn't. Not a garment was removed. Not a word was spoken. Simon moved heavily against me. I stared over his shoulder at the wall, at a pale unsteady circle of light that made me think of sprites and demons, although I knew it was nothing more than the last of the day's light reflecting off the sea. Simon cradled my head in his hands. He lay still. It was finished, whatever it was. Whatever it was supposed to be. He sat up and wiped his face with a corner of the afghan. "There," he said. "Virginity intact."

I sat up. I pulled the end of my ponytail forward and twisted it around my fingers. What happened? I wanted to ask, but didn't dare, in case he got mad, or thought I was unbelievably dumb. Even though Simon was sitting next to me I felt intensely lonely. Had he meant my virginity, or his? He didn't know that I was a virgin, he didn't know that at all.

"How's your drink?" he asked. He picked up my glass and tried to give it to me.

"I don't want it," I said.

"Go on, finish it up like a good girl," he said.

"I can't," I said. I covered my mouth with my hands.

He pulled my hands away and put the glass to my mouth. "Open up," he kept saying. I pressed my hands to my throat and swallowed. I felt sick, panicky, as if I was on the verge of an attack of some kind. Outside, the light was fading away. The little circle of spinning light on the wall was gone. The air felt cooler on my hot skin. My throat burned. I hated the taste of whisky; I despised it.

In August, Dr. Bergius telephoned my mother and invited us to his house for dinner Saturday evening. She accepted for both of us. "Why didn't you tell him you were busy?" I said, exasperated. I had to phone Simon and tell him I couldn't go out with him on his boat. He'd planned what he called a "leisurely cruise," to make up for the earlier fiasco. "Oh, it wasn't that bad," I said, on the phone. Thinking about it, I began to believe this was true. I remembered the rock music from the party travelling with subdued energy across the water. I remembered the boat rocking as if it were a cradle, the blue sky overhead, gulls mewling.

"Oh, come on, it was a disaster," Simon said. "You don't owe your boss your weekends, for Christ's sake." He slammed the phone down. The next morning, he phoned to apologize. He said he'd put the boat trip off until Sunday. "That's if you don't have any important dinner engagements," he said. There was peevishness to his voice that I couldn't help associating with age, with illogical crankiness and permanent bad humour. But I was more concerned that his bad mood was a natural response to my failings, my inadequacies. If I were older, I told myself, my mother wouldn't still be making decisions for me. And then, as if to prove that I was indeed childish,

I took my anger out on Bethany. I told her she'd be sorry — Dr. Bergius was a weirdo, a crank, a madman who quoted poetry all the time. She told me she'd be happy to have dinner with a madman if it meant I'd be with her and not with Simon. Bethany was fanatical; she'd even offered me money if I'd stop seeing Simon. I told her it wasn't enough. It's all I can afford, she'd said, laughing, but close to tears. If you could just try to get home before midnight, she had said. That's all I ask. I don't want you driving home from Venice Bay late at night on that road. And then she said, "Does Simon drive when he's been drinking?"

"No, "I retorted. "Of course not."

I followed her around the garden while she cut an armful of roses to take to Dr. Bergius. I wanted to grab the roses away from her and throw them on the ground. She was wearing a long blue skirt and an eyelet-lace blouse. She had on lipstick the same pale pink as the roses. She looked very pretty. When she scratched her hand on a rose thorn and pressed her hand to her mouth, I wished I could take the pain from her and bear it myself. When I was a little girl, I used to tell Bethany I was going to be rich some day and buy her a beautiful house and a new car. The other dream I had when I was a child was that my father would turn up. He would come home and fall in love with Bethany all over again. He would pick me up and toss me in the air. He was strong and dextrous and cheerful. He'd fix the hinges on the back door and overhaul the furnace when it broke down in the middle of a winter snowstorm.

Dr. Bergius lived at the end of a private drive bordered by tall poplars. Sunlight came fitfully through the leaves, so that Bethany and I seemed to be driving through a more fluid medium than air. The house, when it came into view, was white with a red tile roof. Beyond, there was a pond on which white birds, swans or geese, were floating. It seemed full of hope and possibilities, as if it had once occupied a central place in a story that concluded: *And they lived happily ever after*. It was exactly the kind of splendid property Bethany deserved to have, I thought.

Bethany got out of the car and presented the roses to Dr. Bergius, who had come marching out from behind his house to greet us. He was wearing a long chef's apron over a blue shirt and grey slacks. His silver hair was glistening with some kind of oil. "Why," he said, "look at this. No one ever brings me flowers."

"It's a modern rose," Bethany said. "There are old-fashioned roses and modern ones. The modern ones are bigger and they last longer."

"Ah," said Dr. Bergius. "I didn't know. I'm afraid I have no luck with roses. The leaves turn black. The blossoms turn brown."

"Gardening can break your heart as well as your back," Bethany said. Dr. Bergius laughed uproariously. He shepherded us around to the back of the house, where a picnic table had been set for dinner with green and gold china. Then he disappeared into the house and returned with the roses in a vase, which he set on the table. "Very festive," he said. "A perfect match for my lovely guests."

Bethany shook her head and smiled. "That's very kind," she said.

We ate dinner, which was cold slices of turkey and roast beef with corn on the cob and fresh asparagus and various kinds of salad, and Dr. Bergius questioned Bethany minutely. He wanted to know how she liked her job. Where did she and I live? What was our house like; did we find it comfortable, did we find the noise from the highway intrusive? I could see he wanted to establish himself right away as a good, caring person, like Freud at his most genial. Then he started to describe houses he'd lived in when he was young: the staircases, the windows, the lovely little courtyards.

"This is a wonderful meal," Bethany said, wiping melted butter off her hands and laughing at the mess she'd made with the corn on the cob, and Dr. Bergius smiled and said, "Perhaps Rachel has told you that my late wife, Eva, was a teacher of cookery. I was her keenest pupil. In any case, this is such a pleasure. Not to dine alone. It means a great deal to me."

"Well," said Bethany, "it's a treat for me and Rachel, too, isn't it, Rachel?"

When we'd finished eating, Dr. Bergius went inside to put on the coffee. Bethany and I sat in the dusk, watching the geese. They were domestic geese, Dr. Bergius had said. They did not belong to him, but to a neighbour. I had my back to the house. I began to feel as if someone was watching Bethany and me. I imagined a face at the kitchen window, a cold, superior stare. I imagined someone — perhaps Eva — helping Dr. Bergius set out coffee cups, a small jug of cream. This scene came to me with the clarity and exactitude I remembered from Simon's beloved foreign films. I imagined Eva removing a small silver spoon from a drawer lined with velvet and examining it for signs of tarnish or wear.

Dr. Bergius came to the door and said he didn't know what he was thinking of, leaving us out in the damp air. I didn't think the air was damp; on the contrary, it was a beautiful, mild evening. Nevertheless, we went inside and Dr. Bergius led us through the kitchen, which was perfectly empty, no one else there at all — the coffee maker burbling to itself on the counter, African violets on the windowsill — and into the living room. Here, the furniture seemed to have been shoved to the middle of the room in order to make space for an array of professional-looking recording equipment, including a reel-to-reel tape machine with sound-level meters, much like the one at the radio station. It was the strangest room I had ever seen. Bethany and I sat on the edge of the sofa and Dr. Bergius stood in front of us, his cheeks stained with colour. He began to lecture us in a high-spirited, animated way. He strolled around the room a little. He told us he and his wife Eva had been privileged to hear Stockhausen's *Gruppen* performed in Cologne, Germany, in 1957, shortly before he came to Canada. Imagine three orchestras, Dr. Bergius said — three orchestras contending, as if engaged in battle, then achieving a brief, momentary accord — what we think of as accord, he amended — why, it had changed his life. At the time, Eva's health had been declining; soon after, she was admitted to a sanatorium. His poor mother, also, had been unwell. She'd lost her home during the war, all her treasures, her books. It was a difficult time, he said. As he had listened to the *Gruppen*, he began to understand that everything could be destroyed, and then someone, some brave soul, would begin over, one tentative note at a time, and, with patience and perseverance, there would once again be music and poetry and books. Yes, it could happen. It happened all the time.

Bethany and I sat there stiffly on a fusty old sofa. Through the thin draperies the evening sun cast a mordant glow. We listened — or tried to listen — as Dr. Bergius told us that language came from the mind and the heart, but music came from the soul. Music, like nature, had no language other than colour and design, modalities and tones. In this way it was the language purely of the spirit, the language of wind and light and movement. Finally he sat down — or rather collapsed — on a hassock and put his hands on his knees and drew a breath.

"Rachel writes poetry," Bethany said.

"I do not," I said quickly.

"Ah. And what kind of poetry does Rachel write?" Dr. Bergius said.

"Well, it's very good, I think," Bethany said. "I don't get to see it very often."

"Azure skies, maidens all forlorn?" Dr. Bergius suggested.

"No," I said. "Hardly." I glared at him.

Oh, he said, what in the name of heaven was wrong with him? He'd forgotten the coffee. Never mind, he said. Never mind. He picked relentlessly at the fabric of his pants with a fingernail. Talking of poetry, he said, he had a very special treat for us. He languished a moment more, then rose and made his way across the room to a cabinet, from which he extracted a tape he then threaded onto the tape machine. "Now," he said. "Now. Close your eyes. Listen carefully."

A few scratches. A whispering, a dry, wistful, secretive rustling, as of someone settling in a chair. Then there began a woman's voice, high, reedy, speaking in a foreign tongue. It didn't matter that I couldn't understand the words. I was intent on an image behind my eyes, an inflorescence of bell-shaped flowers on threadlike, waxen stems. The solemn little twinflower, *linnea borealis*, which grew in such profusion near our front gate, in the shade of the tulip tree. Did Bethany see this same image, all mingled with the voice?

"This is my mother. Listen now," Dr. Bergius said. "She's getting impatient with me. 'Karl,' she appeals to me. 'My darling, have I read enough? Can I rest now?' She laughs. I amuse her, obviously. Her little Karl, a grown man, a doctor of medicine, amuses her greatly.

"What is she saying? Let me translate. 'The well — beloved' — no. Wait. I have it: 'The beloved, no more befogged, is coming back! Is coming back!' There you go. Goethe. You see, it is the power of language that returns her to me, all these years later."

Dr. Bergius caught the end of the tape in his hands. "How beautiful the German language is," he exclaimed. "I forget, and then my mother reminds me."

The single word that remained in my mind from that evening was *befogged*, and then it changed into another word: *becalmed*, which seemed perfectly to describe the sorry condition of Simon and his boat. I'd left Simon in the cabin, where he'd been drinking all afternoon and evening and had finally passed out. I wanted more than anything just to get home. I had climbed up the gangway from the wharf to the marina. It was nearly midnight. I had pulled on a sweater, but the night wasn't really cold. Possibly I, too, was a little drunk.

I took a dime out of the pocket of my shorts and used the pay phone in front of the marina, which was closed and dark. After about ten rings, Bethany answered. "Rachel, is that you?" she said. At first, I couldn't convince her I wasn't at home in my bed. "I thought I heard you come home," she said. "I must have been dreaming."

"Yes," I said. "Could you come and get me?" She wanted to know if I was in some kind of trouble, and I told her no, I just needed a ride home right away. "Please hurry," I said.

"Stay where you are," she said. "Don't talk to anyone. I'll be there as soon as I can."

I sat on a curb at the edge of the gravel parking lot. The gentle sloshing of the sea had something in it of Dr. Bergius's mother's voice, which had, on the tape, been accompanied by a faint, insistent, slightly hostile echo, as if the recording had been made in a vast ruined hall. I could picture Dr. Bergius and Eva, the only two people in the audience, their upturned faces shining with pride and apprehension. Distance, absence, loss, all healed by a spirit-voice, a voice from the past, a treat saved up for long, lonely summer evenings, the windows covered, doors left open, white geese swimming on a pond. Was it possible? I wished I could share Dr. Bergius's strange dreams, his vision of a splendid vanished world, but at the time it all seemed troublesome to me, a burden that, once shouldered, couldn't be set aside.

For something to do, I scraped the toe of my running shoe idly back and forth in the gravel. I hugged myself to keep warm, for it was getting cooler as the night advanced. I listened for Bethany's car, but all I heard was the sea lapping at the shore and an occasional odd rustling in the bushes, as if some night animal was scurrying around. I touched my arms, bruised and sore where Simon had grabbed me roughly. He'd been angry because I wouldn't go out with him in his boat. We were ready to go, nearly ready, but it had seemed to me too dark, and the tide was going out, and besides, I thought Simon had had too much to drink. I swore I'd never speak to him again if he untied the boat from the wharf.

He took hold of me. His eyes were watering with rage or drink or remorse, a need for forgiveness and acceptance — not from me, perhaps, but from his wife, Rosemary. Perhaps I was Rosemary to him, at that moment. Then he seemed to see me as I was. He said he hadn't meant to, he hadn't meant to hurt me. He kissed me on my eyelids, on my mouth. He kissed me tenderly with his whiskey-smelling breath and put his hand under my T-shirt, on my bare skin. He ran his fingers up and down my spine. He held me and rocked me in his arms and I rested my head on his chest like a child.

Then he pushed me away. He went a little crazy, smashing around in the confined space of the cabin, hauling tattered old navigating charts out of a locker, trying to spread them out on the already littered table. Whither shall we sail? he kept saying. His speech was slurred. He was unsteady on his feet. At first he frightened me, then he made me laugh.

"I don't know, Simon," I said. "I don't know wither we should sail." There were times when, in spite of everything, I liked him better than anyone I knew. I felt like an adult with Simon. I felt eager to get started on the life I thought I was owed — a life of colour and movement, a life of the heart and mind and spirit, of the wind, the sun. I had another beer, and then another after that. I sat at the table with Simon and we traced out imaginary voyages on the charts, our hands colliding like little lost sailors. If you stay, I'll ravish you, he said. His skin was stretched tight over his cheekbones, his eyes were bright as if with fever, but at a low ebb. Finally, he lapsed into sleep on the nearest bunk. I covered him with a blanket and left him there. It was the exact midpoint of night, the darkest time. And then I waited in the marina parking lot for Bethany. I waited a long time. I imagined the concentration, the care, with which she was negotiating the narrow twisting road, a swath of trees on either side sparking into life in the incendiary rake of headlights. Or was that a picture that didn't occur to me until later, when I tried my best to reconstruct Bethany's journey? I didn't doubt for a moment that she would find me and take me safely home. But I remembered feeling suddenly unsure; cold, overwhelmed with fatigue, nauseous from the beer I'd drunk. I had the thought that if I possessed the nerve, the simple courage, I could reach up and touch the discordant sky with its random covering of stars and planets. I imagined heaven had, that night, a strange texture of its own: coarse, nubby, repellent.

CHILDREN'S GAMES

THE BRICK STEPS THAT LED up to Ben's front porch were slick with
frost the morning Marisa moved in. The leafless trees in the garden
were dusted with snow. On the street below a cyclist raced past, a
couple walked their lanky red-haired dog. Ben's house was in the
Queen Anne Hill neighbourhood of Seattle and looked out over
Puget Sound and the Olympic Mountains. It was an old, gracious
house, with lots of space, lots of rooms. Marisa thought it was a sad
house, containing traces of a vanished life, a life that had belonged
to Ben's former wife, Maureen. Her winter boots, stained with
rainwater, were in the back porch, as if she'd just kicked them off.
Her coats hung at the back of the downstairs hall closet, bunched
together like mourners at a funeral. One day, when she was alone,
Marisa slipped into one — red wool, with gold buttons and a little
half-belt at the back. She brushed a blond hair — Maureen was
blond — off the collar. For the past two years Maureen had been

living in Buenos Aires with her new husband, Luis, but the things she'd left behind, her coats and boots, a gym membership card in a kitchen drawer, her son Logan, made it seem she might walk in at any moment. When Marisa came downstairs in the morning she half-expected to find Maureen in the kitchen, drinking coffee and reading the *Post-Intelligencer*; she'd raise her eyes and give Marisa a bored, incurious glance and think: Ah, the new girlfriend.

Marisa was used to being the new girl. After college she'd taken a number of business courses and for several years had worked for an agency that sent her to fill in when an office was short-staffed or needed reorganizing. She was good at what she did. She liked her peripatetic way of life. When she needed a place to live, she'd sublet an apartment or do a little house sitting. She'd never done this before, though. She'd never moved into a house while it was still occupied. Here was a man and his child. And Logan resented her. He threw his toys at her. For a little kid, his aim was good. "You're stupid, Marisa," he'd shout. "You're stupid and ugly."

"Hey, that's not how we talk to Marisa," Ben would say sternly. He'd order Logan to his bedroom, and Logan would go, but he'd soon be back, unrepentant. He climbed up on the kitchen counter and dunked his feet in a sink full of soapy water. Marisa had been washing a few dishes, because it was Wednesday, Isolde's day off, and the dishwasher was full and she'd forgotten to turn it on. She lifted Logan down and sat him on the kitchen table. She took off his wet slippers and dried his feet on a tea towel.

"I hate you," he said, kicking at her.

"I know you do," she said. "I know you do."

"At the park," he said, "this dog jumped in the pool and the water catched on fire and burned up."

"Oh, one of those dogs," she said. "They think they're so hot, don't they?"

Marisa gave Logan a cookie. That was all she could think to do, feed him apple slices and raisins, as if he were a pet rabbit. He had tantrums that scared her. He sucked his thumb and ate almost nothing. Could this be right, in a child of four? Ben said Logan was doing just fine; he was a fabulous little guy. He missed his mother, but that was to be expected. Ben said Logan knew Maureen still loved him, even if she wasn't here in person.

"Well, yes, I guess so," Marisa had said. Ben was the head of the human resources department at a hospital, which was where they'd met. Marisa had worked as his administrative assistant for six months. In the past, she'd avoided office romances, but she and Ben had become very fond of one another.

Now, for the first time in six years, she was taking a break between assignments. This was all very new to her. It was not easy. She was learning as she went along. With Logan, she tried a little subversion. She told him he was the boss. "What you say goes, Bub," she said.

"You *lady*," he said.

She put some music on. She and Logan danced around the living room — a long, narrow, beautiful room, with dark wainscoting, built-in cabinets, and frosted pink sconces in gold brackets on either side of the fireplace. From the windows Marisa could see pearly clouds drifting across a pale northwest sky. The Olympic Mountains were dark and jagged, crowned with blue-white ice sheets and glaciers. She'd grown up on the Olympic Peninsula. She and her brother, Norman, still owned the old family house. Her parents were dead. Norman was in Europe. She'd neglected to tell Ben any of this. But, so? Marisa was happy. Being happy was a precarious state, she believed, and required not too much vigilance.

Jennifer Warnes sang about how there was no cure, no cure for love. Logan danced in one spot, his legs jittering, his arms held stiffly out. Marisa wondered if *Famous Blue Raincoat* had belonged to Maureen, another discard. Things fell from Maureen's grasp, it seemed. She ran into the night and was seen no more. Marisa kind of suggested Maureen must have left very quickly and Ben said, no, it wasn't like that. Maureen was organized and practical, although toward the end things had got a little fraught. There had been the occasional flare-up of temper, the occasional barb. He hadn't been himself. The day before Maureen left, her mother, Kay, had arrived from Spokane to plead with her not to leave her home, abandon her son. More angry words; more tears. Perhaps as a response to the stress, Logan developed a high fever and had to be taken to the hospital. Then Ben caught the virus and was too sick to be concerned that, while his mother-in-law administered baby Aspirin and alcohol baths to his son, he was driving his wife to the airport so that she could go to her lover. How absurd and intractable life was, Ben said. And how desolate, he added with a smile, until he'd met Marisa.

In the fall, Ben and Logan were going to Buenos Aires so that Logan could see his mother. If he could cancel this trip or even postpone it, Ben would. He wished he and Marisa could take a real holiday and be alone for a time. That, he said, would be ideal. Instead, they were going to spend a week at Serenity Cove, a seaside resort and human development centre. A colleague at work had recommended it to Ben and he wanted to check it out as a possible location for a future administrators' retreat. He'd left it a little late, he said, but they'd found room for him, for all three of them. Also, he'd gone ahead and signed himself up for a course, and now he wasn't sure — had he done the right thing or not?

The day before they left for Serenity Cove, Marisa got a letter from her brother, Norman. It had been forwarded to her from her last address. She ran upstairs with it. Folded in with two sheets of paper covered in Norman's calligraphic hand there was a photograph. Norman was in Poland. He was trying to start up an orthotics factory in the Lodz Special Economic Zone, or, as he'd printed in block letters, the LODZA SPECJALNA STREFA EKONOMICZNA. He flew regularly to Germany, Switzerland, England in search of investors. He was raising lots of lovely Eurodollars, that futuristic currency in which everyone and no one believed. A considerable undertaking, but doable, he believed, if approached with the correct ratio of caution to recklessness: *Watch me, no hands!*

Through the open bedroom window she could hear Ben talking to Logan. Ben had mown the lawn and the smell of freshly-cut grass filled Marisa with a sense of elation and joy. This was her life. This was who she was now.

Norman wrote that he loved Lodz, the California of Poland. The Beijing of Eastern Europe! Incidentally, he added, he'd just got engaged to a woman called Teresa. She was a librarian at the *Bibliotecki Publiczne* in Poland. She was beautiful. He hardly deserved such luck. She had a son, Pawel, aged five. See enclosed photo, Norman wrote.

Marisa picked up the photograph just as Logan ran up the stairs and banged at the bedroom door. "Open the door," he yelled. He wanted a drink. He wanted orange juice. "Hurry, Marisa," he said.

She put the letter and the photograph back in the envelope and slid it under some clothes in her suitcase, which was open on the bed beside her. Then she let Logan into the room.

"What's this?" he demanded, going over to the suitcase.

"You know," she said. "It's a suitcase. I'm getting packed. Then we'll get you packed."

"I'm not going," he said.

"You can't stay by yourself."

"Isolde's staying," he said.

"Isolde is going on holiday, too," Marisa said. "She's going to visit her family in Trinidad." Every morning, except on Wednesdays, Isolde rode her bike up the hill to Ben's house. She made breakfast and took Logan to and from preschool and read Bible stories to him while he ate his lunch. Isolde's husband was a deacon at the Episcopalian church a few blocks away. Isolde was lovely. When she was in the house, everything ran smoothly and Logan was happy.

He threw himself against the side of the bed and slid to the floor, pulling the bedspread with him. Marisa caught the suitcase before it fell.

"I love Isolde the most," Logan said.

"Yes, Logan, I get the message," Marisa said. "But you can't stay with Isolde, because she has to go on holiday with her own family. That's what families do. They go on holiday together."

She sat on the floor beside Logan. Ben had told her Logan was born in this room, in a birthing pool, with the assistance of a midwife. The pool had left water stains on the carpet. Ben said he and Maureen had intended to take it up and have the original wood floor refinished. They'd been in the process of redecorating the entire house, which had been built in 1912, when Maureen had left on a business trip to Argentina. The paint cans and fabric swatches were around somewhere, probably down in the basement. Ben had lost interest in the project. He'd sell the house, if he could, he said, but it didn't actually belong to him. Maureen had inherited it from a great-aunt, a descendant of one of Seattle's pioneer families. She'd signed the house over to Ben in the divorce settlement, with the stipulation that it was to go to Logan when he turned nineteen. That, Ben said, told you everything you needed to know about Maureen: she was impulsive, generous, and crafty as all get out.

Serenity Cove was located on a small island off the east coast of Vancouver Island. It took eleven hours to get there. Marisa had never travelled with a small child before. They stopped at a Macdonald's for a Happy Meal. Then they stopped at a DQ for ice cream, which melted all over Logan's T-shirt, so that Ben had to get fresh clothes for him out of the suitcase in the trunk. Then Logan got carsick (necessitating a second change of clothes) and Ben had to find a drugstore where he could buy some children's Gravol, which meant they missed a ferry sailing. Perhaps it was the arduous nature of the trip, plus the fact that the last time she'd crossed the border she'd been with Norman, just after her father died, that made Marisa feel apprehensive and uneasy. By the time they got to Serenity Cove it was midnight and everything was in darkness. She and Logan stayed in the car while Ben went to locate someone who could give them their room key. Then they got some of their luggage out of the car and made their way along a narrow footpath between trees and little fairy-tale cottages. Their room wasn't in a cottage. It was on the second floor of a fourplex with a long flight of outside steps and a porch light that had burned out. The room itself contained a double bed and a small rollaway cot for Logan. The floor was brown and the walls were a streaky green, as if the room had been briefly submerged and then wrung out.

"Is this the room the bad campers get?" Marisa said after a moment. She put her suitcase down on the floor. "Is this where they send you for failing orienteering or showing poor team spirit or something?" She couldn't help it; she was shaking with fatigue.

"Maybe the guy in the office screwed up," Ben said. "I knew he wasn't paying attention. He was watching some movie on TV."

"It's not that bad," Marisa said. "In the morning it'll look better." She told herself to get a grip. The first night in a strange place was the worst. She knew that. While Ben showered she got Logan into his pyjamas and tucked up in the cot. Perhaps because of the travel sickness medicine, he fell asleep almost at once. She sat on the edge of the bed looking at him. His eyelashes cast shadows on his cheeks. His mouth was slightly parted. His eyes moved behind his closed lids, as if he were already dreaming. Dreaming he was at home. Dreaming of his mother, maybe. He was so small and vulnerable. She felt homesick, which was odd, considering she didn't really have a home. She had a shower and got into bed beside Ben and went to sleep.

In the morning, the room didn't look any better. She and Ben and Logan dressed quickly and went outside, into the bright sun. They joined a crowd of dazed-looking people and walked with them down to the dining room, which was in a low, rambling building just above the beach. They lined up at the door and when their turn came had their names checked off and were given nametags. Then they got in line with trays and helped themselves to breakfast at a long table. Marisa hid her nametag under her plate of toast. Ben pinned his on. "It's just a way of getting to know people," he said. "I know," she said. "But."

Once they were seated in the dining room, she thought her first impression was correct: she didn't especially want to know any of the people here. The look of fragile yearning she saw on everyone's face made her wary. What a homogenous, credulous-looking group, she thought. Everyone alike. Young couples with children. The children were noisy and rambunctious. Logan was very well behaved, by comparison. She diluted his orange juice with water until it got to a colour he was happy with. A woman came into the dining room and introduced herself as Sharon, the program director. She had to speak in a loud voice to be heard, and then suddenly the room went quiet, apart from chair legs scraping on the floor, and she was shrieking about the wonderful week ahead. She smiled and widened her eyes and in a more moderate tone went on to say she hoped their stay at Serenity Cove would prove illuminating and empowering. And a lot of fun, too, of course. "Enjoy your breakfast, eat up, you'll need the energy," she said. There was laughter. There was applause.

Later, as they walked back to their room, Ben said he understood it all had to do with emotional intelligence, the ability to enhance your life skills through knowing how you responded emotionally to people and events. "I think they're working on the assumption that, just as with any kind of intelligence, most people never realize their full potential."

"Well, sadly, I think people do use their full potential," Marisa said. They groped their way into their gloomy room. She picked one of Logan's T-shirts up off the floor and held it close to her.

Logan bent down and started to drive his Thomas the Tank Engine over the rough brown carpet. She knew her despair at the thought of seven days and nights here was giving her voice an edge.

"People do use their intelligence, but it never turns out to be enough, does it?" she said. "Why else do you think we're all so messed up?"

"Marisa," Ben said. "Do you really believe that? That's kind of a bleak view."

"It's realistic," she said. Also, it was the only view she had: a patch of sky, a dull brick wall. Ben didn't know her. He didn't know anything about her. She was a real pessimist. So was Norman. They knew too much about life. When they were kids, they'd loved it that insects, not people, made up the largest living group on earth. How cool, Norman had said. People thought they were so smart, but look at the ants! They had colonies and armies and expeditionary forces. They grew their own food, or some ants did. They had towering cities.

Question: What would you do if you turned into an insect?

Answer: I'd make like a bee and buzz. I'd beetle off.

While Ben was at his first workshop, which was called "The Individual in Relationship" — an irony not lost on Marisa, at least — she and Logan went to the children's play area, which was down a grassy slope from the dining room. There were swings and slides and a little roundabout and a sandbox, where Logan settled in with his beach bucket and shovel.

Marisa found a bench in the shade of a fir tree. From here, she could see most of the buildings that made up Serenity Cove: the residences, the dining room, the office, a building where the workshops and other activities were held. There was also a swimming pool in a glass-walled, flat-roofed building. The buildings were unpainted, weathered wood. Paved walkways meandered around, and here and there planters containing petunias and marigolds were set out. The dining room had a deck that looked out over the sea. That was it, apart from the languorous, disinterested fir and cedar trees that enclosed the grounds.

She got Norman's letter out of her bag. She looked at the photograph of Norman's fiancée, Teresa, and her little boy, Pawel. They were standing in a rose garden outside what looked like a Communist-era apartment block. Teresa was wearing a white blouse and blue Capri pants and sandals. Her straight, light-brown hair was held back with barrettes. She wasn't beautiful, as Norman had said, but she looked intelligent and sensible and pleasant. Her son had a look of Logan about him: the same dark, fine hair, tense little grin. It was as if Norman had honed in on Marisa's whereabouts and learned everything he could about her, then couldn't refrain from launching a few harmless but accurate strikes. Look, she imagined him saying. Look, Marisa, or whatever you call yourself now, you're not so special after all. Even I have someone who loves me. And like your lover, mine too has a little boy for whom I'm playing substitute parent. Of course they were playing. This isn't serious, is it, Norman, she wanted to say to him. In the long run, what does any of this matter?

Whatever you call yourself now. It was true: Marisa wasn't her real name. She'd changed her name, for luck, for euphony, for distance; because she felt like it.

She wished Norman had told her more about his life in Poland, or had at least given her a phone number.

The last time she'd seen Norman was a few months after their father had passed away. Norman had phoned to tell her their father, Jeff, had been found in the house by a friend, and the kind of horrific thing was that Jeff had been dead for several days by that time. Norman said he felt bad Jeff had died alone. He hadn't even been to see him for months. Marisa had said, "I know. Me too."

In July, when Marisa was between jobs and Norman had finished a business course he was taking, they drove up to Vernon with their father's ashes. They'd planned to scatter them in a field near the house where he'd lived as a child, but when they got there the field, with its grass and wild flowers, had been reduced to a barren strip of land between two new housing developments. Norman said they could go back to Jeff's house and scatter the ashes there. Which, now that he thought about it, Jeff might have preferred, anyway. Marisa said she couldn't face another long trip with the ashes in the car. She looked away while Norman opened the box and let the ashes drift onto the sun-baked ground. He asked if they should say a prayer or something. "Dad wasn't religious, was he?" Marisa said.

"How's this?" Norman said. "Good night sweet prince. Ashes to ashes, dust to dust, drink good booze and your pipes won't rust."

"Norman," Marisa protested. But she couldn't help laughing. Norman was funny. He was charming. On the way back, they'd stayed in Victoria. Norman loved the city. He loved the constant wind. In the middle of the sidewalk he spun on his heel, and people had smiled and obligingly detoured around him. He was a good-looking man, slightly built, with fair hair and fine features. He had talked about moving to Victoria. He said technically he and Marisa were Canadians, although that couldn't have been true, since they'd both been born in the U.S. Their father had left his parents' home in Vernon in 1966, when he was twenty, so that he could enlist and get sent to Viet Nam. He'd been a corporal in the Third Battalion, Ninth Marines. He showed Marisa and Norman the shrapnel scars on his arms and described in detail the bad case of "immersion foot" he'd got from slogging through flooded rice paddies. The best time in his life, he said. After the war he became an American citizen. He met their mother, Suzie, and got married.

When Marisa was growing up, Jeff had worked as a car salesman, a delivery truck driver, a school janitor. Whatever job he had, it became a mania to him and then, suddenly, he would quit. During a stint as a trash collector he scavenged things he'd repair and sell from their front yard: old lawnmowers and bicycles and

toaster ovens. Once he'd brought home a set of psychology textbooks, in which Norman had come across something called the
F Test. He and Marisa applied it to their father and discovered that,
yes, as they'd suspected, he met all the criteria; he was a Fascist.
Marisa didn't know what they'd been thinking, unless it was of old
World War II movies or of Colonel Klink in *Hogan's Heroes* reruns
on TV. It was Jeff, too, of course, because he really could act a little off the wall every now and then. He'd fly into rages over nothing
and try to pick a fight with Marisa's mother. She'd shut herself in
the bedroom and then Jeff would turn on Norman and shout at him
and sometimes hit him. After their mother died, Jeff started drinking, or drinking more, with more finesse and dedication, as Norman
said. Life with Jeff was not easy. Norman and then Marisa left
home as soon as they'd finished school. On his own Jeff became
reclusive, suspicious of everyone, sometimes refusing to cash his
government check or go to the store for food. Marisa didn't know
if she and Norman could have prevented any of this. They'd felt as
helpless, perhaps, as Jeff, and as lost.

That July, she and Norman had taken the ferry from Victoria
back to Port Angeles, although they'd bypassed the route that would
have taken them to the house they'd inherited and didn't know what
to do with. They'd driven straight down to Seattle. Norman took her
to the apartment she was subletting. He helped her carry her bags
inside and then he left. She hadn't seen him since. A week later,
she'd started an assignment in the human resources department at a
hospital, where the department head turned out to be a man called
Ben, who, after three months in which both of them pretended they
weren't attracted to each other, they weren't falling in love, he ended
up saying he was sorry, but he just couldn't let her go.

Parents and children were drifting into the playground area, spreading blankets out on the grass to sit on. The women's bright summer
outfits reminded Marisa of how, when she was small, she'd liked

to set her dolls out on the grass on a fine day. She didn't mean to disparage these women by comparing them to dolls. The truth was, they intrigued and intimidated her. Almost, she could envy them. They got to stay in the fairy-tale cottages with their myriad children. Their rings sparkled in the sun, their hair shone. Marisa probably didn't look all that different, but something set her apart. She knew that for a fact.

She closed her eyes and heard, from the direction of the sandbox, a piercing shriek. She got up and stumbled over to Logan, the letter and photograph still clutched in her hand. A little girl screamed that Logan had thrown sand at her. Tears rolled down her red, crumpled face. The little girl's mother hurried over to the sandbox.

"Let me see, Emily," the little girl's mother said. "Are you hurt?"

Hurt? Marisa thought. Hurt, from a little sand?

"Did it get in your eyes?" the woman said. She demanded of Logan: "Did you throw sand at Emily?" Logan squinted up at her. Emily looked fine, apart from a telltale glint of sand in the flawless parting of her yellow hair. Marisa saw Logan's dilemma. There was evidence; there was probably a motive. Still, she thought he'd be wiser not to admit guilt — not here, anyway. She'd talk to him later. Isolde had told her Logan had lots of friends at preschool and, if he wanted, could go on a play date every single day. Remembering Isolde's fondness for Logan made Marisa smile. Emily's mother gave her a suspicious look and wiped Emily's eyes with a tissue. Emily pushed her away.

"Now, don't be like that," Emily's mother said.

She smiled at Marisa. She said her name was Grace. Her skin was pale, her eyes a light glassy blue. She invited Marisa to join her Tai Chi class, at ten in the morning, in the annex behind the swimming pool.

"After class, we go to the dining room for tea. Please come. We'd love to get to know you."

Marisa said, well, she had Logan.

"Oh, there's a drop-in play group. Didn't anyone tell you?" she said.

"No, I missed that," said Marisa. She looked at Logan. He stuck his thumb in his mouth. "Don't do that, Logan," she said. Did everyone guess she was a fraud, neither wife nor mother? "It's okay," she said to Logan. "I used to suck my thumb, too." He was pale, the skin under his eyes bruised-looking. He broke her heart, this kid.

"Five more minutes," she said, "and then we'll go find Daddy."

She went back to the bench and looked again at Norman's letter and the photograph of Teresa and Pawel. Were they real, she wondered? Did they exist? Norman was quite capable of inventing a fiancée and an economic venture, or anything else that suited him.

The dining room had a low ceiling of knotty pine, darkened with age, and a row of small windows smudged and pitted from the sea air, so that even in this bright, clear weather the sky outside appeared overcast and dismal. Emily, the little girl from the sand-box, was in front of Marisa and Ben and Logan in the line-up. Emily was wearing overalls and had pink ribbons in her pigtails. She turned around and pulled a face at Logan and he pushed her. Emily's father glared at Logan. He put his arm around Emily and leaned over, as if shielding her from harm. According to his nametag, he was Mike.

"Emily," he said, "you stay here with Daddy."

"Logan," Marisa said, "you stay with me." She spooned some green beans onto his plate. She talked him into having a little salad. A little mashed potato? she suggested. He shook his head. "That's enough, lady," he kept saying. "No problem, Bub," she said.

Marisa heard Emily saying that mashed potatoes made her throw up. She only liked spaghetti.

"There isn't any spaghetti," Mike said. "There are just these nice potatoes. See, you put a teeny bit of butter on them, like this."

Someone touched Marisa's arm. It was Grace. She stepped into line with her tray. She speared a slice of ham and said, "Marisa, I didn't see you in my Tai Chi class."

"I know," Marisa said. "I'm sorry."

"Oh, don't," Grace said. "Don't say sorry. Come sit with us for dinner. We'll have a chance to talk."

Marisa smiled and nodded. She poured gravy on her mashed potatoes, because what the heck, carbohydrates might calm her nerves. But, hey, how could you not love these things? The fatigue, the frayed nerves, the ennui followed by a sudden combative urge. Not to mention the paper banner on the wall that proclaimed: *Healing the Family Week!!* How could you not love it?

Marisa and Ben took their trays out onto the deck and sat at a table shaded by a green umbrella that swivelled every now and then in the on-shore breeze. They swatted wasps away from their food and tried to keep the paper napkins from blowing away.

Marisa waved at Grace and shrugged, as if to say, sorry, we just couldn't find a table near you; everyone had come outside to eat, due to the stifling heat in the dining room. Next to Marisa and Ben sat Sharon, the program director, in vivid turquoise shorts and top, crimson polish on her toenails. The man sitting with her was someone Marisa often saw striding across the lawns with books and papers under his arm, head down, dark glasses concealing his eyes. His name was Garth, Ben had told Marisa, and he was a popular motivational speaker. Ben had seen him once or twice on public television. Garth was also a director at Serenity Cove, or, rumour had it, the owner. He wore khaki shorts and a black T-shirt that revealed his muscular chest and shoulders. He was tall and had a Celtic cross tattooed on his forearm. Later, when the meal was more or less over, people drew their chairs closer to Garth. He waited for quiet and then opened a book, held it at a solemn distance, and read: "'From my own voice resonant — singing the phallus. Singing the song of procreation ..."" He paused, then went on, in a strong, authoritative, agreeable voice: "'Singing the need of superb children, and therein superb grown people.'"

The words of the poem, which seemed to emanate not from Garth but from a benevolent and disembodied source, washed over Marisa as if they came from the depths of the sea. The spell cast by the words was shattered, however, when Mike said, "That's so cool." Grace said, "I know. That's Whitman, isn't it?"

"Yes," said Garth. "It's Whitman. 'Singing the need of superb children, and therein superb grown people.' That's us, wouldn't you say?"

"Yes," said the others. "Oh, yes, that's us, definitely."

Marisa leaned closer to Ben and said, "I love a little poetry after dinner." Ben smiled thinly. A wasp zeroed in on Logan's dish of ice cream and Logan, startled, threw his spoon into the air and it landed on the deck, which made him cry. Marisa picked it up and said she'd get him a clean spoon, but in the dining room the cutlery tray was empty. She went to the kitchen door and asked if she could rinse the spoon off at the sink. Without a word a young man removed the spoon from her hand. The staff at Serenity Cove worked with a negative energy she found irresistible. They crashed dishes around in the sink and dropped knives on the floor and kicked them out of the way and left the fridge door open. They were, she understood, recruited from the island's year-round population, and in all probability resented being underpaid and overworked. She'd seen the coldly disdainful looks they gave the guests, the same kind of look she caught when the spoon, washed and dried, was returned to her.

In the kitchen the air was humid and thick with the smell of cooked meat and boiled potatoes and induced in Marisa a kind of torpor, so that she was unable to move.

"Can I get you anything?" a young woman asked her.

"No," Marisa said. "No, that's okay." Her thoughts were all churned up. *The needs of superb children*, she thought. She leaned against the doorframe. So this was it, she thought: everything about this place reminded her of the church-run camp she'd been sent to the summer her mother's health got worse. At Camp Zaragoza, she'd made lists: *flowers, hearts, sand-dollars*, silly, inconsequential things, carefully printed on a scrap of paper, to help keep her thoughts pinned-down and orderly, instead of flying around in her head like bats. She'd had to take a Bible with her. It was on another list — an official list — along with two bathing suits, insect repellent, a flashlight. Her mother had got out of bed and had gone down to the basement, where she'd found a Bible in a box of old books. Marisa remembered her mother wiping the dust off the Bible. Before handing it to Marisa she had opened it and had read: *In the beginning*, as if the words surprised her. The Bible had print so tiny the words appeared sly, furtive, guarded. Marisa had liked it, though, the way it smelled, of dust and antiquity, and the small weight of it in her hands, and the fact that her mother had given it to her. Unfortunately, it turned out everyone at Camp Zaragoza had a new Bible written in a plainer style, with coloured maps of The Holy Land. The woman in charge, who was called Senorita, because she'd been a missionary in Mexico, took the old Bible away from Marisa and loaned her one with large clear print. Then she was assigned to a class for kids who'd flunked the test in Bible knowledge, where she was given multiple-choice tests: *Abraham was willing to sacrifice his son Isaac: a) on a mountain in the land of Moriah, b) on Mount Ararat, c) beside the pyramids in Egypt.*

She'd hated Camp Zaragoza. And here it was again. The sun was beating in the kitchen windows and in the middle of the room flies circled furiously. When she went outside to the deck with the spoon, Ben was gathering up their plates, because the wasps were frightening Logan.

That evening, games of horseshoes and tag and hide-and-go-seek were organized on the lawn above the beach. After the games a fire was lit in the fire pit below the dining room, in front of the beach. Everyone sat around in a circle and roasted marshmallows and sang "Row, Row, Row Your Boat," and "If I Had a Hammer." Logan sang along. His chin was gooey with melted marshmallow. He and Emily sat on the grass in front of Marisa, who stared into the flames.

She was far away, in a different place, thinking about her last day at Camp Zaragoza, when Senorita had called her into her office and said she had something very serious to tell her. She still couldn't think about it without feeling chilled and weak. Senorita had told Marisa her mother had gone to be with the angels. Then she'd made her sit down and lower her head and then someone, one of the camp counsellors, brought her a glass of warm ginger ale. What Senorita had told her had seemed outrageous. Her mother would never leave her. Marisa had tried to impress on her the truth: her mother did at times get sick, she'd have a fever and go to bed, but she always got better. She and Norman would make her weak tea, the kind she liked, with cinnamon and a little milk. Their mother said it did her good. She always got better. This was what Marisa wanted to tell Senorita.

In Senorita's office there was a metal table with an electric kettle, a teacup, and a jar of instant coffee on it. On the wall there was a calendar with a picture of the Holy Spirit dove-like over a Midwestern wheat field. At Sunday morning services, Senorita spoke in tongues, which sent Marisa and some other girls from the remedial Bible class into fits of giggling: another strange, uncontrollable visitation. Later, they were punished by being confined to their cabins or given Bible verses to memorize. In Senorita's office all that seemed forgiven, if not forgotten. Senorita held Marisa, enveloping her in surprisingly spongy and yielding flesh that smelled of harsh soap, cafeteria food, and the dusty, fragile pages of the old Bible, returned to her by Senorita before she left the office. Later,

Senorita instructed all the campers to join hands in a circle with Marisa. They recited the Lord's Prayer and sang, "Just a Closer Walk with Thee." Marisa felt nothing. Her heart was a little stone thing. For the rest of the day she waited for her father to come and get her. She had her sleeping bag baled with twine, her clothes packed in a gym bag. She slipped her lists of words into the old Bible, marking the story of Abraham and Isaac alone on the mountain in the land of Moriah, the two of them laid waste by intention and capitulation and devotion.

Every time she thought about it, Marisa remembered the ride home differently. It was pouring with rain, it was a sunny day, it was the dead of night. There were frogs leaping across the road. Lightning split a tree and it crashed to the road in front of the truck. Her father was silent, morose; he drank a can of beer as he drove. Norman was reading; he had his feet up on the dash. Or he was asleep. Or perhaps he wasn't in the truck; perhaps he'd stayed at home, and was waiting for Marisa on the porch, in the dark, alone.

Don't think about it, she told herself. Banish it. But she couldn't. It was being here, at Serenity Cove. It's not fair, she thought. I'm not registered in a workshop; I don't even have a therapist.

She and Logan went down to the beach and Logan waved at a seaplane as it banked and gained altitude and headed toward the Coast Mountains.

"*Bienvenido,*" Logan shouted. He looked at her uncertainly and said, "He didn't hear me."

"He might have," said Marisa. "I think for sure he saw you."

Logan said he was going in a plane to see his mother. A big plane, he said, holding his arms wide. He was going to sit with the pilot. The pilot knew where his mother lived. "I'm going there," he said. "I'm going to Argentina."

"I know you are," Marisa said. "You're going to see your mommy."

"Are you coming, too?" he said.

"No, I don't think so," she said. She pointed out a heron standing in the shallows. A duck paddling around a log floating in the water, two people gliding past in a kayak. Logan gave these things a critical look, as if he considered their existence debatable. The beach was not sand, but sandstone.

Sandstone, she told Logan, was a kind of sedimentary rock, shaped by the tide and storms into all these interesting whirls and loops. "It looks like a birthday cake, doesn't it?" she said, running her hands over the rock. "It looks like cake batter."

He appeared dubious. "A black cake?" he said. "A cake that's made of rock?"

"Sure," she said. "Why not?"

Marisa jumped from one outcropping of sandstone to another, nearly losing her balance once. Logan tried to do the same, but he got scared. "Stop, Marisa," he cried, and she did stop. He took her hand. She smiled at him. They were friends, she thought. She wanted to tell Logan that she'd lost her mother, too, but in her case the loss was permanent and deep as a well, and she didn't know how to explain that to herself, never mind to a child. He'd figure it out, of course, just from knowing her, because it was part of her, like the shape of her hands.

Early that morning Logan had crawled out of his cot and into bed with Ben and Marisa. He wanted to know: if it was morning here, what time was it in Buenos Aires, where his mommy lived? Ben told Logan his mommy would have had lunch by now. She'd go for a walk in the garden or she'd watch a movie, or go out to see a play. Whatever she did, though, wherever she went, she'd be thinking of Logan.

Ben told Logan about the wind in Argentina, a magnificent warm wind called the Zonda that swept from the Pacific over the Andes and down to the plains, where it ripened the grapes in the vineyards. He told Logan about the haciendas and the gauchos and the fact that Argentina was the eighth largest country in the world. His mother was learning to speak Spanish, Ben said to Logan, but when she dreamed of him, she dreamed in English, just as Logan did. As he spoke, Ben seemed sad. He sounded to Marisa as if he, too, had just woken from dreams of the absent Maureen.

Maureen had met Luis when she'd gone to Argentina on behalf of the travel agency she worked for. (A travel agent, Ben said, so naturally she'd named her son after an airport.) Luis's adopted twenty-four-year-old son had met Maureen in the city of Mendoza, where he was to show Maureen's group an old rail line between Mendoza and Chile that was in the process of being restored as a tourist attraction. Something happened there, Maureen was taken ill, she thought a poisonous spider had bitten her, and the son had arranged for Maureen to recuperate at his father's home in Buenos Aires. Luis was made aware of their imminent arrival. He called his own personal physician. He hired a private nurse. Luis, too, had an adventurous spirit, it seemed. He'd gone ice climbing in Banff, spelunking in Indonesia — or Malaysia, or somewhere — and had crossed a desert in North Africa on a camel. In any case, he had captivated Maureen, this Luis. She did return home, as soon as she'd made a complete recovery, but she knew she wouldn't stay. There was a divorce; there was a marriage. That was the story, Ben said.

For a long time, Ben said, he'd felt bitter and angry. He'd found himself plotting something crazy, like burning down Maureen's great-aunt's house, relocating to an entirely different part of the world and making sure she never again saw Logan. That phase had, mercifully, passed. He was reconciled; he was learning to let go. That was partly why he'd come here, to Serenity Cove. "It must be that, don't you think?" he said. "It can't be the food."

The tide was coming in; the sea lapped at the rocks. It was pale on the surface and filled with light, but darker beneath. Marisa thought of the times she and Norman and their mother used to go to

Dungeness Spit. Their mother would draw stick figures in the wet sand: Norman and Marissa and her, hands linked, round smiling faces. She kicked off her shoes and went and stood in the water, shading her eyes with her hand, as if she could see a ship sailing in. The wind blew her hair around. Every time she took them to Dungeness, she said, "We are at this moment standing on the northernmost point of the contiguous United States. And every year more sand accumulates and the point reaches farther and farther to the north." She loved facts, historical and scientific facts: names and dates. When she'd met Jeff, she'd been an art student. On the kitchen wall she'd hung some of her favourite paintings, including one Marisa remembered clearly. The painting was by Pieter Bruegel the Elder. It was called "Children's Games." Her mother had cut it out of a library book. Norman had said, "Ma, you can't do that to a library book." He'd bent over the desecrated book, a thin, serious boy, his elbows cupped in his hands, as if he, as well as the book, had sustained an injury. "I know, I know," their mother had said. "This is a bad thing I'm doing. But I love this painting. It's a crazy, wonderful painting."

She used a razor blade to remove the colour plate from the book. She worked slowly, taking a break to flex her fingers and hold her hair out of the way.

"How many games can you find?" she asked Marisa.

"Blindman's bluff," Marisa said. "Tag, leapfrog, tug of war." The figures in the painting were riding hobbyhorses and rolling hoops. They were playing tug of war and climbing trees and getting dunked in a stream. They were tossing bones, gambling, trying to beat the odds. From what she remembered, it was the adults at play more than the children. The adults had usurped the children's games. Tiny, squat figures, with faces like clay, little, sullen, smudged mouths, eyes like beans. The games, the rules of the games, wouldn't let them go, and dusk was coming on. In the distance there were buildings, church spires, green, sunlit fields, a little Medieval Flemish village, the promise of custom and safety, reward for labour, a simple meal, but no one dared stop the games to look. That was how Marisa saw it. She used to stare at the picture until the figures in the painting dragged her into the village square, into the waning light. The air smelled of rain, the earth was stirred up with the passage of wheeled carts and horses and feet. Everything was suffused with an ancient, golden light that dimmed or annihilated sight and sharpened other, more immediate senses, making her feel a little like a dumb beast that rocked unsteadily on its four legs. The people laughed and pulled her along, prodded her, but they weren't being mean. It was like being resuscitated after a long period of dormancy or something. The last time she'd visited her father the painting had still been on the kitchen wall. She should go and get it. Children's games, she thought. Wasn't that what this was all about: the same scene, the same probing, febrile games, people acting like children, defenceless, trying to laugh, aching to learn something true and enduring. The sense of something to be won or lost.

Not long before her father took her to Camp Zaragoza, he told her and Norman that their mother had leukemia and she wasn't going to get well. She wasn't ever going to get well.

How long did she have? Norman had asked in a thin voice. Their father said he didn't have a clue. He said the doctors and radiologists and haematologists clammed up when he questioned them. He knew they thought he was a jackass for being persistent and expecting them to actually do something. He stopped. He said from what he understood she didn't have long; days or weeks.

Marisa remembered Norman picking assiduously at a hangnail, his eyes brimming. She had wished her father could have comforted her and Norman. Why couldn't he? He should have talked to them. He was too full of his own pain. That day he walked out on them. He went to the bar. He drove around in his truck. She didn't know what he did. He just wasn't there.

Marisa and Logan found Ben sitting with Mike and Grace at a picnic table near the playground. They were discussing the last session of the workshop Ben and Mike had been in, which had been more of a work*out*, Mike said, if you asked him. In the workshop they'd got into an intense discussion of what was meant by the term unconditional love. Marisa got down on the grass with Logan and Emily and Emily's little plastic zoo animals. She became aware that the grass was crawling with ants. She put her hand down and an ant crawled onto it, scurried around, fell into the cool green world it knew best.

Grace pulled the tab off a can of Diet Coke and took a drink. She said she didn't get it. As far as she could see, love had to be conditional on something, otherwise it became indiscriminate and lost its value. Mike said it didn't have to be that complicated. What it meant, he thought, was not giving up on someone because they'd done something you didn't especially like or approve of. "Although, you're right," he said. "We do pick who we love, don't we, even if we don't do it consciously, which kind of undermines the whole concept, doesn't it?"

"I think," Ben said, "that what Garth meant was that we grow — we achieve some kind of growth — when we're capable of loving people who are different from us, people who don't conform to our expectations or our way of life. That's what I understood, anyway."

Grace put her head down with a little thunk on the picnic table. "I have needs," she said, "and my needs are not being met."

"Poor baby," Mike said. He rubbed her back.

Grace sat up. She turned around and touched Marisa with the toe of her sandal. "You never did make it to my Tai Chi class, did you?" she said. "Oh, well. Maybe next year."

That night, Marisa and Ben stood on the porch outside their room. Logan was in his cot, asleep. The wind in the trees and the waves along the shore made a sound like subterranean breathing, as if the sleeping people in the little cottages were all dreaming the same inescapable dream. Ben said they'd never do this again; they'd never spend a week like this, together but apart. "My word," he said. "What was I thinking, coming here with you? Here," he said. "Come here. Put your arms around me. Let me hold you."

She touched Ben's face. In the dark he seemed real to her. He seemed like a dear man. Serenity Cove, she told Ben, reminded her of another place, a summer camp she'd gone to as a child.

"No kidding," Ben said. "Every vacation I ever went on as a kid was to a place like this. A doctor's family, you know: holidays got taken very seriously. So anyway, then what do I do? I come here to shed a little light on my life as a child and as an adult."

"A superb adult."

"Yeah, well, I don't know about that. Anyway, maybe there is no light bright enough. When I try to understand all the shit that's happened to me lately, the divorce, juggling Logan's preschool with Isolde's schedule, the house, the job, it all begins to seem immaterial — unreal, you know — like something I invented for some nefarious purpose I didn't in the least comprehend. But why should the circumstances of my life mystify me? That's the question. Or maybe, God forbid, the answer."

But he had to say he couldn't imagine being here without her. Who else would have been so patient with Logan? And with him, for that matter. She'd been a real trooper.

"That's me," she said.

No, no, he didn't mean it that way, Ben said. She understood. She was water, Ben was stone. He was constant, as constant as anything could be, given the duress of wind and waves and time. One of the first things he'd told her, when she'd started work in his department at the hospital, was that his parents had counted on his being a doctor, like his father, but he'd failed a mandatory pre-med course and the rest was, as they said, history. This is me, he seemed to be saying. This is who I am. In the office, he rolled up his shirt-sleeves and made the coffee. He believed in long, rigorous staff meetings, with plenty of coffee and soft drinks and pizza. He believed in dialogues and discourse and give and take. He was the boss and the rebellious wisecracking underling at the same time. He tried harder than anyone Marisa had ever known. But what Marisa saw in his eyes sometimes was fear. Stalking him was fear, the fear of being alone, of losing more than he'd already lost. But he stayed just ahead of this fear. He pretended it had no power over him. Years from now, Ben would still be saying jokingly: this is the room where my son was born. These are my ex-wife's coats taking up all the space in the hall closet. She gave me this house, but I have to live in it for a hundred years, like a prince in a tower. What a character my ex was, he would say. What a riot.

In the morning, on the ferry, they got out of the car and stood on the deck. The sun was shining on the water. Gulls flew level with the boat, their beaks open, their pink vulnerable-looking throats curiously exposed. Ben lifted Logan in his arms and they all looked back at the island they were leaving, the rocky shore, the dark canopy of the forest, here and there a roof peak, a chimney, a little dock, a moored boat. They were wearing sunglasses, sunhats. They looked like the other families standing at the rail. *Healing the Family Week*, Marisa thought. Nametags and mashed potatoes, dead wasps floating in soft drinks, croquet, swimming, poetry. *Superb grown people*, as they dared to think of themselves.

She'd been the one who'd travelled farthest, she thought now. But she was going back to the same place she'd left from, and that was remarkable, she had to admit. For a time, at least, she was going back. She watched as the ferry's wake unspooled like a length of silk on the pale sea. Soon the island got smaller and less distinct, its edges blurring into the outlines of other islands, then it just slipped away, as if she'd had it on a string and the wind took it.

When they got home, she and Ben took Logan shopping for new clothes, for kindergarten. They picked all the runner beans in the garden and packaged them up in little plastic bags and put them in the freezer. With Isolde's help, they threw a magnificent party in honour of Logan's fifth birthday, in August. At the same time, Marisa got a job in a law office, not quite full-time, but a permanent position. The hours were good; it was possible for her to pick Logan up at his afternoon kindergarten and at the same time do a little shopping for the evening meal.

In December Ben took Logan to Buenos Aires, to spend Christmas with Maureen. While he was away, Marisa heard from Norman. He had flown in to Los Angeles and then up to Seattle. She picked him up at the airport and brought him to Ben's house. They had lunch and she kept saying, "I missed you. I can't believe you're here, Norman." It was true. She had to keep looking at him to make sure he was real. He talked about how completely, unexpectedly like a stranger he felt, in America. Together they cleared away the lunch dishes and Marisa made coffee, which they took into the living room. When Marisa asked Norman about the orthotics factory, he looked blank, then sort of snapped to and said, yes, well, for a while he'd believed it would be a way of helping people and building a profitable business at the same time. Now he was considering other ventures. He was involved, along with several others — another American, two Poles, a German — in developing a new enterprise, a rock café, with a stage and seating for maybe a hundred. It would, he believed, be a big success. "Is this in Lodz?" Marisa asked. "Yes," he said. "Yes, it is."

He asked if she'd got the picture of Teresa, and Marisa said yes, she had, and Teresa and Pawel looked lovely. How lucky he was, she said. When he got back to Poland, Norman said, he and Teresa were going to get married. "I'd like you to be there, Marisa," he said. "In fact, you have to be there. I won't go ahead without you." He smiled.

"At least you're doing all right for yourself," he said, indicating with a slight nod the room, the frosted pink sconces on the wall, and the little prisms of light refracted through the leaded-glass of the windows. Not bad at all, he said. And Marisa shocked herself a little by taking a cool, considered look around and saying, yes, it's nice, isn't it? Almost discounting her right to be in the house, demoting herself to the position of house sitter, casual but trusted acquaintance of an absent family. It was as if she were striving to remain a little detached, as if she were asking herself: Did she belong here? How could she deserve all this, the beautiful room, the four walls, the splendid old house on its hill above the city?

THE JOY OF LIFE

ONCE, IN WALES, a man named Felix Curtis spoke to Alex about the "persistence of vision." He was quoting Claudius Ptolemy, he said, but he was also speaking of his own view of individual immortality. Did she understand his gist? Yes, she said, although she was, at the same time, trying to hear what Désirée and Robin were saying to one another. Felix Curtis said, an image, a scene, a particular face captivates the mind. For the peace of the soul, it must be preserved; it must be made sense of, however fleeting it is. It must be used in making art. But perhaps she was not interested?

"Oh, yes," she said. "I am. I'm very interested."

It was a summer night and it was raining and a coal fire was burning in the hearth. These images, of the fire and the room with its restless shadows along the walls and its more or less static occupants were to remain in Alex's mind over the years, persistently, just as Felix Curtis and Ptolemy before him had said.

In a small art gallery located about a block and a half up from Pier 69 on the Seattle waterfront, on a fine afternoon in early September nearly fifty years later, Alex stands in front of a painting of a picnic. Unharmed by time — looking, in fact, as if the paint has just been freshly applied, as if the artist has just put down her brush and wandered off for a moment of respite — its grandness astonishes Alex. Such effort, she thinks, such a task. Light positively shines out of every object: the purple lupines and the blue delphiniums, the slate roof and narrow green front door of the house. The painting shimmers in the still, cold air of the gallery. Alex waits for a suitable response to occur within her. She waits receptively, as if the painting is an icon she is praying to. What she wants, she thinks, is a powerful surge of memory, an elegiac, romantically vivid memory of that time and place, which is to say the verdant front garden at Grove's End, in West Glamorgan, Wales. In June 1957.

Désirée's painting of the picnic looks something like this: a luminous blue wash of sky above green hills and austere grey mountains, and in the foreground a garden, and in the garden, spread out on the green grass, a plaid blanket with a group of people carefully disposed on its surface. Désirée, who can't bear, ever, to be left out of anything, has painted herself in next to Robin Pritchard. Her hand is touching his arm, as if she has just thought of something she wants to say to him. Loren, Désirée's daughter, is resting her hand lightly on the back of a small brown dog with a tail like a feather duster. Alex, in the painting, is seated, her legs tucked under her. Like the other figures she appears solid, solemn, yet also languorous, somnolent, and strangely blind, her downcast eyes merely suggested by violet shadows. No one, except possibly the dog, who has a friendly, eager expression, is smiling.

Alex stops next in front of a painting of a young woman leaning against a tree in a grove. I don't want to see this, she thinks. But she keeps looking. The woman in the painting is her. And yet it is not; she didn't ever look that cowed, that meek, surely? Not even when she was young and unhappy and far from home. What's happened is that Désirée, in the process of painting, has altered her face, pinched it in, made her features appear elongated and neurotic, sulky. (Alex has nurtured, over the years, a small nagging fear that this was done spitefully. Or worse, that the paintings is, after all, an accurate likeness.) In the painting, she has her arms full of lupines and daisies, which she remembers as being dusty with pollen and rank smelling, as if pulled out of a swamp. At the dark centre of each flower is a restless corona of extremely small black insects, some of which had started creeping inexorably up her bare arms. She swore they were biting her. Désirée told her not to be squeamish. Ignore them, she said. She was mixing paints on her palette, absorbed, businesslike, and then squinting at Alex, sizing her up. She began to sing a rousing, martial tune. *Bright-eyed freedom stands before ye, hear ye not her call?* "Man of Harlech," she said, smiling. Less than a month in a new country and she'd assimilated the culture, the music, the mood and temper of the people, the vagaries of the climate. Whatever was novel and immediate enthralled her, Alex realized. When it ceased being novel, she would yearn for release.

Alex remembers how, while she was posing for this painting, a shiny green beetle with long, delicately jointed legs plopped onto a leaf right in front of her face. There she was, pressed up against the rough, raw bark of a tree, a woodland nymph undergoing a painful metamorphosis into a more rudimentary, natural state. While all she truly wanted, or so she remembers thinking, was to go back to the house for a nice hot cup of tea. She felt awkward, self-conscious, alternately too hot and too cold, and Désirée had skilfully caught all this. She had portrayed with great precision the splotches of colour on Alex's cheeks, the agitation in her eyes, even the thirst in her throat. She made Alex look as if she were about to run away or go mad or make, suddenly, a strange appalling confession. (Which, in Alex's case, would go something like this: I am in love with a man, another woman's husband. I dream of him. I have carved his name into the trunk of a tree in this very grove and I did it with such precision, in such a fine script, that no one will ever discover it, least of all you, Désirée.)

Désirée said that she'd just realized that when she was painting someone, she understood that person better than anyone else did. Better, in fact, than the subject understood himself, or herself. For example, everything Alex thought and felt was clear to her, *at that very moment.* "It's true," Désirée said. "I see all your most secret thoughts."

"Then I guess you know," Alex said, "that I'm hungry and bored and I want a cup of tea and I want to sit down. I want to go back to the house. But you didn't know, did you, until I told you? Because no one can read minds."

"Oh, you'd be surprised," Désirée said, unperturbed. "You'd be surprised at what I can do."

Désirée's art has the power to supplant memory, Alex now realizes. Or at least to recast it in a new form. When she looks at these paintings, she is seeing the past through Désirée's eyes, not her own. Alex thinks the daisies were crawling with insects, but maybe they weren't; she thinks she felt the tree pressing uncomfortably into her back, but was that true? She thinks she saw a beetle on a leaf. How far can she trust such evanescent minutiae? Not very far, she decides. She can't even be sure if she looked like the young woman in the painting: petulant, cross, tired, homesick. She hopes she didn't. It is Désirée's memory, not hers, that is present in each painting, like some kind of fixative applied to the surface. This is the artist's power, solely, Alex thinks, as she stares at herself, the self she may or may not have been at that time.

In 1957, Alex, Désirée, and Désirée's daughter Loren, then four years old, travelled to Wales, so that Désirée could stay at Grove's End, which was a kind of retreat, or refuge, for artists, owned by a man named Felix Curtis. This Felix Curtis — Alex was never comfortable calling him either Felix or Mr. Curtis — had set up Grove's End as a place where artists of all kinds — painters, writers, poets — could work in peace, without distractions, for a certain amount of time. They paid for room and board, and were expected to contribute toward housekeeping, but the costs were reasonable and there were funds available from various foundations and patrons, Désirée explained. Felix Curtis had been a successful businessman, in some unspecified enterprise, and had inherited money, she believed. Perhaps he was a lord of the realm in disguise, she suggested. Anyway, she'd been writing to him. He'd mailed her a printed list of references, testimonials. Some of the artists on the list had amazing reputations, Désirée said. Their work sold for thousands of dollars. Or thousands of pounds, she should say. In the brochure, these artists, and others, as yet not so famous, praised the salubrious atmosphere at Grove's End. She handed the brochure to Alex. "See what it says about the home-like environment, the pastoral setting? Fields of grazing sheep, the mountain paths, waterfalls, wild flowers. Go on, read it." Obediently, Alex read the brochure. Désirée said she saw Grove's End as her salvation. She needed time to paint every day, without the constant interruptions of having to look after Loren and be a good wife to Tom, or try to be a good wife, not to mention doing the shopping and cooking and laundry. She spoke in such a dispirited tone that Alex had to laugh. What else could she do, with Désirée, but laugh?

"I want you to come with me," she said to Alex. "I can't leave Loren, she's not old enough. Tom wouldn't know what to do with her. And anyway, he wouldn't be able to leave the nursery. Summer is his busiest season. Without you, Alex, I won't be able to go.

Please say yes, Alex. It'll be a holiday for you. And we'll be together."

Once she was there, once they were settled in at Grove's End, Désirée did begin to work. She poured over art books Felix Curtis supplied her with, books on technique, biographies of artists; she went out in the morning and sketched landscapes in charcoal; she experimented with watercolours; she did as she pleased, as she said, from morning until night. And because this was also meant to be "like a holiday," she planned picnics, like the one in the painting.

On that day, Alex remembers — and she does remember this, it is her own memory, she is sure, not Désirée's — Désirée woke up very early, before it was even properly light, and ran downstairs in her dressing gown to put a chicken in the oven to roast. Then she ran back upstairs and rapped sharply on Alex's bedroom door, and on Robin's bedroom door, which was at the end of the hall. "Come on, you two, I need help," she was saying. "I need a picnic brigade, on the double." By the time Alex dressed, and got Loren dressed, and the two of them went down to the kitchen, Désirée had scones baking in the oven. She put Alex to work chopping up potatoes to boil for potato salad and preparing the devilled eggs. Loren wanted to help, so Alex let her kneel on a chair at the table and sprinkle paprika on the eggs. Robin came downstairs and poured himself tea and sat at the table and moaned, "Look at the time. It's dawn. I am not at peace with this savage hour, Désirée."

"That's too bad," Désirée said. "Too bad for you. It is the best time. I love morning." In passing, she touched the back of his neck with her hand, leaving a floury mark. She never missed a chance, Alex thought, marvelling. Her own hand, stirring sugar into her tea, was only a few inches from Robin Pritchard's hand, but she would never, never. However, if she did, if she felt capable of being that bold, she could well imagine the sensation: a fine tingling warmth along the skin, her pulse racing. A hotness, in her face, betraying her. Désirée wasn't shy, she never blushed, her head was not foolishly transparent, like Alex's.

Although not apparent in Désirée's painting, a white mist, caused by the warmth of the sun on the wet ground, had been rising from the grass that day. It made Alex think of souls, the souls of the wild flowers, perhaps, rising toward heaven. (Being at Grove's End encouraged such images, it seemed.) The effect of this mist, gauzy and indeterminate, was lovely, as was the softly filtered sunlight in the grove of ancient oak trees — there really was a grove at Grove's End. Birch trees, white-skinned and stately. Oaks and mountain ash trees. Robin told them one of the ancient Welsh gods, none other than Gwydion, god of the arts, he believed, slept curled around the roots of the trees and would one day awaken and make everyone at Grove's End immortal. Robin lay on his back on a plaid rug Désirée had spread on the ground, his head propped on his arm, and smiled up at Désirée. He had a book with him and he put it face down, open, on his chest. That morning, he told her, he had written two fine long poems. Later, he would read them again, he said, and undoubtedly discover — to his sorrow — that they were rubbish.

The grass, as Alex could feel through the soles of her shoes, was damp. More than damp — soggy. Not surprisingly, since it had been raining for days.

"It isn't really a lawn, is it?" Désirée said. "It's more of a bog. Never mind, at least the sun is warm."

Désirée opened the wicker basket and took out a plate of chicken. She said it would taste better chilled, but without a proper refrigerator what could you do? She set out bowls of green salad and potato salad and devilled eggs, crimson with paprika, and also not quite cold enough for her liking. "What lovely red eggs!" she said to Loren. She unwrapped a loaf of crusty bread and passed it to Robin, who tore off a piece and put it on his plate. When the dog, a great scrounger who had managed to insinuate himself into the picnic, began to whine, Robin broke off a few more pieces and tossed them to him. Loren then wanted to do the same.

"The bread is for people, not dogs," Désirée told her. "You're setting a bad example," she said to Robin, reaching over and swatting his hand. He said, "Ah, but the child is enjoying herself, aren't you Loren, *bach*?" He gave Loren a piece of bread, so she could feed the dog. "Watch that the doggie doesn't nip your fingers," Alex said, a small, sensible warning in her opinion, but it came out sounding neurotic, tedious, dull. Désirée said, "That dog wouldn't bite anyone. It hasn't got any teeth, poor old bugger. Why are you always looking for the worst to happen, Alex?"

"I'm not," Alex said. "I don't mean to." She poured Loren a drink of lemonade. "Don't spill it," she cautioned and Désirée laughed and moved a little closer to Robin and there were the three of them, Robin and Loren and Désirée. Robin held up the book he was reading. "Albert Camus writes: 'It is normal to give away a little of one's life in order not to lose it all.' I like that very much," Robin said. "It could be applied to the bread. It's normal to give away a little of what you have, even if it's your last scrap and it is only to a dog."

If Robin Pritchard had not turned up at Grove's End, nothing would have happened, Alex believed. Nothing, that was, other than a great deal of talk about art and lots of walks in the mountains and the valley, and getting used to a high-carbohydrate tea at four o'clock in the afternoon, with sausage rolls and ham sandwiches and, occasionally, rice pudding with currants as a treat for Loren. But Robin Pritchard was inevitable, Alex could see, or at least came to believe. He was a Welsh poet, a dark figure straight out of Welsh bardic history, from the Mabinogeon. Désirée had heard some former residents at Grove's End, who occasionally dropped in for tea, talking about the poet. He was in the vicinity, she told Alex, and might even put in an appearance and then they'd get to meet him. They would get to meet Robin Pritchard, she said excitedly. They were in the front hall, on their way out, and Felix Curtis was just coming in the door, returning from a walk. His eyes were bright and his face was rosy. He took off his cap and hung it on a hook. "Ah, Robin Pritchard," he said, rubbing his hands. "I know him. I know him well. He's a marvel, is Robin Pritchard. Not a word of a lie, now; he's devilishly good, an individual of real talent. Nearly as good as Dylan Thomas. Well, no, perhaps not. He's entirely unique. He's his own sort of poet."

He had stood aside with a flourish to let them pass. Outside, Désirée had imitated Felix Curtis. She had gripped the lapels of her coat and strutted around, her feet squelching in the mud, saying, "Devilishly good; quite the man; quite the thing, old girl. Quite the bloody marvel."

They were on their way to get Loren from her nursery school. They were walking through this alien, beautiful landscape as if they belonged here, Alex thought. They were in Cambria. They were in the ancient land of Myrddin, who was Merlin, she believed, and of King Arthur, and of men with coal-blackened faces who lifted up their voices and sang as they walked home from the mines.

Alex and Désirée didn't meet Robin Pritchard at Grove's End. They came upon him in a bookshop, by chance, one rainy afternoon. The name of the bookshop was Madog's Corner, and the poet, about to read from his own work, was saying, "Madog, impartial protector and defender of all manner of poets, those significant and those highly forgettable. How suitable the name, is it not? This lovely bookshop, preserve of the wild-eyed poet."

"Good Lord," Désirée said to Alex, under cover of a shuffling of feet and backsides on chairs and an appreciative wave of self-conscious laughter.

Robin Pritchard looked, Alex thought, more like Rupert Brooke than Dylan Thomas. Alex had loved Rupert Brooke since she'd studied Literature at teacher's college and had come across his picture in an anthology. He had died in 1915, after Gallipoli, and because of this she hated war and was a Pacifist, which to her meant being patient and kind and not raising her voice in anger. Robin

Pritchard was not as handsome as Rupert Brooke, but he was good looking, she conceded, glancing at him covertly. His thick black hair curled over his high white forehead. His eyes were luminous, dark. She watched him while pretending oblivion, browsing through the cookbooks. Désirée, on the other hand, was plainly intrigued. Her eyes were bright, her lips parted in the slightest of smiles. Alex tightened her grip on a book of Welsh recipes. *Teisen Nionod*, she read, required two pounds of thinly-sliced potatoes and one pound of onion. *Bara Sinsir* was gingerbread with black treacle and brown sugar, although minus ginger. How curious, Alex thought. Loren tugged on her coat sleeve.

"Yes, yes, in a minute, love," she whispered to the child.

She watched Désirée taking books from the shelves, opening them, shutting them, putting them back.

"I want to go," Loren said.

"Yes, we will go," Alex said. "We are going, right now." Alex shelved the recipe book.

It was warm in the bookshop. Loren's face was flushed and her nose was running. Alex glanced at the women in their navy blue macs and tweed skirts perched on folding chairs in front of the poet. It seemed to her there were two groups of women in attendance, of different ages, one group middle-aged and attentive, the other young, dreamy, full of smiles, equally attentive perhaps, but more to the poet's fine eyes than to his words. Very cleverly, by not taking a seat, by appearing not even to listen particularly, Désirée avoided joining either group. She simply leaned over one of the women while Robin Pritchard was reading and casually plucked a copy of his book from a stack on the table.

"Excuse me," Alex heard her say, while she held her hair away from her face. Wordlessly she paid for the book, tucked it under her arm, and then walked out of the bookshop with Alex and Loren trotting after her. They went down the street and got into Felix Curtis's grey Hillman Minx, which they had borrowed for the afternoon.

"Well. I am full of admiration," Alex said to Désirée. Désirée smiled, shook her head a little, and bumped a front wheel up over the curb. "Whoops. Daydreaming," she said. She pulled out into the road and shifted gears. "I beg your pardon, Alex?" she said. "What are you talking about now? Admiration for what?"

"You know," Alex said. "You know what I mean."

Later that same day, Robin Pritchard appeared in the dining room at Grove's End, his hair dripping wet and hanging in his eyes, his shoes, which he had removed and was holding in his hand, soaked. "Good evening. Where shall I put these?" he began, and Felix Curtis, from his place at the head of the table, said, "Robin. Dear boy. Welcome, welcome. Put them on the radiator, there's a good man, and do, please, join us. Have a cup of nice hot tea."

Désirée said, "Pour Robin a cup of tea, Alex."

Alex had been buttering bread fingers for Loren to dip into her soft-boiled egg. She wiped her hands and poured the tea. It was black and not very warm. She handed it to him. All roads evidently led directly to Grove's End. All poets, writers, artists, stonemasons too, for that matter, she shouldn't be surprised, ended up here. Felix Curtis, patron of the arts, gathered them in and found them a warm pile of straw.

Robin Pritchard said hadn't he seen Alex and Désirée earlier, in the bookshop? "I saw you with your little girl," he said to Alex, and, before she could correct him, Désirée began saying how much she'd enjoyed listening to him. "I bought your book, by the way. I love poetry. I'm going to read it tonight," she said.

"I think we shall have to persuade Robin to give us a private reading," Felix Curtis said. He was feeding his dog scraps of meat under the table. The dog's jaws kept snapping shut with loud cracks, like breaking crockery.

"It would be an honour," Robin Pritchard said, smiling at Désirée and turning his teacup around in its saucer.

Seven of Désirée's paintings in the Seattle exhibition were completed during that summer at Grove's End, and were actually referred to, in a pamphlet Alex picked up at the front door, as The Grove's End Paintings. There are also some pencil sketches from the same time, and a few oil pastels of Loren, which are Alex's favourites, and which, it seems to her, ought to belong to Loren.

The pamphlet also points out that, sadly, Désirée didn't produce a great deal in her brief life, her tragically short life, and Alex thinks wryly that yes, that was true enough, Désirée's life was brief, but not, she thought, tragic, and if she hadn't produced a great deal, it had as much to do with her habit of tearing up or otherwise destroying her work if it didn't please her, as with anything else. In fact, the wastebaskets and dustbins at Grove's End were always brimming over, and not only with Désirée's discards. Artistic dissatisfaction was greatly in vogue, it seemed to Alex, in 1957. No one was ever pleased with what she accomplished. There was always some writer or poet striding maniacally around the low-ceilinged rooms or else slumped, greatly despondent, in an armchair.

Désirée had said to Alex: "Oh, God, what am I doing here? I'm surprised I haven't been kicked out already. Alex, I'm a dabbler, a dilettante, an amateur."

"You know that's not true," Alex said automatically. She said again, with more enthusiasm, "You are definitely not a dabbler." She picked up some sewing. She was mending the hem in one of Loren's dresses. Loren was sitting on the floor, taking the apron off a doll in Welsh national costume that Felix Curtis had given her. It occurred to Alex that she had learned to absorb Désirée's rages and doubts as placidly as if she were a pool of water, the same pool into which Narcissus had stared with such devotion, such need. This was her role in life; it was a role she had willingly taken upon herself, immersed herself in. Désirée needed her; Loren needed her. But perhaps she was the one being too intense, too analytical. Perhaps she was simply *here*. She squinted, trying to thread her needle.

"Do you want to go home?" she said, knowing what the answer would be, and Désirée, purged by now of her distress, replied, "No, I don't. You'd like to, wouldn't you? But I'm not ready to give up yet. It's just that it's so hard. You have no idea, Alex. It takes everything, all the strength I've got, which is never, ever enough."

Alex and Désirée had been friends long before Désirée married Tom. They were friends at school. They lived in the same town. They were intent on experiencing everything possible, as quickly as possible — why else were they alive, Désirée had said — including fast cars, cigarettes, hard liquor, haunting love affairs with men who would be almost strangers to them, and in whom, indeed, they'd profess more interest than they felt. At least, they had dreamed of these things. Mostly, they had driven up and down the coastal highways in Désirée's battered red MG. And then they began making detours in order to call on Désirée's friend Tom, who managed his parents' nursery on several acres of former farmland in Washington State, overlooking Puget Sound. This was where Désirée wanted to paint, she'd said at the time. This was her landscape. She wanted to try to capture the fog shrouding the opposite shore, its reflection a milky stain on the water. And then the sun suddenly breaking through and the rain-drenched air gold and silver, the finest, noblest of elements.

Désirée kept saying, jokingly, that Tom was perfect for Alex. He was quiet, home loving, honourable — oh, yes, a truly honourable individual — with an abiding, innate love for the soil, the family, the community, his country. "A real square," she had said, laughing. "Exactly your kind."

Alex had to agree; he was her kind. She respected Tom's honourable nature. She liked him very much. This did her no good, however; she knew that, when Désirée was there, and she always was there, Tom didn't see her at all.

"It's *you* he likes," Alex said. "If he does like me, as you say, it's a shame," Désirée said. "He's wasting his time." She wasn't getting serious about anyone, she said; in fact, she planned never to marry. Once a woman married, she didn't have anything of herself left over. You had to choose: was it going to be a career as an artist, or was it going to be marriage? In her opinion one excluded the other, and she'd made her decision: she was wedded to her art. "Oh, yes?" Alex said, laughing. Was it possible, she sometimes wondered, that Désirée believed the things she said? Did she even hear what she was saying?

They spent a lot of time that summer hanging around the nursery. They volunteered to help out. They learned to pinch back the growing tips on geraniums, and to transplant tender young seedlings from flats into pots filled with vermiculite and peat moss, which they mixed together according to Tom's instructions, and at the same time they watched Tom as he worked at the far end of the greenhouse. He was tall, lean, with fine, light-brown hair and the slightest limp, acquired not in the war (he had enlisted several months before the war's end, on his eighteenth birthday), but from an injury to the ligaments of the knee in a football game the previous fall. They knew that he liked fried chicken, vanilla ice cream, and preferred coffee to tea. He admired — how was this possible, Désirée and Alex laughingly asked each other — John Foster Dulles. He thought Doris Day was cute.

"Well, she is cute, I suppose," Désirée said. "Cuter than John Foster Dulles, anyway."

"Ask him if he has any snapshots of himself we could have," Désirée said. "No, you," Alex said.

"No, you," Désirée said. They laughed and chased each other, spilling a bag of potting mixture on the floor of the greenhouse. Tom pretended he couldn't see or hear them. He pushed a wheelbarrow piled high with flats of petunias out of the greenhouse. "Piers Plowman," Désirée said. "You're evil," Alex said. "You're just plain evil."

The thing was, artists had to experience every thing that life had to offer. That was what Désirée began to say. Why should this or that way of life be considered superior? Maybe she needed to consider that point of view, for a change. The true artist was able to make use of everything, including love, marriage, even children. She certainly didn't want to be an old maid living in a boarding house and going around with dried paint under her fingernails and one of those beret things stuck on her head, did she?

When Désirée married Tom, Alex was her bridesmaid. And exactly a year later she was godmother to Désirée's infant daughter, Loren Alexandra. On the day of her baptism, the baby lay stiff as a china doll in Alex's arms. Then she took a gulp of air and began to shriek. She cried all the way home from the church, and for a good part of every day and night in the weeks that followed. Alex walked up and down with her; she patted her back and tried singing to her.

Désirée couldn't cope. She cried more helplessly than the baby. "Babies do cry a lot, at first," Alex said. "But they get over it."

"No, they don't," Désirée said. "They just go from one thing to another. I think she's coming down with a cold now. I don't know what to do with her. She doesn't even like me." Désirée used to throw herself down on the floor in the living room after Alex had finally got Loren to sleep. She would say that she couldn't survive. "I'm so tired," she said. "This isn't natural. I must be sick. I must be dying. I'm so tired I wouldn't care if I died."

"Don't say that," Tom said, trying to pull her up from the floor. "That's a terrible thing to say."

Leave her alone, Alex wanted to say. Leave her alone; she'll get fed up with herself. Instead, she offered to stay and see to the baby during the night, and Désirée said, Oh would you Alex, are you sure you don't mind? I truly don't mind, Alex had said. I truly don't.

Alex was good with babies, even babies as ornery — Tom's word — as her godchild. Alex had always been able to get by on very little sleep. She enjoyed helping out where she was needed. That was what she told herself. She tried very hard not to covet what

Désirée had. The truth was, when Alex had first seen Loren, only an hour or so after the birth, her heart had become molten. Tears had sprung to her eyes. She had lightly, reverently, brushed her fingers across the baby's head, along the side of her face. In the shape of her eyes, the dimple in her chin, the fine brown hair, she was a small replica of Tom. She had to force herself to hand the baby back to Désirée. "Be careful, don't drop her," she had actually said. What was happening to her? She wanted this baby and she wanted Tom and she wanted Tom's house — a white house with green shutters at every window — and she wanted the view of Puget Sound, and the smell of the sea and the soft grey fog manifesting itself all at once in place of the clear sky. She wanted to be a nurseryman's wife. Yes, let her be honest: she wanted all this, and at the same time she felt horribly ashamed and impatient and angry with herself. She kept thinking, But what shall I do?

Soon after they'd arrived at Grove's End, Désirée enrolled Loren in a Montessori kindergarten in the village and then sent her off every morning with Alex. The teacher was Mrs. Clara Fradkin. The children called her "Mama Clara" and happily followed her around the schoolroom like ducklings. Loren, who even at the age of four still cried easily and often, as if this was, for her, the most natural form of expression, cried when it was time to go home.

"This is the exact opposite of what usually happens," Mrs. Fradkin said severely, removing Loren's hands from her skirt. "Usually the child wants to go home to its mother. This is a very unusual situation. Do you have good rapport with Loren?" she asked of Alex, who explained once again that she was not the child's mother, she was only a friend, a close friend.

"I'm an aunt, really. I'm Aunt Alex, aren't I, Loren?" she said. "I am her godmother," she said.

Loren buried her face in the folds of Mrs. Fradkin's substantial skirts. Mrs. Fradkin wore black cloth slippers and print dresses under voluminous aprons and her plentiful grey hair was twisted in thick braids around her head.

"Perhaps the mother should come for Loren, then," she said to Alex.

Alex agreed. She thought Loren would like very much to have her mother come to the school. She imagined Désirée would be delighted to have a closer look at this schoolroom, with its long wood tables and its easels and paint pots and flowers in jam jars and its scarred wood floor. Surely, if Désirée could see Mrs. Fradkin as Alex saw her, she would immediately reach for her paintbrushes. She would have Mrs. Fradkin sit with her feet in a bucket of steamy water. Or knitting, with a fluffy cat asleep on her lap. She would have her sit in the cold blue light from a window reading an antique leather-bound book. The furrows in Mrs. Fradkin's intelligent, sensible face would be accentuated. The mole beside her upper lip would be pre-eminent. Alex, seeing this painting in her mind, became quite excited. She wanted to pick up a brush and begin work on it herself.

"Loren's mother would come for Loren if she could, but she is very busy," Alex explained, trying to grasp Loren's hot, damp hand in hers and discretely disentangle her from the teacher. "She's at Grove's End," she reminded Mrs. Fradkin, but Mrs. Fradkin, unimpressed, merely said, "I think the mother should at least on some occasions call for the child. It is the child that matters, after all."

"Mrs. Fradkin does not approve of you," Alex later told Désirée.

"The club is always looking for new members," Désirée said. "Let her join. It's not exclusive, believe me." She was sitting on her bed, drinking a glass of red wine. She had a letter from Tom in her hand and she waved the sheets of paper at Alex. "He wants us to come home," she said. "Well, he wants me and Loren to come home, I don't suppose even Tom would presume to make the same demands of you. He misses me. He's offering to take me on a holiday if I come home now, this minute. Mexico, Jamaica. He says he thinks I'd probably enjoy painting or sketching in the Caribbean, from what he's heard of it." She let the letter slide from her hand to the floor.

"I would love to go to Jamaica," she said. "Some day. I just don't like it that he puts conditions on everything. If I come home now, he says. If I'm a good girl." She picked up the wine bottle from her night table and refilled her glass. "Want some?" she said. Alex shook her head. Désirée said: "Robin is taking me to Pembrokeshire, to see the town where he used to live. Where he had a house. Or his parents had a house. I think it was before the war. I meant to ask, would you mind looking after Loren while I'm gone?"

"No, I wouldn't mind," said Alex, not meeting Désirée's eyes.

"We could take her along, but she'd be bored. So this would be a better arrangement, wouldn't it?"

"Oh, yes," Alex said. "I suppose it would."

"I know what you're thinking," Désirée said, lifting the wine glass in the air and studying its contents. "I know what Alex is thinking. You're thinking I'm a married woman and I shouldn't be going to Pembrokeshire with Robin Pritchard or any other man. Aren't you?"

"No, I'm not. Oh, Désirée, I don't know," said Alex. "It's up to you, isn't it? You know what you're doing. I don't mind, I'm happy to look after Loren."

"Well, then. You're a good friend, Alex. But I don't want you to judge me. I don't want you to think badly of me, either." She got off the bed. She went to the window. "I want some happiness out of life *now*. Not always later, later. Not that I wasn't happy before. I was. I think I was. But this is different, isn't it? This is unexpected and precious to me." She moved away from the window and put her wine glass down on the night table. "Do you know who I saw outside just now? Robin. He's walking up the lane. In two seconds he's going to come in the front door. There. What did I tell you?" She smiled at Alex, a sunny smile, full of complicity, as if they were girls again, students cutting classes, preparing for another adventure on the road in Désirée's red MG.

On the kitchen wall at Grove's End there was a copy of a painting by Henri Matisse: *The Joy of Life*. It was a scene of nude figures lying around in what seemed to Alex a post-apocalyptic garden. Was that what Désirée meant? Alex's first impression was that the figures had, in a sense, all turned their faces to the wall. They had finished with being actively in life; now they were preoccupied with what they could learn through their senses, through the tips of their fingers, or by gazing for timeless moments at the closed lids of their eyes. In her opinion, at least to begin with, the painting was immoral, or did she mean amoral? She tried to explain this to Désirée, who laughed and said, "Oh, Alex, you are a strange one, aren't you?"

Désirée took the print down from the wall and wiped a cobweb from the backing. She propped it up closer to the window and studied it avidly.

"Well, I don't care for it," Alex said. "I don't think I like the colours. They're harsh."

"You know, it's not about life," Désirée said. "It's not really about the joy of ordinary life. It's about the joy of art, I think. It's about the sheer joy that can be attained through art. Through the simplicity of art. Which is, oh, I don't know, seeing with perfectly innocent eyes. Does that make sense?"

Look how delicate the figures were, how insubstantial, she said. Above them the great massed dream-shapes of the trees, and the clouds, and the sea.

"It's decadent, though," Alex said. "How can you see decadence through innocent eyes? It's strained, in a way, that whole scene. As if the artist is reaching for something he can't quite grasp."

"Well, maybe that's what painting is all about," Désirée said. "Maybe that's where the joy comes in. Working at something so hard you almost die of it." She smiled, as if Alex couldn't be expected to understand or to share in this vision. Sometimes it seemed to Alex that everyone at Grove's End gave her the same look. She made them all feel superior, she supposed. She didn't care. She knew she wasn't an artist, or a poet. She was only there to look after Loren while Désirée painted. There had been trouble about this at first. Felix Curtis had told Désirée he was very sorry, but, no, there wasn't room for a friend and certainly not for a child. He said this in a letter, before they left America. I can't come without my daughter, Désirée had written back. She said she had no choice but to withdraw her application. Felix Curtis had replied immediately, by telephone. He had said he would make room for Désirée's daughter and for Alex. He would sleep in the garage, if necessary. On the floor in the garage, where he'd catch his death of cold, no doubt, but for her he would take that chance. When she finished talking to him, Désirée had said to Alex, "I think he's mad."

When they arrived at Grove's End, Felix Curtis had presented Loren with the Welsh doll, in its apron and tall black hat. Why, how sweet of him, Alex had thought, in surprise. He was older than she'd expected. He was slight, with narrow shoulders and a thin neck and odd, almost unnaturally large, flat, glistening eyes. He kept a tin of toffees especially for Loren on the mantelpiece. "Would you like a sweetie?" he would say. "Only one, that's a good girl. You don't want to spoil your tea."

In the evenings at Grove's End, everyone gathered around Felix Curtis. They would wait (there were generally three or four writers or painters staying there at a time), seemingly mildly amused at their own eagerness, for Felix Curtis to say something tantalizing or provocative. And he, obviously relishing the moment, would lean back with his pipe clamped between his teeth and his dog curled at his feet. (There was a watercolour of Felix Curtis, done by Désirée, in this exact pose: firelight flickering across his face, his eyes darker than ever, more lustrous, a cartoonishly ardent group crouched at his feet, and in the recesses of the room shelves of books, paintings askew on the rough plaster walls.)

Not long after Robin arrived at Grove's End, he told Alex and Désirée that he firmly believed Felix Curtis was a reincarnation of Madog ap Maredudd, manifesting all over again that mighty warrior's special fondness and regard for poets. "Madog and Felix. They are one and the same entity, in my opinion," he said. Désirée said she didn't know about Madog ap Whatever-his-name-was, but she certainly felt that Felix Curtis was an extraordinary person. Her salvation. She worshipped him. He was like a religious figure to her, she said, a priest or a saint. Once, he had casually informed her that he was actually given to visions of angels and demons, which appeared at his window by starlight and made their claim on his spirit, in spite of the fact that he was not religious in any orthodox sense. It was something in his brain that caused this, he had said: a bit of loose wiring.

"Now, let me put this question," Felix Curtis was saying. "Can we afford art? What are we doing, when we indulge ourselves with our personal, narrow *artistic* interpretations of history, of nature, of humanity?" And what, he wondered, did art specifically have to do with memory? With the psychology of memory? With the "persistence of vision," if he could use that term? Those impressions the eye recorded for one-tenth of a second and then relinquished: how would they be remembered, if they were not immortalized by the artist? He winked at Alex: Now there was a question, he said to her. And here was another: How did the artist deal with the strictures of bourgeois life, which as everyone knew hampered more promising careers than did any other factor?

Hah, Alex thought. She had just finished washing up a sink full of dirty dishes that had been ignored by everyone else. What about the strictures of Bohemian life? she wanted to ask. But Désirée agreed with Felix.

"Yes," she said. "That is exactly the question. If I weren't here, I wouldn't be working. By now, I would have given up. I wouldn't have produced any work this year. Not a thing."

"I don't believe that," said Robin. "I don't believe that for a moment. You're an artist. Artists create as others breathe." He was sitting at Désirée's side, on a hassock. He had helped himself to a toffee from the tin on the mantelpiece and was unwrapping it thoughtfully. Désirée was half-reclining in a chair, her head back, her legs crossed, one foot swinging. She was wearing sandals and a blue dress, and her hair, which she hadn't had cut since coming to Wales, was held in place with one of Loren's hair ribbons. She put out her hand and Robin caught it in his and as they smiled at each other. Alex felt a disturbance, like an electric shock, pass through her, and, she imagined, through the walls of the house. At the same time she saw the look of surprise, of recognition, on Felix Curtis's face, followed at once by a pleased, and even proud smile, as if he were saying to himself, Well, it is all happening just as I planned.

One day when Alex went to pick up Loren, Mrs. Fradkin told her how much she, and the children, enjoyed Loren's songs.

"Her songs?" Alex said.

"Indeed, yes. Loren invents the loveliest little songs. She sings them for us. But you must know this. The songs are little ballads about Loren's daily life, the little things that happen. She sings about you. And about her mother. She sings about a little brown dog that likes to eat bread."

Alex bent down and began helping Loren into her sweater. Her cardigan, Loren called it, in her new, shy, quick Welsh voice. She, too, had the gift of assimilation, it seemed. "I didn't know you liked singing, Loren," Alex said to her. "Is it a secret? Are you going to sing for me and Mummy when we get home?"

Loren shrugged out of Alex's grasp. She wanted to do up her own buttons, she said. She knew how: Mama Clara had taught her.

After school, Loren had lunch and then a nap. When she woke, Alex took her on another walk into the village, this time to a green-grocer's, where the proprietor, a Mr. Jones, let her use the telephone to place a collect call to Tom. This was a clandestine arrangement she and Tom had made. Of course, he also heard from Désirée, but she often forgot to call, and when she did call she didn't seem interested in discussing practical matters, according to Tom. Or anything else. She didn't tell him how she liked Wales or how she spent her days. She didn't tell him what he wanted to hear. Was Désirée working? he said. Was she working better in Wales than at home? He would like to know if this arrangement was of benefit to her or not. Actually, he'd like her to come home. He wished she'd be more specific about her plans. Didn't he have a right to know? Tom asked. Did Alex have any idea?

Alex telephoned at about three in the afternoon, when it was early morning in Washington State and Tom was sure to be at home still. (It took some time for the call to be completed, and while she waited she tried to picture Tom sitting at his kitchen table with a cup of coffee, his eye on the telephone, but instead she'd see him striding happily, purposefully through the glassy humid air of the greenhouse, between flats of recently misted plants, which was how she liked to remember him.)

As soon as Alex heard Tom's voice, she pressed the phone to Loren's ear.

"Say hello to Daddy," she prompted. Loren became too shy to speak. Her eyes sparkled and she smiled in delight, but she wouldn't say a word.

Alex took the phone back and told Tom that evidently Loren was a singing star. "She's never sung a note of music in my presence, but Mrs. Fradkin assures me she makes up whole songs, long stories set to music. Today at school, she made a puppet out of a hankie. It has wool hair and button eyes, one red and one black. She won't let go of it."

"That sounds like Loren," Tom said. And then, "I find this situation intolerable, to tell you the truth. I had it in mind that Désirée would be on her way home by now. Has she said anything to you?"

"I'm not sure," Alex said. "I don't think so." This was on a Friday, when Désirée was in fact at Grove's End packing an overnight bag for the weekend trip to Pembrokeshire with Robin Pritchard. Alex thought: I could tell him where she's going, what she's up to. I could say I had no choice but to tell him because I'm concerned about Loren's well-being. I'm genuinely worried that Loren will find out that her mother behaves like a perfect little slut and that she has no respect for herself or for her marriage, Alex thought, tightening her grip on the telephone receiver and glancing at Mr. Jones, who was placing leeks in a tidy row on the counter, and listening, no doubt, to every word. Even without Mr. Jones, Alex wouldn't have the courage to say that there seemed to be a certain amount of creeping about at night, floorboards creaking, doors opening and closing, up on the second floor at Grove's End. Secret (supposedly) kisses on the stairs. Conversations that halted in mid-sentence when Alex entered a room. She stared at a glass jar containing pink rock candy beside the cash register. She was mute. She was weak with anger. She knew she wouldn't say anything. She couldn't hurt Tom or Désirée. Never a harsh or unkind word, she reminded herself; that was her credo.

"Do you want to try talking to Loren again?" Alex said. She put the phone against Loren's ear. Loren pressed her puppet against her mouth and scrunched her face up in concentration.

"She loves hearing your voice, but she just isn't going to say anything, I guess," Alex said. "She isn't going to sing, either. Well, who knows? Maybe she's going to turn out to be a poet." She waited, as if Tom were going to be able to pick up on the coded message. Poet, get it? Robin Pritchard? A weekend in Pembrokeshire?

"And how are you doing?" Tom asked.

"Oh, I'm well, thank you," Alex said. "Homesick, to be honest. I'm looking forward to coming home."

This art show Alex is attending is being held in a large warehouse-like room that obviously once served as a dance studio, with bars along the walls, springy wood floors, mirrors. There are other people here, a few, women mostly, standing transfixed in front of the paintings, murmuring amongst themselves. They don't see Alex; she has reached an age, she thinks, when she's invisible to the young. She overhears a young woman saying that Désirée's paintings are beautiful, perhaps too beautiful: sentimental. "Well, definitely beautiful, but not sentimental, I don't think," her friend says, pointing at the picture of Alex languishing in the grove of trees. "She looks scared, to me. Lost. Makes you wonder what happened to her next. Maybe she was running away from some creep. Her husband or boyfriend, maybe. She looks like a victim."

"No, she doesn't. What makes you say that? Who was she? Does it say?" The other young woman consulted the brochure. "A friend, that's all it says. Painting of a friend. What kind of a friend, I wonder? They should tell you more in this thing," she gave the brochure an impatient shake and walked to the next painting.

The ceiling is very high. Sound echoes. The wood floor is elastic under Alex's feet. Loren took ballet lessons once. Alex had wanted Loren to have everything: dance lessons, perfect birthday parties, a bed with a white lace canopy, dolls, pretty dresses. On the plane coming home from Grove's End, Alex had tried to distract Loren by drawing stick figures. She tried to draw the Welsh doll, but it ended up looking like Mama Clara with her limp dresses and her pinafores. Her mouth, a smudged pencil mark, spoke clearly enough to Alex: *It is always better if the mother comes for the child.* Loren had tucked her hand inside her cloth puppet and pressed its mismatched button eyes against the window, so that it too could look out on the featureless grey sky above the Atlantic.

Alex sits down on a bench, facing Désirée's paintings. Now that they are at a distance from her, she feels a little less overwhelmed, although the figures in the painting of the picnic seem to have assumed colossal proportions. They dwarf the sky, the garden, the house itself. The figures tower, strange, surprised, wonderful, above Alex. Why, she wonders, did Désirée choose to do this particular painting on such a vast scale? All of her paintings, the ones here in this gallery, are possessed of such vividness, indeed such urgency, that Alex finds herself feeling oddly enervated. She wonders if Désirée hovers, an unseen yet discernible presence in the room. Or perhaps Alex's sudden discomfiture is simply a result of not being used to art shows. She and Tom didn't ordinarily visit art galleries, even when they were able to get around more than they do now. They used to sail. They loved gardening, of course. She didn't tell Tom about this show. She didn't want to upset him; his health is frail. Even now he can't speak easily of Désirée. It was Loren who told Alex about the retrospective. She had been present at the opening of the show. "I hope you can get down to see Désirée's paintings," she had said. "I think it would be sad if you missed them."

It suddenly occurs to Alex that she's put a lot of energy into her life. In a way, she has been the real artist. Or sculptor, perhaps. She's worked with stone, with the immovable weight of time and circumstance and personality. She has achieved one perfect work of art. That is, she's managed to get what she desired, what she most desired, which is Tom and his handsome white house overlooking Puget Sound. She has been married to Tom for nearly forty-six years, although it doesn't seem that long, it seems no time at all. She has three grown children, including Loren, who is now nearly twice the age Alex and Désirée were when they travelled to Wales. Loren is married and has two children. She is a primary teacher, inspired, perhaps, by the early example of Mrs. Clara Fradkin.

Loren has already visited the gallery to see her mother's paintings. "They're utterly amazing," she said on the phone. "I was so moved by them. And I kept thinking how hard it must have been for a woman to work as an artist in the 1950s. My mother must have been an incredibly determined woman to accomplish so much. She must have been very brave." Had she known how brave she was? Loren asked Alex.

In the late summer of 1957, when she and Loren arrived home from Britain, Tom was waiting for them at the airport. Alex had impulsively, gently, put her arms around him, in the manner of Mrs. Fradkin comforting one of her baby ducklings. She and Tom were courteously silent with one another; the one subject of consequence between them at that time was Désirée, who had chosen to stay behind. How could they possibly speak of her, how could they mention her name, when they both knew that she was in an openly adulterous relationship with Robin Pritchard? (That was the way people talked in those days; that was the word they used.)

Désirée wrote to Tom asking for a little more time. She told him everything. She said, I don't want to hurt you, my dear, dear Tom. Don't give up on me, please. Tom read portions of these letters to Alex. Sometimes he let her read them herself. Then he took them back and tore them up and burned them.

I'm so afraid, Désirée wrote to Alex, that if I come home I won't be able to paint and I won't be happy ever again. It is too late. I think I am happy here, Alex; I do think I am.

Alex had her own ideas, her own fears, and has them still: that Désirée unwittingly made herself noticeable to one of those incandescent jealous gods, the kind with a keen eye for anyone who dares to set herself apart. Hiking in the mountains of Snowdownia with Robin, Désirée became lost. Or rather, both she and Robin became lost. It began to snow. This was in early spring, the weather cruelly changeable. Robin decided that he would go on alone, in the hope of sighting the shore of a certain lake, which he thought would help him get his bearings. Désirée must have got tired of waiting, or had begun to feel frightened, desperate, perhaps, and had tried to make her own way down the mountain. The storm worsened. Snow could be completely disorienting; it transfigured the landscape almost at once, Robin wrote. Désirée walked, Robin theorized, until she was more lost than ever and simply too tired to go on. She found a place to rest and in resting was overcome.

Alex knows all this because Robin wrote to her. He wrote several letters, heartbroken and strangely lyrical, full of descriptions of snow and frost. Alex felt as if she were reading a fairy tale.

How can she believe that Désirée's life ended in the monochromatic white noise of a snowstorm, all colour and warmth drained from the world around her? Of course she can't. She prefers to think of Désirée (and why shouldn't this be true?) living under an assumed name in a comfortable cottage somewhere in the Welsh countryside, her vision clear, unclouded, persistent. At the end of each day she cleans the paint from her brushes and sets them neatly aside, in preparation for the next day's labour. The air smells of linseed oil and turpentine and lilac. (A lilac tree grows outside the windows, Alex is sure.) Désirée has given away every single thing that mattered to her so that she can work in peace. She paints from pure memory, her colours light and clear. Outside her cottage is a grove where Welsh gods, all of whom bear a startling family resemblance to Felix Curtis, sleep curled at the roots of ancient trees, clutching to them the gift of individual immortality.

The idea comes to Alex that she and Désirée have shared a life between them. This idea slips perfectly, unexpectedly, into her mind as she walks around the gallery again and looks perhaps for the last time at Désirée's paintings. It is, Alex thinks, as if she has taken up the life Désirée set aside, the life Désirée abjured. She is a practical and, she hopes, graceful custodian. Linked, she and Désirée have managed to discover joy, more than separately they deserved or could have achieved, its strength and radiance running through the delicate yet reliable veins of one singular form.

THE READING ELVIS

THE DAY BEFORE Graham and Sarah were to fly to Costa Rica for spring vacation, Graham received word that his mother had died peacefully in her sleep. The news wasn't entirely unexpected, yet to Graham it seemed profoundly in error, the wrong message for the wrong person. He found himself waiting for a second call that would confirm a mistake had been made, but that call didn't come. Sarah got her two dogs out of the boarding kennel and cancelled their flights and hotel reservations. Graham went to the nursing home where his mother had lived for the last seven years of her life — seven years to the month, like one of those nonnegotiable spells in a fairy tale — and began cleaning out her room. A few romance paperbacks, books about reincarnation and life after death, a jumble of cosmetics, cheap jewellery: the possessions of an optimistic, determined teenager. He gave her television and her walker to the nursing home. Her clothes he could donate to some charity. But did anyone wear that style of dresses anymore? Dresses with gauzy ruffles around the neck and tiny rhinestone-encrusted buttons, frothy layers of chiffon, silk that was friable and papery to the touch as dead leaves.

The room was much too warm. He shifted his mother's clothes and blankets to one end of the bed and sat down. He read a letter she'd left for him, in which she set out instructions for a funeral mass in the Orthodox Russian tradition. *Dear Graham, Go to the Church of St. Michael the Archangel,* she wrote. *There's enough money set aside for this. I've already talked to the priest. He came to see me. He doesn't care I'm not very religious. He cares about me, who I am, and about my Immortal Soul. All my love to you and Sarah — Renate.*

The funeral was held a week later. Recumbent in her white and gold coffin, a phaeton minus the wheels, his mother resembled the ancient remains of a once-beautiful queen, a comparison that would have pleased her, except for the ancient part. The priest, Father Dimitri, a slender, bearded young man with luminous brown eyes, informed Graham and Sarah that the church observed a period of remembrance lasting forty days, the length of time the soul remained on earth, close to those it loved. When Graham heard this, a shiver raced down his spine and he took an involuntary step back. He wanted to tell Father Dimitri that his mother had never loved him and had never forgiven his father for deserting her and Graham. The only thing she'd seemed to believe in, as an article of faith, was a story that her own mother had, as a girl, worked in the household of the last tsarina and had bathed her forehead and held her hand in childbirth. Also, for as long as Graham could remember his mother had treasured a fake Fabergé egg on a little stand of its own, and a set of garishly painted Russian nesting dolls she'd got from a mail-order catalogue. But rather than causing offence, these facts would no doubt have made the priest's beautiful eyes moist with compassion. As it was, he gently blessed Graham and Sarah and sent them out into a light rain that cleaved like oil to the face and hands.

His mother's death, and the funeral liturgy, which seemed to take place in a richer, more festive time than the present, affected Graham in ways he hardly understood, and when he returned to the classroom he felt as if he'd been somewhere far more distant than Costa Rica. In his absence there had been changes: the principal had gone on stress-related sick leave, and the acting principal was Kathleen Shaw. No one had warned him. He walked into the staff room and there she was. She was peeling an orange and the smell took him back to the interior of the church of St. Michael the Archangel, where, near the altar, a bowl of overripe oranges perfumed the still air. Once again he was approaching the coffin to gaze on his mother's beautiful, ravaged face, a paper ribbon printed with a prayer affixed to her forehead, like a child's party favour.

Kathleen stood and took his hand. She offered her condolences. He thanked her warmly, his voice unsteady. After touching her hand, he, too, smelled of oranges. He asked her how she was and she said, "Oh, well, you know, I'm on the bridge, I'm ready for action. You know me." He did know Kathleen. This new reality, however, Kathleen once again in his life, was almost too much for him. He was in a fragile state. His emotions were all over the place. As he went around his classroom checking homework assignments, he thought he saw his mother watching him, her hair arranged on top of her head like the round, braided loaf of bread at the church, which, according to Father Dimitri, symbolized eternal life. A shock went through him. He felt faint. Then he saw it wasn't his mother. Of course it wasn't. It was the overhead lighting reflecting off a poster of a young Elvis Presley seated on a porch swing outside a vine-draped antebellum mansion, reading *The Sound and the Fury*, by William Faulkner. "The Three R's: Rock and Roll and Reading," read the caption. Graham's grade sevens generally saw through this at once, or thought they did, the ones who knew who

Elvis was, and there were fewer of those every year, it seemed. Elvis didn't sit around reading, they'd say scornfully. He didn't waste his time on books. Graham would say, "Well, people, here's some Elvis trivia for you: Elvis was a reader. The story is, he was in the bathroom reading when he died."

"That's *gross*," the kids said.

"No," Graham said. "It's not gross. It's human. Reading is a human activity and so is dying, when you think about it."

Of course, he suspected Elvis didn't read a lot of William Faulkner, in spite of their both being Southerners who'd achieved a sort of immortality. Faulkner more so than Elvis. Or was it the other way around?

Graham had come across the poster years ago, rolled up with an elastic band and stashed behind some AV equipment in a supply cupboard, and he'd immediately claimed it as his own, although he was really more of a Bob Dylan, Leonard Cohen kind of guy. The poster was amazing, though. What a find. There was Elvis, in jeans, an open-necked white shirt, loafers with white socks — so sixties, Graham had thought fondly — looking insolent, sexy, iconic, and young, so young. The scene was fabricated, no doubt, and by the time the poster was printed Elvis must have been dead for decades, yet Graham felt a deep sense of peace emanating from it. He'd pinned the poster up in his classroom and, magically, Elvis's soulful dark eyes had sought him out wherever he stood. He was just about to call Kathleen to see this phenomenon, when she walked in. In those days, they'd taught at the same school, and her classroom was just across the hall from his.

"Where did you get that?" she'd demanded. "You can't have it. It's mine." She'd left it behind last summer, she said, and the janitor must have put it away in the supply cupboard. She yanked out a thumbtack and a corner of the poster snapped up, tearing the paper a little.

"Hey, you can't do that," Graham had protested, and she'd said, "I certainly can, it's mine, I can do what I want." She'd tried to shove him away. He took hold of her wrist, gently, astonished anew at the tensile strength of her, her steadfast resistance to him, to any form of persuasion. She backed away. She pushed a chair under a desk and shelved a misplaced science textbook. Her colour was high. He'd yearned to hold her, but they were assiduous about not showing affection at school. He said if the poster was hers, she must take it. She'd said, no, if it meant that much to him, he could keep it. He couldn't win. He knew the dispute over the poster was merely an outward manifestation of a long-standing grievance. The problem was that Kathleen thought he neglected her in favour of his children. She'd said he let them run his life and that he was overprotective and cloying, as a parent. Her remark had stung. Even if true, it was surprisingly mean-spirited, coming from Kathleen. He'd told her rather stiffly that when Annette had died he'd promised himself his girls would have a normal, happy life, and if that made him cloying, so be it.

"I want someone I don't have to share," Kathleen had said, on another occasion, when he was at her apartment. She had leaned away from him into the clasp of her own thin arms. "If it's not your daughters," she said, "it's your mother. It's just never me, is it?"

He remembered staring at the pure angles of her neck and shoulders, the intransigence of her. A desire to offer comfort and an urge to say something hurtful had warred in him briefly, neither winning, in the end. What could he say? You're wrong. You demand too much, I'm only human.

He'd opened the apartment door — Kathleen was wearing a silk robe, her hair fanned out around her shoulders, her eyes were cold yet beseeching — and he'd stepped almost against his will into the hall, where a patterned carpet seemed to ascend and descend simultaneously, like a trick staircase in an Escher print, so that he didn't know what to do, keep going or turn back to Kathleen. That remedial moment had existed, it could have been grasped, but he'd kept walking, his crepe-soled teacher-shoes catching on the illusory steps he was either climbing or descending, he couldn't tell which, and if he couldn't tell, who could? He assured himself Kathleen would get over this and they'd grow together, as couples did. He rode the elevator down to the car park. He remembered an autumn storm, rain battering the windshield, leaves skidding across the road. It seemed a miracle when his house, its lighted windows sailing eerily through utter darkness, was suddenly there, in front of him. His daughters had baked chocolate brownies, although he'd asked them not to use the oven when he was out, but when did they ever listen to him? Their homework books were spread out on the kitchen table and the radio was on. He turned it off and helped himself to a brownie, then he ran upstairs. He found the girls in Debbie's room, which reeked of ammonia because Debbie had just dyed her hair a surreal magenta shade. Marty was painting her toenails. She told him that Grandma had phoned six times, maybe more, and was she ever mad at him.

"We told her you were at a staff meeting," Debbie said.

He sat on the edge of the bed. "You were trying to be helpful, I know. But you shouldn't tell lies," he said.

"We didn't lie," Marty said.

"No, technically, we didn't," Debbie said. "You were with Kathleen. And you're both teachers, aren't you? So it was kind of like a staff meeting, wasn't it?" She ran a comb through her wet hair. She was older than her sister by eighteen months. She was the one who looked like him. She had his mouth, the shape of his eyes. Marty looked like her mother. Every year he noticed the resemblance more and took comfort in it, even when it made his heart ache.

This, he thought, was the true way the dead returned, gently, obliquely, without warning. At university he'd read something by Nietzsche, in a book that didn't belong to him, but to his roommate, and — it was, if he remembered correctly, that God was a vicious circle. How grimly satisfying he'd found those words. He was nineteen, with shoulder-length hair, two pairs of jeans and three sweaters to his name. He smoked, he drank, he wrote impassioned political tracts for an alternative student newspaper on a rickety old typewriter and signed them *Aravin*, which was not Russian, as he'd thought, but Georgian, for "no one." Aravin was no one because his father had vanished when Graham was a child, for a reason his mother had never articulated to him. His mother had kept him in the dark and it was a big darkness, it took over. Time was infinite, while individuals were finite and appeared repeatedly. *Again and again he makes himself necessary to himself.* So said Nietzsche. Graham's father, however, had slipped into a wormhole of time. Or, rather, he'd transferred to his company's head office in Toronto. That was all Graham knew. He'd thumbed through phone books and directories at the public library — this was long before the Internet — until he turned up a possible home address for Rice, C. R., in Brampton. But he did nothing. Wasn't it, he thought, up to his father?

In the end, Graham had written a brief note in which he said he'd be very pleased to hear from his father. The note had sounded paltry and insufficient, like a veiled threat or a request for money. He did get as far as buying a stamp at the post office, and while there had seen a job posting for temporary letter carriers. He applied and got hired. He met Annette, a permanent, full-time employee. She had the uniform, the cute Canada Post shorts, woolly socks, hiking boots. She had cornflower blue eyes and masses of unruly hair she tucked up under her peaked cap. She'd loved working outdoors and chatting to everyone she'd met. At the end of her shift a taxi had picked her up and then had swung by to collect Graham when he'd finished his route. He remembered how she'd taken off her cap and rested it on her tanned knees. She'd smelled of the summer wind and sunlight. She was twenty years old. They fell in love. They got married. They were happy.

Graham found he could talk to Sarah about Annette. He could tell her what pretty people they were, how young and strong. They only got stoned on weekends. They were hippies, flower children, with the additional security of an income from his teaching job. He and Annette were married twelve years. Then a terrible thing happened. Sarah told him it was good for him to talk about it rather than brood over it. He wasn't sure if this were true or not. It hurt him afresh, either way. He told Sarah that Annette was driving home from the store and there was a collision. Never could he forget the circumstances surrounding the accident, the way they accumulated and bore down one on the other with a terrible inevitability: the sudden heavy rainfall, the slick roads, the chip truck with bad brakes, the two-lane highway that, back then, didn't have a left-hand turn lane. He kept asking himself: Why hadn't he been the one? Why hadn't he gone to the store in Annette's place? He felt such a burden of guilt. Sarah said it was not unreasonable for him to believe he'd had a choice. Not at all unreasonable to think he could have saved Annette. Sarah had lost people, too. Her parents; a man she'd loved. She understood grief was bitter and tenacious and necessary, sometimes the only true thing left.

He'd taken a six month leave of absence. He stayed home with Marty and Debbie. He prepared meals, made school lunches, drove the girls to piano and ballet lessons and orthodontist's appointments. He learned to do French braids and where to shop for hair ribbons and leotards. Without Annette, time had no measure or quality; seasons loped past like small fleet animals. First one year passed, then two, then three. Marty and Debbie got older and needed him a little less. It wasn't true that he got over what had happened. He never would. It just began to seem okay, at some point, for him to ask Kathleen out. He didn't tell Sarah about Kathleen. He didn't know how to tell her. It was such a dismal, failed affair, in the final analysis. He remembered the time Kathleen had invited him to go skiing with her at her parents' condo at Whistler. Her whole family was going to be there, she'd told him. They were so excited about getting to meet him, at last, she said. This was planned for the long Easter weekend, and of course he'd had to say he couldn't go. "But I want you to," she'd kept saying. "It's important to me." He said he couldn't possibly leave his daughters alone on a holiday weekend. What were they supposed to do, cook their own turkey dinner? Hide their own Easter eggs?

He'd waited for Kathleen to invite the girls along, but she never did. She'd given up on the ski trip instead and had come to his house for dinner. Marty and Debbie had made a giant floral arrangement for the table, with daffodils and forsythia. All through the meal they'd kept fussing with it, moving it around, petals drifting like dirty snow into the serving dishes. He saw Kathleen grow tight-lipped and grim and headachy, or at least she gave that impression, listlessly prodding at the turkey on her plate. Pressing her fingers to her temples. But she was a teacher, he reminded himself; she knew what kids were like. He remembered how he'd kept watching her, gauging her reaction. He'd waited for a little affirmation: *What a fine job you're doing here, Graham. Your daughters are a delight.* He could see she was trying her best. After dinner, she applauded Marty's halting piano rendition of a Beethoven sonata. She let the girls lounge on the arms of her chair in the living room, while she and Graham tried to talk. She even let Marty thread a few soggy pale daffodils from the centrepiece into her hair. The flowers were still there, jauntily wilted, when Graham walked her out to her car and they said goodbye.

"Miss Pennyfeather," Marty and Debbie called her. They held their heads and clutched their stomachs and said, "Please remove that revolting food from my plate. Oh, I have a headache. Please, please children, do try not to be so noisy."

"When is Miss Pennyfeather coming again," they said. "We do so miss her."

"Are you going to marry Kathleen?" Marty wanted to know.

"No," he said. "I'm not. Anyway, it's none of your beeswax."

"Sneezewax," said Marty. "Beeswax, kneeswax, fleaswax."

After his daughters had finished school and left home, Debbie to study nursing at university and Marty to hike with friends around Europe, Graham had found, to his surprise, that he had no tolerance for a solitary life. His house was out in the bush, at the end of a lonely dead-end road. He had no neighbours. He'd dreaded the long winter evenings, when the forest had seemed to creep closer to the windows and there were noises out there in the dark he couldn't account for. He became obsessed with the idea that if anything happened to him, if he fell down the stairs, say, or were taken ill, no one would find him, perhaps for days. He couldn't sleep, he never bothered to eat. He marked papers and wrote report cards and stared at the walls. It got so bad he'd considered asking his mother to move in with him, but she needed more care, by that time, than he could give her. The house, with its stairs and long narrow halls, would be completely unsuitable. Besides, he knew she'd relish the chance to tell her friends that her middle-aged schoolteacher son was afraid to be alone. Finally he'd decided to sell up and move into town. When his realtor brought a young couple to view his property, however, he'd panicked and cancelled the listing. In response, the prospective buyers dispatched their own realtor to reason with him. That was how he met Sarah. One Sunday morning she drove into his front yard in a mud-splattered old grey Peugeot station wagon, two massive dogs barely contained in the cargo area. Graham had gone outside to talk to her. He noticed her hair was pulled back in a ponytail and she was wearing jeans and a red sweater and little pearl earrings, luminous as snowberries. She gazed around at the garden, the trees, and at the house, with its wide veranda and dormer windows. He began to see himself through her eyes, the owner of a fine house set on fifteen-plus acres of mostly second-growth forest, with a pristine creek that never dried up, and stands of alder, maple, wild fuchsia, not to mention the rare and inestimable attributes of privacy and quiet and clean, unsullied air.

"I have to tell you," Sarah was saying. "My clients are both lawyers. I don't mean to intimidate you, but they're threatening to sue if you renege on the deal."

"There is no deal. The deal is off. Let them sue." He'd squared his shoulders. From the beginning he'd liked arguing with Sarah. It made him feel as if he'd run a hard, fast race and come in first. Even when he kept losing the arguments, he still liked it.

In the end, he hadn't sold and Sarah's clients hadn't sued. To make up for the trouble he'd caused her, he'd taken Sarah to dinner. Afterwards, they'd gone to Sarah's house, where he'd spent the night. The next morning he went directly from her place to school, exhausted, euphoric, his clothes scratchy with dog hairs, his shirt collar buttoned to hide the little blotches Sarah's teeth had left, nipping at him repeatedly, like a badly trained puppy. Two months later, she'd sold her house and moved in with him. She painted the living room celery-green and put an antique rosewood table with a plant on it in the front hall, at the foot of the stairs, to keep the good fortune from flying out the door. That was the thing about Sarah: she was forthright and energetic and did what she liked.

Last summer, ten months after they'd met, he and Sarah were married. The ceremony was held in the garden behind his house, beneath a hastily constructed rose arbour. Graham's mother, in a cream linen dress and matching duster, was the guest of honour. Marty hammered out "Mendelssohn's Wedding March" on the old piano in the living room with the doors and windows thrown wide open, so the music would carry outside. Sarah's dogs wore little blue bow ties and went around sniffing at crotches and demanding a share of the smoked salmon canapés. Sarah admonished them, saying, sit, sit, but they refused to sit. They acted like it was their big day. When Graham kissed Sarah, the dogs growled menacingly. The wedding guests laughed nervously and stepped out of the way.

"Doggy people," his mother had commented, when he drove her back to the nursing home. "They're not like normal people, are they? They let their dogs jump up on people and piss on everything. I have always been suspicious of May-December marriages. I just hope you know what you're doing, Graham."

One day in April when Graham got home from school, he saw the dogs were penned up in the dog run, pacing in tense little circles, like stranded commuters. Sarah's car was not in its usual place in front of the garage, either. Graham went into the house, he put his briefcase on the kitchen floor. He took off his jacket and hung it on the back of a chair, he got a beer out of the fridge. He checked the answering machine, but there were no messages. He finished the beer and opened another.

The book he'd been reading at breakfast was on the table. It was a present from Sarah, something she knew he'd like because it was set in South America. He'd told her he always regretted not having travelled to South and Central American years ago, but when they'd had to cancel their trip to Costa Rica, he'd been secretly relieved. He was almost happier picking up second-hand travel guides at flea markets and simply reading about places like Costa Rica, one of his favourite imagined destinations because it had no army and ranked third in the world for longevity, due to a traditional diet of fish, fruit, and rice. Sarah had vacationed there once. She'd gone white-water rafting and had got an infected mosquito bite, even though she'd been assured there were no mosquitoes in Costa Rica. She'd seen a three-toed sloth in the branches of a trumpet tree, or at least that was what the guide had told her she was seeing. The rest of the trip was a kind of blur, she said; it was too much crammed into too few days. It's no big deal, she kept telling him; everyone goes to Costa Rica.

Yes, he'd said. But to him travel *was* a big deal. Tourism, in his opinion, disrupted fragile ecosystems and violated habitat. He didn't especially want to see a tour guide's version of a country. He wanted simply to wake one morning in an isolated, unspoiled village, in a small room containing a cot and maybe a chair, one window, one door.

He opened the novel, leafing through a few pages. What he liked was that much of what happened in it was realistic, but then something fabulous and unnatural occurred, and these events were made to seem infinitely more acceptable and satisfying than ordinary life. Beautiful, fragile women gave birth to precocious, delicate children who survived against the odds and had the ability to see everything, in every corner of the house, as if the walls were negligible, transparent. The men were gangsters, priests, poets. Hardly ever, it seemed, were they schoolteachers. Nevertheless, Graham had the feeling the book was, in a way, about him. He, too, had a house full of memories; he, too, had a sense of impending doom, which he carried with him always, like a piece of costly, unlucky jewellery he couldn't bear to part with.

In the jacket photograph, Graham noticed, the author bore a striking resemblance to Elvis Presley, if, say, Elvis had survived into late middle age and had studied creative writing at some southern university.

He tried Sarah's cell phone, but she didn't have it turned on. The kitchen was very clean. The dishwasher had been run and emptied, everything put away, and there was an unmistakeable sense of absence, of someone who should be here gone. He drummed his fingers on the counter. He went outside and let the dogs out of the run. They circled him suspiciously and began to gallop around, chasing leaves and the shadows of birds. They kept glancing down the lane, as if expecting Sarah to appear. Graham found himself doing the same thing. He thought he heard the phone ringing and raced into the house, but he was too late, there was no one there. He stood in the front hall for a moment, staring at the telephone, a little nauseous with anxiety and a gut full of beer. Then he roused himself and went back outside, letting the screen door slam shut behind him. The dogs Sarah called *baby* and *precious* and hand-fed buttered toast were not there. They had gone.

The dogs were Rhodesian Ridgebacks, powerful, golden beasts Sarah had got through a rescue society in San Diego. They were abused once, abused and neglected, and they were still mistrustful and a little unstable, puppies one minute and big, neurotic dogs the next. They looked at Graham with their animal eyes and he looked back with his human eyes and tried to convey a sense of command without condescension, kindness without undue meekness. Their names were Hamlet and Quinn. Hamlet was older and bigger than Quinn. Quinn was shyer than Hamlet, and even less predictable. As a boy, Graham had once stolen a dog from a backyard. He and the dog had spent most of a day together, roaming the streets and nearby fields. He remembered the way the dog had hunkered down with him in the shade of a tree, panting, its eyes bright with curiosity and fear and what looked like deep sadness, an exact mirror of the tumult in Graham's own heart. He threw a stick and the dog brought it back to him. He gave him a drink from a water fountain in a park. Late in the afternoon, as he and the dog had started walking back to town, a gang of boys had appeared and trailed them, shouting insults and obscenities and every now and then making a run at Graham. One of the boys threw a rock that caught Graham in the shoulder and he spun around in time to see a bigger rock strike the dog hard in the flank, causing his hindquarters to collapse. The dog wore a collar with a tag that said Jake, but Graham had already given him a new name: Pedro. Graham had charged headlong at the boys. He was outnumbered, but the boys were unbelievably stupid. He could kill them all with his bare hands, if he wanted, and he realized he wanted to do just that. He anticipated the satisfying crunch his knuckles would make as they smashed into someone's teeth. Maybe the boys could see how angry he was, or it could have been the sudden appearance of two men on the other side of the street, but the boys turned and ran. Graham walked back to Pedro. The dog looked up at him, cowering. He thumped his tail ingratiatingly on the sidewalk. It's okay, Graham had assured the dog, petting him. But they both knew it wasn't okay, the world was basically a shitty place and for animals the situation was worse than for people.

Pedro had been an affable golden retriever, a different species, practically, from Sarah's dogs, which seemed to Graham more closely related to the gang of two-legged brutes that had attacked him and Pedro. Sarah was always telling him, in a prideful way, that if her dogs ever got loose they'd run until they caught up to something warm-blooded and they'd rip it to pieces.

Graham stood at the edge of the forest. The piercing whistle he'd perfected in years of P.E. classes got no response and neither did his no-nonsense teacher voice. He hesitated to walk into the woods at this late hour. Darkness fell quickly in April, and the nights were still cold. The dogs would get hungry and come home soon of their own accord, anyway, he thought.

Last Sunday he and Sarah had mulched the flowerbeds and spread lime on the grass, and then, as part of his ongoing, environmentally friendly battle against incursions by woodland insects, he'd sprayed insecticidal soap on the Japanese plum trees. Sarah stood at the foot of his stepladder and held up her hand for him to see her blister. "Look at this," she said. "This is too much work. For two people this is just crazy." She said perhaps, while the market was hot, he might want to reconsider selling.

"I'm not selling," he said. "Not as long as I live."

"People always say that," Sarah said, picking at her blister. "You'd be surprised how many people say that. But sooner or later, they sell. They always do."

"Not me," Graham said. "I'm staying here. I'm never leaving."

"You think you won't leave," Sarah said. "But you will. You'll see."

"If you'd wear gloves," he said, "you wouldn't get blisters."

"I lost them," she said. "They wore out." She picked up the rake. Graham got off the ladder and started carrying it toward the garage. One of the dogs was stretched out on the grass next to Sarah, the other rooted around nearby in the tulip bed. Those dogs adored Sarah. She'd once told Graham they were her family. And now he'd lost them.

In the house he sat down with his book, turning pages, unable to concentrate. At ten o'clock, Sarah phoned. He clutched the phone. All this time he'd feared a knock at the door with bad news: we regret to tell you. Thank God it wasn't bad news. Sarah was in North Vancouver, with Darla, who'd called that morning to say she'd just undergone emergency outpatient surgery for an ovarian cyst. "Poor Darla, she's still groggy from the anaesthetic," Sarah said. "I'm going to stay with her tonight. I'm going to try to get her to eat something. Graham, are you there? How are Hamlet and Quinn?"

"They're fine, I guess," he said. He hesitated. In the mirror above the telephone his image surged up, dank and full of deceit. You little liar, Marty and Debbie used to accuse each other.

"You guess." Sarah laughed. "What does that mean? Have you given them their dinner? Did you take them for a walk?"

"They've had some exercise, yes," he said.

"Don't forget to bring them inside tonight, okay? Tell them I'll be home soon. Are you there, Graham?"

"I'm here. I miss you," he said.

"I miss you, too, sweetheart," Sarah said. "See you Saturday. I'll let you know what ferry I'm taking."

During the night he woke. He went to the window and saw the dogs in the yard. In the moonlight, they appeared pale and insubstantial, yet they were real enough. He raised the window; they stared up at him, their eyes glinting in the moonlight. Or perhaps it wasn't moonlight. Perhaps this was the light of dawn. He staggered back to bed. He told himself the dogs would be on the front porch in the morning, waiting to be let in. But when morning arrived and he went downstairs, he found they had, once again, disappeared.

He read to his class the poem "Ozymandias," by Percy Bysshe Shelley: "The lone and level sands stretch far away." What this poem tells us, he said, is that even our most enduring monuments crumble and dissolve into nothing. Given time, all things will end. The Earth and its creatures and Earth's brightest star, the sun, and even the universe, unimaginably immense as it is, will wind down, run out of energy, cease to exist, at least in any recognizable form. He told his class that when the news came on the radio that Elvis had died, he was finishing work on a deck he'd built on the back of his house. His wife, Annette, had gone into the kitchen for a couple of cold beers and when she came out she told him: Elvis is dead. And they had both sat there, disbelieving. August 16, 1977.

Another thing: the poet Shelley died at sea, in Italy, in a sudden squall. His friends cremated his body on a beach. At the last moment someone leapt forward and plucked the poet's heart — which must have seemed immortal, or at least capable of immortality — from the flames. It was also said that an Englishwoman who'd known Shelley later met him on a street in a little Italian seaside village. He had looked well and cheerful, she'd reported and had smiled graciously as he passed by.

Graham sat at his desk with his head in his hands, picturing the dogs, the damned dogs, *at that very moment* loping home with burrs in their coats, their tongues hanging out, flecks of foam on their muzzles. *If he willed it to be so, it would be so.* They would have had some kind of doggy adventure and then, satiated, their animal lusts for space and distance and conquest satisfied, they would have returned home and even now, even now, they would be sleeping on the porch in the morning sun.

He'd phoned Marty — she lived not far away — and asked her to call by the house later this morning and let the dogs in. I'm pretty sure they'll be there, he'd said, and Marty had said they'd better be, hadn't they, and he'd said yes, they had.

Kathleen walked into his classroom and took a look at him and said, "Graham. Are you okay?"

"I'm okay," he said. He tried to smile at her.

"Are you sure? You don't look so good."

"Well," he said. He began to tell her everything, not leaving out the painful fact that he'd seen the dogs at dawn and had failed to bring them inside.

"Have you phoned the animal shelter?" Kathleen said. "The police? Did you talk to your neighbours?"

He picked up his pen as if to make a note of her suggestions. "The animal shelter," he said. "Yes, of course. I don't really have any neighbours."

"Animals," Kathleen was saying. "They rely on us and we always let them down, don't we? We always do. When I was a little girl I had a guinea pig. It was one of those longhaired guinea pigs, all fluffy and soft, like a dandelion puff. One day I came home from school and it was gone. In its place on my dresser there was a goldfish in a bowl. I knew it was my fault. My mother had warned me enough times that if I didn't clean out its cage she'd take my guinea pig to the animal shelter, but I didn't believe her. For kids the hardest thing is developing a sense of responsibility, isn't it? The goldfish died, too. The bowl was too small, I guess."

Graham looked at Kathleen, at her translucent skin, her slight overbite, the delicate curve of her neck.

"It took me a long time to forgive my mother," she said. "Maybe I didn't ever forgive her."

He got up and wrote the date on the chalkboard, pressing too hard, so that the chalk snapped and flew into the air and landed at Kathleen's feet. She picked it up. He walked around her and sharpened a pencil in the electric pencil sharpener. The playground was beginning to fill up. Kids were chasing each other around. They were dressed in bright summer clothes, although the wind was cold and there was a feeling that, in spite of the clear sky, rain was on the way. He glanced at Kathleen, who was staring at the chalk she held between her fingers, like a cigarette. He could see the perfect part in her hair, the clean white of her scalp. She went over to the Elvis poster and ran her thumbnail over the yellowing sticky tape he'd used to mend the small tear in the corner. "I can't believe you still have this," she said. "I can't believe it. Do you remember," she said, "when people used to see him all the time, at a fast-food restaurant or a laundromat?"

"A laundromat?"

"Yes. And at motels, airports, and, you know, hitchhiking at the side of some interstate highway in the rain or something, with an old suede hat pulled down low so you could barely make out his face. But, still, people seemed to know who he was. In real life, of course, they would never have seen him, not unless they bought tickets. But when he was dead, he was everywhere. He belonged to everyone."

"Yes," Graham said. "He did." He looked at Elvis's pomaded hair gleaming in sunlight filtered through bougainvillea leaves. If he moved slightly, his arm would touch Kathleen's arm. Her hair smelled of flowers and he recalled the feel of it, silky and cool, and how it used to catch on his shirt buttons or his watch strap and Kathleen would pretend to be annoyed, but she wasn't, not really.

She handed him the chalk. "I hope it turns out well for you," she said, before walking out into the hall. Somewhere in the distance a door slammed. He heard children's voices, laughter, a teacher calling out that there was no running in the halls, no running allowed, then silence. All morning he couldn't stop thinking about what Kathleen had said. How true, he thought, how amazing: what had vanished forever would always be in some sense more vivid, more real and accessible, than what in fact existed.

That night he made himself a simple meal of scrambled eggs and toast and ate slowly, with a reserved, almost finicky grace. He had a sudden vision of his mother eating in the same fashion, taking little fastidious bites, chewing furiously, her hand curled tight around a balled-up napkin as if for ballast. He remembered how unfair he'd thought it, that he had to make do with this life, that the body he occupied was his body, and the woman at the table was his mother, and that was how she ate now, alone, making lightning-fast stabs with her fork, like something mean and sneaky far down on the food chain.

Graham's father had been a pharmaceutical company salesman whose visits home had become increasingly rare events, like the questionable return of an unstable comet, nothing but gas and ice particles and an insufficient quantity of vivifying dust. Graham used to carry around in his head a stark yet strangely satisfying image of his father in the one place he never actually saw him: alone in a hotel room in the evenings, sitting on the edge of the bed, methodically sampling the goods. A little Valium, a little Librium, onward and upward through the Phenobarbitals, then inexorably down again, a trombone player inching toward a risky tremolo, a moody indigo riff.

Why not blame the drugs? Why not be generous and blame the drugs? He'd been there himself. He remembered his mother saying, in a flat, angry voice: I always knew he'd leave, I always knew. They'd kept moving west, he and his mother, until they reached Vancouver Island and there was nowhere else to go. Renata got a job, a series of jobs. She called herself a widow. When she was mad at Graham, when she hated him for just being there with his big feet and his acne and his rock music, she would scream at him that he was just like his father. When in fact he was nothing like his father.

He thought of his mother's gold hair, gold to the day she died; her cigarettes, her bangles and sparkly rings. When his first daughter was born, his mother came to stay for a few weeks with him and Annette. She held the baby as if it were a live charge. Then, like the wicked jealous queen in a fairy tale, she turned to Graham and announced: "I had such a strange dream! You and the baby were left on your own. Just you and a motherless child. It was the saddest thing." As she spoke, she gave Annette a sly, sidelong glance. That was his mother: tactless, cruel, prescient.

Years later, he and Kathleen had stayed behind after a staff gathering at a pub. He'd started to talk about his mother. He told Kathleen about the awful little jobs his mother had taken, cleaning houses, addressing envelopes, selling lingerie. He talked about the mean places they'd lived, the sleazy apartments, the meals of toast and tea. He heard himself sounding amused and bitter and ironically distant. It was the beginning of the Christmas holidays. Kathleen was wearing a corsage her grade-five class had made for her, construction-paper holly leaves dusted with gold. Some of the glitter had rubbed off on her chin. She told him she had a wonderful family, the best parents in the world. Her father was a dentist. Her mother was a teacher. She had two brothers, two nephews and a niece. "I just don't have anyone of my own," she said, savagely pinching a few drops of lemon juice into her Diet Coke. "But maybe that will come."

"Of course it will," he said. He covered her hand with his. He told her what his mother had said to Annette, years before Annette had died. "It was like a curse," he said. "It was the wicked fairy's last gasp, a poisoned arrow, the ace of spades."

"Well, you don't have to believe that," Kathleen said. "You don't have to believe garbage like that. Your mother didn't have the power to make someone die. She wouldn't have wanted you to think that."

"You don't think so?"

"I don't," Kathleen said stoutly. He touched her hand. He remembered feeling such gratitude, as if she'd absolved him of a grievous sin. Together they'd gone out to the parking lot and there, as a few wet snowflakes fell from a low sky tinged pink by overhead arc lights, they clung to each other and kissed in a wild, desperate, hurtful fashion, their teeth clashing, gold glitter adhering to Graham's mouth, a sharp metallic tang. At last they tore themselves apart and said goodnight, goodnight, and kissed again, this time tenderly, lingeringly, and drove away in their separate vehicles.

And then there was a time of waiting, of waiting for some indication from Kathleen that she wanted to see him, or for some inspired act of reconciliation on his part, but neither occurred, and that year Kathleen transferred to another school. For her, the staircase was always ascending. It always led to another, more spacious realm. She used to tell Graham he needed to decide what it was he wanted out of life, meaning, he thought, that he had to choose between his devotion to his daughters and his love for her. Quite possibly, however, there was a wider implication to her remark: namely that, on close inspection, his life didn't stand up all that well; it consisted of fractured, isolated fragments that maybe matched and maybe didn't. Here he was as a moody, disadvantaged, fatherless adolescent. Here he was as a young husband building a house in an enchanted forest, except the enchantment was thin and permeable, no protection at all, really. Here he was as a widower with two high-spirited young daughters, and here he was in his current phase, married for the second time (Dad, are you sure you want to marry Sarah, or is it just sex or something, because it's not too late, you can still change your mind, you know), and now Sarah, his dearest Sarah, was in North Vancouver and her beloved dogs were out there somewhere in the waning light and plainly his sole task was to retrieve them for her.

In the living room he turned on a lamp, although it was early evening, not yet dark. Beside the lamp, on a small table, stood his mother's Matryoshka dolls, which Sarah, who tended to be claustrophobic, had arranged in a row so they wouldn't suffocate, trapped one inside the other. Their painted eyes glittered mockingly at him.

He remembered sitting with his mother in her room at the nursing home on a hot day in July, watching television news coverage of the return to St. Petersburg of the remains of the last tsar and tsarina of Russia. His mother had wiped her eyes and had said look, look how small the coffins are. He, too, had felt moved, although he kept telling himself if he'd been there he would have been on the side of the Bolsheviks. He'd never believed his mother's stories of White Russian ancestry, and why should he; his mother had been born in Moose Jaw in 1919. But he was beginning to understand this: for his mother it had been Russia, Imperial Russia, a pale winter sun glinting off the frozen Neva, horse-drawn sleighs gliding across a gold-tinted bridge, while for him it was South America, or it was Costa Rica, a beautiful green jewel of a country — but in both cases, he now saw, these visions came out of a desperate yearning for an unknown landscape, a place where it was possible to begin over and just maybe, with luck, get it right this time and thus avoid being irredeemably damaged by the simple process of living and making choices. But possibly such dreams had a thinning effect — by which he meant they dulled the mind and diverted attention away from what really mattered.

He got a jacket and a flashlight and took the dogs' leashes from a hook by the kitchen door. He went outside and walked across the lawn to the edge of the forest. He loved the hour before twilight, long blue shadows across the ground, his own shadow supine at his side. He knew he looked like his mother: the same long, thin nose with a bump, the same slightly prim mouth and narrow down-turning eyes. It was almost as if he had inherited nothing from his absent father, and yet in many ways his father had been a powerful influence in his life. He used to dream of his return. In the dream his father wore an open raincoat over a dark suit and carried an attaché case he kept shifting from one hand to the other, saying he had only thirty minutes to spare before his flight departed. Graham had to talk fast, trying to convey to his father how much he regretted not having known him better and how at school he'd got into a little trouble with drinking and so-called soft drugs, and other, less soft drugs, and had indulged in way too much partying, but then he'd married a lovely girl and had two daughters and he'd done all right, all things considered. His father gave him a smooth, unperturbed look. He consulted his watch. Graham wanted to grab him and shake him, but even in a dream he couldn't do that. His father had died more than a decade ago, in Ottawa, where he'd retired with his second wife, information Graham had gleaned from a newspaper clipping a former employer of his mother had slipped inside a Christmas card.

Graham walked around the yard, stooping for a closer look at what appeared to be fresh prints in the bark mulch. Were the dogs nearby, taunting him? He stood, thinking of how Sarah had driven from San Diego with two strange dogs in the car breathing down her neck and getting carsick and losing their balance whenever she turned a corner or accelerated. Near Bellingham, she'd detoured to the town of Fairhaven and had gone into a restaurant beneath a bookstore. She'd ordered something to eat and had sat near a window, where she could keep an eye on her car. Then she'd gone upstairs and browsed quickly through the books, on the lookout for new names for the dogs. They had names already, but those names were inextricably linked to their unfortunate prior histories and were, she believed, no longer suitable. Finally she'd settled on Hamlet, from Shakespeare, and Quinn, from a romance novel she'd nearly bought, then decided against, because it had seemed to her the owner of dogs like Hamlet and Quinn wouldn't read paperback romances. She could feel herself morphing into a new creature, a new being. She'd described it as a truly physical process: it gave her little electrical sparkly feelings on the back of her hands. She went outside and got the dogs out of the car and took them for a walk. A wind was blowing and the sea was all churned up. The dogs tugged at their leashes, tangling her up, and she laughed at the picture they must have made. Sometimes Graham could see this scene so clearly it was as if he'd been there, too.

In the evening light his house was beautiful, the proportions pleasing to the eye, the front door appealingly recessed, the pitch of the roof precisely right. He'd cleared just enough land to hold it, like a bird in a cage. He remembered the raw wood taking shape, the roof timbers against a clear sky. Every nail he'd hammered in place himself, or he and Annette had, the two of them working side by side. He dreamed of travel, yet there was nowhere else he wanted to be.

In the forest there was a cold mist rising from the damp ground, a smell like incense. The last time he'd made it this far into the woods, scouting for fallen trees to use as firewood, he'd discovered a crude circle of stones around a pile of ash, tin cans, a couple of plastic water bottles. Someone had constructed a shelter, branches and boughs leaning against the trunk of a Douglas fir, a tarp to keep out the rain. Furious, he'd kicked the rocks and ashes around and shoved the lean-to over. If he'd asked, whoever he was, Graham would have said go ahead and live in the woods, make yourself at home, just don't leave garbage around or start a forest fire. Sometimes Graham had the odd feeling the squatter in the woods was in fact a younger, hardier version of himself, a self that had somehow sheared off after Annette died and had established a risky ephemeral independence, refusing to participate in a world he didn't understand or like. And how did you exorcise a ghost like that, even supposing you wanted to? A ghost named *Aravin*; no one.

Graham made it as far as the ravine, a strange geological feature, an abruption cutting deep into the earth. He was looking down at huge moss-covered erratics, rocks deposited here centuries ago, at the end of the last ice age, and luxuriant bracken fern, downed trees, mossy and rotten — nursery trees, they were called — host to an astonishing variety of life forms: hemlock and maple seedlings, ferns and lichens and fungus. How beautiful, he thought. What a beautiful, holy place, even to an agnostic like him. He crept closer to the edge. It had rained earlier, a brief downpour, and then the sky had quickly cleared, but the ground was still wet, and his foot must have slipped. Before he knew what had happened, he was falling. His arm struck a tree, or rather the tree struck him, the pain astonishing, as if the arm had been ripped from the socket, and then he almost landed on a rock shaped like an anvil, which just might have given him a platform he could use to climb back up from, but he merely grazed it, and he was still falling and he kept thinking this couldn't be happening, and at the same time he knew it was.

He came to rest on a relatively unencumbered stretch of ground, but still the impact must have knocked him out briefly, because there was a gap in his consciousness, and the next thing he knew he was looking up at a scrap of dusky sky as from the bottom of a well. With a little effort, he sat up. He feared his arm was broken, a simple fracture, nothing that would impede him too badly, as long as he did the impossible and ignored the pain. He rested a while, concentrating on breathing and staying calm. He'd lost the flashlight and the leashes. He didn't blame the dogs for any of this. Let the dogs be in charge of the world, for a change. Let them have their way. He waited, gathering his resources. Then he began making his way up the face of the ravine, gaining a foothold in rocks, on branches, trying to use his legs and his one good arm-although even his good arm hurt like hell. His ascent acquired a workable rhythm and he marvelled at how quickly he was able to adapt to such strenuous, unaccustomed labour, and to the pain, which had acquired the mass and solidity of another being, a truculent, unshakeable companion.

There was a time when he actually thought he had it made. All he had to do was hoist himself somehow up and over the embankment and onto solid ground. But when he took hold of a root to use as leverage, he precipitated a shower of dirt and rocks. What looked solid was fragile, tenuous. He rubbed at his eyes, to clear them of grit. Just to survive until morning — nothing else was required. In the morning Sarah would look for him. The dogs would return home, their little game ended, and they'd lead Sarah here and he'd be rescued.

He thought of extinction, what it meant when the place you'd taken up in the world was empty, when there was nothing there. He was looking at his life and he saw the value of it, its irreplaceable fugitive nature. He thought of Annette, her smile, her dark curls tumbling around her pale face. Kathleen. Sarah. His daughters. His mother, Renate. He thought of Father Dimitri, with his compassionate smile and kind eyes. Forty days, he had said, before the soul severed its connections with the living. He thought of how people came into his life and enthralled him with their laughter, their neediness and kindness. He thought of the forest drifting above him, like an elevated, sleeping city.

Each year his students would get in the habit of lightly tapping the Elvis poster, before an exam or a basketball game, for luck. Perhaps he, too, should pray to Elvis, the reading Elvis, his surprisingly delicate-looking hand resting on the open page, the text made blindingly plain to him, the words an avenue of escape, a way up into another world: *Some days I would rather read than sing.*

He thought of Elvis. Elvis back on Earth. He thought of Elvis walking up and down on the face of the Earth. He thought of the Earth going about its process of subtraction and addition, taking away, building up, taking away, a planet that operated like a god, hoarding and spending, and people trying and failing and trying again to accommodate themselves to this process. For a moment he thought he glimpsed his mother in the trees, her dress leaf-green, dappled with the last faint rays of evening light, her hand stretched forth, saying: *Why are you always afraid, Graham? What is there to fear?*

ACKNOWLEDGEMENTS

I wish to thank Thora Howell and Kathryn Mulders for their encouragement and assistance, and thanks also to Irene Mock, Kim Goldberg, Joan Skogan, Jennifer O'Rourke, Cynthia Cecil. Special thanks to the Canada Council for financial support with the writing of these stories.

"What Saffi Knows" received a *Western Magazine* Award for Fiction, appeared in *Event* and *Best Canadian Stories*; "Felt Skies," appeared in *Event*; "The Joy of Life" appeared in *Paper Guitar: 27 writers celebrate 25 years of Descant Magazine*, edited by Karen Mulhallen.